"Was the village Susanna's idea?"

Now bent over his work, Justice shrugged. "It was a group plan." The hint of red coloring his ears betrayed him.

"It was your idea."

He shrugged again, this time adding a little smile as though pleased she'd uncovered the truth.

"How clever, Justice. A_____ something like _____ *since you have none* _____ r heart ache. Des_____ ord had blessed her _____

"It's not somethi___ __ __p with on my own." He cleared his throat. "I saw villages like this one in Germany the Christmas I spent in Europe." A frown replaced his smile, and he hunched over the bench as though finished with the conversation.

She longed to touch his shoulder, to give it a reassuring squeeze as she did Gerard's or Isabelle's when they needed encouragement. But this was no child, however boyish his eagerness to please the children of Esperanza. This was the man who could arrest her and send her back to her debtors.

Florida author **Louise M. Gouge** writes historical fiction for Harlequin's Love Inspired Historical line. She received the prestigious Inspirational Readers' Choice Award in 2005 and placed in 2011 and 2015; she also placed in the Laurel Wreath contest in 2012. When she isn't writing, she and her husband, David, enjoy visiting historical sites and museums. Please visit her website at blog.louisemgouge.com.

Visit the Author Profile page at Harlequin.com for more titles.

LOUISE M. GOUGE

Cowboy Lawman's Christmas Reunion

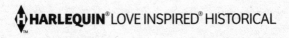

HARLEQUIN® LOVE INSPIRED® HISTORICAL

REL
G

PLEASE RECYCLE

THIS PRODUCT IS RECYCLABLE

Recycling programs
for this product may
not exist in your area.

LOVE INSPIRED BOOKS

ISBN-13: 978-0-373-42543-3

Cowboy Lawman's Christmas Reunion

Copyright © 2017 by Louise M. Gouge

www.Harlequin.com

Printed in U.S.A.

And be ye kind one to another,
tenderhearted, forgiving one another,
even as God for Christ's sake hath forgiven you.
—*Ephesians* 4:32

This book series is dedicated to the intrepid pioneers who settled the San Luis Valley of Colorado in the mid- to late 1800s. They could not have found a more beautiful place to make their homes than in this vast 7,500-foot-high valley situated between the majestic Sangre de Cristo and San Juan mountain ranges.

Thanks go to my beloved husband of fifty-three years, David Gouge, for his loving support as I pursue my dream of writing love stories to honor the Lord Jesus Christ. I would also like to thank my editor extraordinaire, Shana Asaro, who always makes my stories better.

Chapter One

Friday, October 14, 1887
Esperanza, Colorado

Sheriff Justice Gareau ducked around the corner of the Esperanza train depot, hoping he hadn't been spotted by the woman who'd stepped off the train. He felt downright foolish. Usually people hid from him if they'd done something wrong, and he sure hadn't done anything wrong. No, it was that woman who'd done wrong by him and ruined his life. Well, *ruined* was perhaps too harsh a word, because he had a pretty good life these days. But she'd sure broken his heart. A heart he was determined never to give to a woman ever again.

What was Evangeline Benoit doing in this remote Colorado town anyway? And why did her sudden appearance turn him into a bumbling chump? Because once, long ago back in New Orleans, she'd been his childhood sweetheart and, eventually, his fiancée. Only she'd broken their engagement to marry a wealthy older man the very day Justice needed her most.

He wondered if she'd come looking for him. Perhaps Lucius Benoit wasn't supporting her in the style she'd chosen over what Justice could have given her as the son of a bankrupt businessman.

"Howdy, Sheriff." Charlie Williams, the telegraph operator, walked toward him, carrying some of his wife Pam's wild gooseberry pie. Pam ran the Williams's Café, where Justice ate most of his meals, unless somebody took pity on his bachelor status and invited him to dinner. How he kept from getting fat and lazy on her fine cooking was a mystery to him. "You waiting for me?"

"Nope. Just holding up this wall." Justice leaned one hand against the yellow clapboard siding and gave Charlie a practiced easy grin, one he'd learned from his mentor in the Texas Rangers, where he'd served for four years before coming to Colorado. "Seemed a little wobbly after all that wind yesterday."

Charlie chuckled. "You let me know if you need anything." He entered the building and closed the door.

Justice pulled his tan Stetson lower over his eyes and stuck his head around the corner to see which direction Mrs. Benoit—he couldn't allow himself to call her Evangeline, since she was another man's wife—had gone. To his disappointment, or so he told himself, she still stood on the platform and was now enfolded in the arms of Mrs. Susanna Northam.

"Hey, Sheriff." Nate Northam clapped Justice on

the shoulder, nearly startling him out of his wits. "What're you doing? Holding up that wall?"

Once again, Justice managed an indifferent shrug. "Just meeting the morning train, as usual." Which didn't make sense even to him, seeing as how he was hiding around the corner from said train.

Not fooled at all, Nate laughed, and his green eyes lit up with humor. As the eldest son of town founder Colonel Frank Northam, he ran Four Stones Ranch with his brother Rand, while their youngest brother, Bartholomew, owned the law office next to the jail-house.

"Come meet my wife's cousin." Nate took hold of Justice's arm, as only a close friend would do to a lawman, and urged him forward.

Susanna's cousin. Justice's feet refused to move toward her, while his mind raced wildly in the other direction. In all of the Lord's beautiful creation, couldn't He have sent Justice some other place than one where he'd eventually be forced to meet up with Evangeline…Mrs. Benoit?

"Now, come on, before Susanna scolds me for being late." Nate gave Justice a little shove. "Besides, you know my sweet wife will be trying to find a husband for her widowed cousin, so you may as well be first in line so you can beat out all the cowboys in these parts."

"Uh, no." Justice dug the heels of his boots into the boardwalk and tried to twist away. "I'm not planning to get married anytime soon." So Evangeline was a widow. What happened to the wily old rascal who'd turned her head and stolen her heart with his riches?

Nate laughed again. "That's what we all said, all of us used-to-be confirmed bachelors." Somehow he managed to force Justice's feet forward. "Come on. Let's get this over with. I'll try to make it as painless as possible for you."

No matter what Nate said, seeing Evangeline again could only bring pain. He had no choice though, what with a man nearly as tall and every bit as brawny as he pushing him toward his doom. He tugged his hat down farther in the futile hope she wouldn't recognize him. After all, eleven years was a long time. He'd added a few inches in height and considerably more in shoulder width. Maybe—

"We're here, Susanna." Releasing Justice, Nate bent down to give his pretty little wife a peck on the cheek before turning to Evangeline. "And you must be our cousin from New Orleans." Yankee though he was, he bowed over her offered hand with the grace of a Southern gentleman. "We're mighty pleased to have you come to stay with us."

"Thank you, Nathaniel." Her musical voice generated bittersweet memories for Justice.

While the others traded the usual pleasantries, Justice peeked out from under the brim of his hat. Up close like this, she appeared much more womanly than the seventeen-year-old girl who'd jilted him, but every bit as beautiful, maybe even more so. Her blond hair, swept up in a fancy do and topped with a stylish brown hat, still looked like spun honey. Her once bright blue eyes, however, wore a tired look that bespoke more than travel weariness. Behind her, a flaxen-haired girl and a sandy-haired boy watched her anxiously. Her children? Only one way to find out. Justice nudged Nate, who grinned, obviously misunderstanding his intent. He was concerned about an old friend, nothing more.

"Cousin Evangeline, I'd like to present Sheriff Justice Gareau, one of our town's most eligible bachelors."

"Nate!" Susanna smacked his arm and laughed. "For shame. If you're trying to help me with my matchmaking, at least be a little subtler."

While she spoke, Evangeline's ivory complexion grew even paler, those blue eyes widened and, before Justice could catch her, she dropped in a heap on the wooden platform.

Even in her hazy awareness, Evangeline understood at last why she'd come to Esperanza. The Lord hadn't sent her to Susanna to escape justice, but to encounter Justice. But how had he known where she was? How had he arrived here before her? What irony. Her creditors had sent the only man she'd ever loved to arrest her. And from the stern look she'd seen on his face before she fainted, he felt no pity for her, despite his youthful declarations of love. She couldn't blame him. Papa had forbidden her to see him, had broken their engagement himself so she'd had no chance to explain herself to Justice. Nor had Justice come to rescue her, despite her plea through his father, proving his love for her had turned cold. *Ah, yes, my dear. The opposite of love is not hate, but indifference.* Or so Lucius had often told her as he'd traipsed off to enjoy his many vices.

The sound of sobbing reached her ears. Her poor children. Evangeline forced herself to awaken even as heat flooded her face. She'd fainted few times in her life and then only because Lucius had… She would not think about those frightening times. Lucius was gone forever, and now she must face the cruel future he'd laid out before her. At least her children would have a home with their cousin after Justice arrested her.

"Evie. Evie, dear." Susanna's plaintive voice cut through Evangeline's muddled musings. "Oh, Nate, do something."

But it was Justice who scooped her up from the wooden platform. For the few brief moments he carried her, she could rest her head against his broad, solid chest, her cheek touching the tin star that proclaimed him a lawman, and pretend their lives had turned out the way they'd dreamed of when they were young.

She opened her eyes to a shaded room inside the train depot, where Justice set her down on a bench and sat beside her, one arm still supporting her. She blinked to clear away the last of her fogginess. A telegraph operator sat by his machine, his kindly old face filled with concern. Susanna held on to Evangeline's children. All three bore frightened expressions, with Isabelle and Susanna sharing their family resemblance and Gerard wearing his father's anxious scowl.

"You see, children, Mama's going to be all right." Susanna released them and sat beside Evangeline, touching her forehead and then gripping her hand. "No fever, thank the Lord. I'm sure you're exhausted from your travels, but Nate went for the doctor just the same."

"Thank you." Evangeline continued to lean against Justice, unwilling to end her fantasy.

He still hadn't spoken, but she could feel his heartbeat, its rapid pace saying volumes. So he was not without some feeling for her.

She looked up into that beloved face. The years had been good to him, for he was even more handsome, more manly, than he'd once been. As she regarded him, the concern written there quickly disappeared, replaced by a hard facade. Yes, he was indeed going to arrest her.

"Hello, Justice." She moved away from him.

He touched the brim of his hat, a surprising courtesy toward someone he must consider a criminal. "Mrs. Benoit."

She managed a wobbly smile. "So formal."

"What on earth?" Susanna practically bounced where she sat, not the ladylike behavior they'd learned as girls. "Do you mean to tell me you two know each other?" She laughed. "No wonder you fainted, Evie. You must be shocked to see someone you know way out here in Colorado." She stared meaningfully into Evangeline's eyes.

Dear Susanna. She'd understood Evangeline's desperate letter asking for a secret place to rear her children. As girls meeting each summer for family holidays, they'd devised a code to say more than plain words. What she hadn't told her cousin was that her desperation stemmed from Lucius's impossible debts to his cousin, Hugo Giles, which she must repay, and the debts he claimed she owed to several New Orleans merchants. And then there were Hugo's other, more unthinkable threats. Her flight from him might have been enough for Susanna, or at least Nathaniel, to withhold their generous invitation to live at their ranch. She'd tell them, of course, when the time was right and it wouldn't sound like a plea for money.

"Well." Susanna, always so cheerful, now looked at Justice. "Sheriff, you simply must come with us to the hotel for dinner so you and Evie can get re-acquainted."

"Uh, I have some paperwork—"

"Nonsense. You have to eat." While Susanna continued reasoning with him, a wild sense of relief flooded Evangeline and almost brought on another, much different sort of fainting spell.

Meeting him at the train had only been a coincidence. Justice didn't mean to arrest her after all. Perhaps he didn't even know about her flight from Hugo.

He moved a few inches from her, his face a study in misery. "Susanna's not going to let up until I say yes. Do you mind if I join you?"

"Not at all." She copied Susanna's bright tone as much as her fatigue permitted. "That is, if you'll agree to address me as Evangeline, as you once did." He'd always claimed it was the most beautiful name he'd ever heard.

The ripple of his clenched jaw both thrilled and worried her. "I'll join you if you insist."

"Well…" Evangeline must set him free, since he didn't want her company.

"Of course we insist." Susanna stood. "Now, let's leave so Charlie can go back to work." She gave the telegraph operator a friendly wave. "Come along, children." She reached out to Isabelle and Gerard, both of whom pulled back. "Aren't you hungry?"

"Mama?" Isabelle sent Evangeline a questioning look.

Gerard merely scowled, nothing new for him. He'd been unreceptive to every suggestion she'd made since his father died, despite Lucius never giving either child a modicum of affection.

"Yes, of course." Evangeline stood, swaying slightly before she regained her balance, and gripped each child by the hand. "Come along. I'm sure you're as hungry as I am." She smiled over her shoulder at Justice, whose face once again became a granite facade.

If he wasn't here to arrest her, couldn't he at least return a smile for old times' sake?

What a foolish question. She must expect nothing from a man who'd refused to rescue her from a forced marriage to a man whom he knew to be cruel.

Justice trailed after the ladies and children as they made their way down the boardwalk toward the hotel. If it wouldn't look like cowardice, he'd quietly change his course and return to his office. Or slip into Williams's Café, a step ahead on the right. Too late. He'd already passed the door. Besides, a quick glance through the window showed all the café tables were occupied, and he didn't see anyone he'd want to eat with in his current mood.

He glanced up at Evangeline's back. She'd actually had the nerve to smile at him, although it had seemed sad rather than flirtatious. If she'd played the coquette, he'd have left right away, and none of Susanna's cajoling would have stopped him. On the other hand, as much as he wanted to remain indifferent to Evangeline, he worried about her fainting. Susanna was right. Evangeline must be exhausted from her travels. She'd probably fainted in relief over arriving safely to her cousin's care.

No, not true. She'd been all smiles and enthusiasm when greeting Susanna and Nate by the train. It was when she'd seen Justice that she'd wilted like a cactus flower in hot summer wind.

Admit it, Gareau. It felt good to hold her in your arms.

No, he must not allow such thoughts. While he couldn't deny enjoying her feminine closeness and the scent of gardenias wafting from her hair, memories of eleven years of slowly receding pain shocked him back to reality. Just when he'd begun to consider looking for a wife, even praying the Lord would send him a companion to share his lonely evenings, Evangeline came along to remind him that giving a woman his heart brought nothing but misery. If he married, it would be merely for companionship, not for some foolish interest in love. Loving a woman only brought pain.

Nate and Doc Henshaw met them at the corner of Main Street and the southbound highway, and across the street from the Esperanza Arms. After introductions, they trooped into the hotel lobby, where Doc sat Evangeline down to check her pulse and heart.

"Because of the high altitude here in the San Luis Valley, many folks suffer lightheadedness for a while when they first arrive." Doc tucked his stethoscope back into his black leather satchel. "Come see me if it persists beyond a few weeks. In the meantime, don't rush into too much activity." He eyed the two children. "You youngsters help your mother, understand?"

"Yes, sir." The little girl, Isabelle, nodded solemnly and moved nearer Evangeline, putting a protective hand on her shoulder.

The boy, Gerard, scowled and shifted his eyes around like a cornered cougar. Justice's lawman senses went on alert. Something wasn't right with the boy, probably because he looked like his father, that scoundrel Lucius Benoit, who'd embezzled Justice's father's money and stolen Evangeline's heart with his wealth. Justice would try to be fair, but the boy needed to be watched.

After pronouncing Evangeline well, Doc made his exit.

"Come on, now." Susanna herded everyone toward the large hotel dining room. "Let's eat. That should make Evie feel better."

As elegantly appointed as the best New Orleans hotels Justice recalled from his youth, the Esperanza Arms boasted a talented French chef and an expert English pastry maker. He rarely ate here because he preferred the homier cooking at Williams's Café. Still, it wasn't good for a sheriff to show favoritism, so he made occasional visits, more to chat with the owners, Garrick and Rosamond Wakefield, than for the food. Rosamond was Nate Northam's sister, and their whole clan had done much to build this community without trying to control the citizens, one reason Justice accepted the post of sheriff. True to his name, if there was anything he couldn't tolerate, it was *in*justice, sleazy politics and men trying to control other men. Reminded of his past with Evan-

geline, he added something else to his list: people
who didn't keep their promises.

Seated at either end of the long table as though
hosting one of their formal dinner parties, Nate and
Susanna oversaw the ordering and serving of dinner.
Justice sat beside the boy and across from Evangeline
and her daughter. From there he could observe the
others, a habit he'd picked up in the Texas Rangers.
A lawman learned a lot about folks by watching and
listening. Yet, as much as he tried to remain indifferent, when Susanna questioned her cousin about
various topics, he listened even more intently. Maybe
he was trying to recapture memories of their happy
childhood in New Orleans, when their fathers had
been partners in a coffee import business, along with
Lucius Benoit. More likely, against all that made
sense in his lawman's mind, he wanted to know what
Evangeline had been doing these past eleven years
and what had happened to her scoundrel husband,
who'd stolen her heart all those years ago or, more
likely, bought it with his money.

"Oh, it's not terribly interesting." Evangeline gave
Susanna a meaningful look, praying she'd understand. When her cousin returned a blank stare, Evangeline tilted her head toward Isabelle, then Gerard
and blinked her right eye and then her left, their signal for "later."

"Oh." Susanna sat back. "Well, honey, please let
me say how sorry I am for your loss. As my daddy
can tell you, widowhood is so difficult, especially
when you've had a good marriage." She gave a sad

smile to each of the children. "I'm sure you miss your papa."

While seven-year-old Isabelle stared down at her plate and pushed the food around with her fork, Gerard snorted before shoveling a large bite of potatoes into his mouth. Evangeline glared at him across the table until she noticed how intently Justice was watching her.

"Manners, Gerard." She spoke sweetly but gave her son a tight smile.

Gerard scowled at her. Justice appeared about to correct the boy, but Nate beat him to it.

"Son, your mother reminded you about your manners. You say 'yes, ma'am' and do what she says."

As she'd feared, Gerard slammed down his fork and sat back, arms folded over his slender chest. "Make me." Although he was only ten years old, his growl sounded horribly similar to Lucius's when he'd been angry, which was often.

Nate questioned Evangeline with one raised eyebrow, perhaps asking permission to correct her son, but Justice took action. He leaned his considerable height over Gerard and gave him a menacing look that made Evangeline shudder. Any criminal would tremble at that look.

"Son, your mother reminded you about your manners." He repeated Nate's words in a cool tone. "You say 'yes, ma'am' and do what she says." He spared Evangeline a glance before going on. "In this town, we don't tolerate recalcitrant conduct among our young folks. Believe me, you don't want to know how we deal with any boy who disrupts the peace around here."

Gerard blinked a few times, and his jaw dropped. He glanced at Justice then at Nate, looking trapped. Evangeline could almost laugh at Justice's choice of a grown-up word like *recalcitrant* if her son's recent behavior weren't one of her biggest heartaches.

"What do you say?" Justice moved an inch closer to Gerard.

Eyes wide, her son stared up at him. "Yes, ma'am."

"Say it to your mother."

Gerard gulped and looked at Evangeline. "Yes, ma'am."

"Good." Justice sat back and cut into his thick, juicy steak as though nothing had happened.

Nate and Susanna also resumed eating and chatting. But Evangeline saw the rebellion, perhaps even hatred, returning to Gerard's eyes as he glared at Justice. She could never figure out what was behind those angry eyes, and her son certainly never told her what he was thinking.

"Evie, I'm so thrilled to have you here." Susanna appeared determined to keep the conversation pleasant. "Once you settle in, I'm going to put you to work on my latest project for the community."

For the first time since seeing Justice at the train depot, Evangeline felt a spark of hope. "Well, aren't you the clever one. Do tell, what is your project?"

Susanna smiled at Nate. "We've recently finished building a lending library. That is, we constructed the building and the shelves, and we already have several boxes of books donated. What with harvest and roundup and all going on in the fall, nobody's had time to organize them." She gave Evangeline a sly smile. "You can be our librarian. What do you think?"

Her pulse racing, Evangeline considered the possibilities. She and Susanna both loved books and had spent many a summer day reading together. Yet she'd been forced to sneak away from New Orleans, not able to keep a single book from Lucius's vast library he'd inherited from his father but never used. As she tried to visualize working in the Esperanza library, another thought leaped to mind.

"What will I do with the children?" Isabelle would be a big help in the library, but Gerard might prove an insurmountable problem.

"Why, school, of course," Susanna said. "We have an excellent grammar school. Over the weekend, we'll let them catch their breath from their long trip, but we'll enroll them on Monday."

"Yes, of course." Evangeline hadn't thought that far ahead. Escape had been her sole focus when she'd fled her home city.

"And of course you'll receive a salary." Susanna gave her a smug smile, pleased with her own plan.

Evangeline was pleased with it, too. Now she wouldn't have to burden her cousin financially. And what a lovely way to spend her days, far better than anything she could hope for. "Then I would be delighted to accept the post."

At the other end of the table, Justice and Nate spoke quietly, their faces serious. Were they talking about her? No, she mustn't assume she was the topic of private conversations, as often was the case among her supposed friends back home. Once Lucius went broke and fell from society's good opinion and then died at the hands of a fellow gambler, once their lavish home and furnishings—including his books—went on the auction block, everyone had turned away from her. No one believed her innocent or unaware of Lucius's shady business dealings. No one believed she hadn't run up those debts with various merchants. When at last the house had been sold and she and the children moved into a tiny shack, where creditors came to hound her for the staggering debts, society entirely cut her off. Those who knew nothing of her husband's gambling and licentious lifestyle assumed she'd spent her husband into poverty and ruin.

"You'll have to excuse me." Justice stood, his sudden movement and awe-inspiring height startling Evangeline from her musings. "My paperwork won't finish itself."

"Sit down, Justice." Susanna waved him down. "I'm not finished."

A pained look on his face, he obeyed her. "Yes, ma'am. How can I help you?"

Instead of answering, Susanna looked at her husband. "Nate, I'm sure these little ones would like to visit our town's ice-cream parlor. Why don't you take them down the street?"

Nate chuckled. "Yes, ma'am." His knowing smile indicated he understood why his wife made the request.

Once he and the children left—even Gerard couldn't resist ice cream—Susanna gleefully began her explanation. "Evie, Justice has been working on a special project."

Justice shook his head and exhaled through pursed lips. "Susanna—"

"Now, Justice, you can't build that entire Christmas village all by yourself. Evie is a brilliant artist. She can help you."

Evangeline stared at her cousin. "What on earth are you talking about?" The last thing she wanted was to work with Justice. "What Christmas village?"

Susanna appeared more than pleased with herself. "Every year we have a big Christmas pageant at the church, with a party for the children afterward. Every child receives a toy, usually a carved soldier or doll, which our talented cowboys make. This year, we're adding another special gift for the whole community, but especially the children. Justice is making a miniature village with a church, houses, trees and all sorts of things." She shot Justice a smile, which he did not return. "Because there's so much traffic at the jailhouse, he can't work on it there because it's supposed to be a surprise for everyone. That's why he's working on it in the library's locked back room, where no one can see it." She sat back, grinning. "So that's settled. You'll work on it together."

Her heart dropping, Evangeline could only stare at Justice to see his reaction. He looked trapped, the same way she felt.

Once again, he stood. "You ladies will have to excuse me. I still need to—"

"Yes, of course." Susanna gave him a gracious nod. "Don't forget we're expecting you for Sunday dinner."

"Thank you, ma'am." He gave her another pained

look and nod of resignation, and then bowed to Evangeline. "Ma'am."

While his unsmiling face sent her heart plunging, the woman within couldn't keep from admiring his masculine form as he strode from the dining room. Why? From everything she'd seen so far, he wasn't the least bit happy she would be living in his town. And he certainly wasn't any more pleased than she was to have Susanna manipulate them into working together on the Christmas village.

Which shouldn't bother her as much as it did. After all, she'd come here to save her children from the shame and poverty, or even worse, brought on by their father's evil deeds. To save herself from a lifetime of repaying close to four thousand dollars to an unscrupulous man whose only claim to the money came from beating and probably cheating Lucius at card games, and whose only evidence was his bank's IOUs supposedly signed in her husband's shaky hand. Hugo hounded her for the money, which threw her life into torment. But when he threatened to have her declared incompetent so he could take guardianship of her children, she knew she must escape.

Justice didn't need to know those details of her life. Having an occupation, she could hold her head up in this town. Perhaps by working on the Christmas surprise, she would gain a measure of respect she'd lost long ago back home. And eventually, she'd gather the courage to tell Susanna and Nate everything.

Justice shuffled the papers on his desk, trying to find some task to add credence to his claim of needing to work. In truth, he had little work to do in Esperanza, which was exactly the way he liked it. He'd joined the Texas Rangers nine years ago to protect innocent folks and imprison lawbreakers. Seeing what wicked men had done to his father, sanctioned all the way by unscrupulous lawmen and politicians, he'd vowed to punish evildoers wherever the Lord sent him.

After four years with the Rangers, he'd felt the Lord call him farther west, and he'd spent a couple of years in Creede, a town way up in the San Juan Mountains near the headwaters of the Rio Grande. The Lord had blessed that time above all expectations, but Justice got restless again. Then his former mentor in the Rangers put him in contact with the owner of the Esperanza Bank, Nolan Means, who needed a bodyguard due to threats from vengeful outlaws. Once the gang was taken down, Justice accepted the post of deputy with the former sheriff, Abel Lawson. Lawson retired shortly thereafter, and the town hired Justice as their sheriff.

Justice was honored by the town's trust and prayed he'd never do anything to let them down. His goal in life was to develop the reputation of being a no-nonsense lawman whom outlaws feared so much they'd never come near Esperanza. So far, so good. A few suspicious-looking sorts sometimes drifted through town on their travels to the silver and gold mines up near Creede, but he always encouraged them not to linger. While one or two offered resistance, a quick display of his two handiest weapons, his lariat and his Colt .45 Peacemaker, soon sent them on their way.

People seemed to appreciate his approach and supported his methods, and in turn he respected them. Among other sensible laws, the town charter stated anyone setting up a business or even buying property for a home must sign a temperance pledge. No alcohol was permitted in the town limits other than Doc's medicinal alcohol—a law that kept out the drunks and the troubles they brought.

The only trouble in town, if one could call it that, was a few unruly schoolboys, most of whom straightened up after he gave them a good talking to. He still had his eye on a few of those lads.

Lord, please don't let Evangeline's boy get involved with Deely Pine and Cart Fendel. Those two would steer Gerard onto a worse path than he was already headed for with his sullen, rebellious attitude. Justice would try not to think too harshly of the boy. He'd lost his father, a bitter situation Justice understood all too well. And if his mother sought a home with relatives, she probably didn't have much money, if any. Justice might have to—

Whoa! No use riding down that trail. Unless Gerard did something destructive to someone's property, Justice wasn't about to involve himself with Evangeline's son. Closely resembling his father, he reminded Justice too much of his own past griefs. Let Nate handle the boy out at Four Stones Ranch. Justice needed to stay as far as possible from anything to do with Evangeline and her youngsters.

The plan wouldn't be easy to follow, thanks to Susanna Northam. Justice was more than content to work on the Christmas village by himself. While on his Grand Tour of Europe, he'd seen many such displays in Germany, had seen how they delighted the children of the towns he visited. Now building one himself, he found the project filled a hunger in him, a longing to do something for Esperanza's children, since he had none of his own and probably never would have. As she'd said, the back room of the library was the only place in town where he could keep his work hidden from prying eyes. True, he did sometimes wonder if he'd finish in time for the Christmas Eve pageant and party, so a little help would be appreciated. But with the town so quiet, he had little else to do. He couldn't have known Susanna would hire Evangeline to work in the library and then suggest he needed her help. What a nightmare. He liked Susanna, but sometimes she could be meddlesome when she got a bee in her bonnet. Thanks to her, he'd have to see Evangeline every day whether he wanted to or not.

Irritated with his own thoughts, not at all pleased at being reminded of the most painful events of his life, Justice snatched up a pile of wanted posters from his desk and started thumbing through them for about the fifth time.

"Howdy, boss." Sean O'Shea, Justice's deputy, entered the office and whipped off his hat, hung it on a peg by the door, then ruffled a hand through his fiery red hair. "Say, I thought you said you'd never take up old Sheriff Lawson's habit." He nodded toward the posters. "You said reading those more than once was a waste of time. Haven't you read 'em at least three times already?"

"Mind your own business." Justice's tone came out much harsher than he intended.

Sean held up his hands in surrender. "Yes, boss."

"And don't call me boss."

Sean snorted out a laugh and sat at his smaller desk across the room. "Must be a woman," he muttered.

Which almost earned him getting lassoed and dragged across the room.

Except he was absolutely right.

Chapter Two

After supper at Susanna's house, Evangeline and her cousin settled the children into bed in the rooms they'd share with the three Northam children. At nine years old, Lizzie displayed her mother's gift for hospitality, welcoming Isabelle as the younger sister she'd always wanted. Gerard actually behaved himself with six-year-old Natty, otherwise known as Nathaniel Junior, and two-year-old Frankie. Gerard probably behaved because the smaller boys looked up to him. Once they all fell asleep, Evangeline and Susanna joined Nate in their lovely parlor.

The moment she sat in the pink-flowered brocade chair Susanna indicated, emotion overtook her, and she burst into tears, as much to her own surprise as to her hosts'. Susanna rushed to her, knelt and pulled her into a comforting embrace.

"There, there, Evie, don't cry. You're here now, and everything's going to be all right."

Evangeline shook her head. "N-no it won't be."

"Nonsense. You're just tired—"

"Sweetheart," Nate said patiently, "let her speak. I'd imagine she has a lot to tell us."

"Oh. Oh, yes, of course." Susanna stood and drew Evangeline over to the settee where they could link arms. Her warm contact brought much-welcomed comfort. "All right, honey, you talk. I promise not to interrupt." She sent Nate a sweet smile.

Envying their beautiful marriage, Evangeline shed a few more tears before dabbing her cheeks with the handkerchief her cousin offered. "Where to begin?"

"Well, I've been wanting to know…" Susanna sent Nate a sheepish grin. "I promised not to interrupt, but this is important. You could have knocked me over with a feather when you and our Justice Gareau recognized each other, so now I have to know. Is he the secret beau you used to talk about when we were girls? Wouldn't that be romantic? And here you'll be working with him on the Christmas village."

"That was a long time ago and a world away." Evangeline dried a few more tears. Dear Susanna. She was not only her cousin but the dearest, truest friend she'd ever had. Kindness personified. Would she still love Evangeline once she knew the truth about her flight from New Orleans?

With many pauses to control her emotions, she managed to tell her story, or at least as much as she could bring herself to say. Above all, she didn't want to sound as though she were begging for pity or help.

"I'm sure you remember our last summer together," she told Susanna. "The year we both turned seventeen." She added the detail for Nate's benefit. "Mama died shortly after we went home to New Orleans." She wouldn't add that Mama had discovered

Papa's shady business dealings and had become sick with shame, dying soon afterward.

"Papa arranged my marriage to Lucius Benoit, an older man who'd recently become his business partner." Papa hadn't given her any choice in the matter. Still, she wouldn't recount how much she'd loved Justice and how her father's cruel intervention had nearly destroyed her.

"Gerard was born the first year, and Isabelle three years later. After that, Lucius became involved in his work, as men do, so we rarely saw him." She wouldn't speak of Lucius's brutality. Near the end, before he was shot, he admitted he'd married her for Papa's money. But Papa had no money. He'd arranged the marriage thinking Lucius's supposed fortune would pull their business out of debt. What a bitter irony for both men. And she'd been the pawn in the middle. While Lucius made her pay for it, shame over his beatings kept her silent about them.

"When he died—" she wouldn't tell them how he'd met his end "—he left a few debts, which I plan to pay back over time."

"How much debt?" Nate leaned toward her, perhaps to offer help. She couldn't let him.

"Oh, not much in the grand scheme of things." She waved a hand dismissively to deflect further questions. After all, it was her business, and hers alone, how much she owed Lucius's cousin, Hugo. The other supposed debts from various merchants hadn't been hers at all, but Hugo claimed they were, claimed he possessed notes she'd signed for gowns and hats and shoes. She couldn't fight against such false charges when no one believed her. If Justice learned she'd fled her supposed creditors, he would surely arrest her.

Nate sat back, his forehead furrowed. "Last winter was pretty harsh, and we lost a lot of cattle, but we expect this year's herd to put us on the road to financial recovery. If you need help, we might be able to work something out."

"You're very kind, but you really needn't bother. Now with my job at the library—" she squeezed Susanna's hand in gratitude "—I'll start putting away money. And the children can work as they get older." She managed a teasing smile. "Maybe you could teach Gerard to be a cowboy."

Nate winced and studied his hands. "Maybe I could. We'll see."

Evangeline dabbed her damp cheeks again. "Please promise me you won't tell anyone about this, especially Justice."

While Susanna gave her an enthusiastic nod, Nate ran a hand down his cheek.

"I don't know." His eyes revealed his disapproval. "Since you haven't done anything wrong, I don't suppose Justice needs to know, at least not right now. But you should probably tell him someday for the sake of your old friendship."

"I'm sure you're right." Evangeline wouldn't correct him about not having done anything wrong, or he might change his mind. As difficult as her past had been, her only goal now was to rear her precious children in safety and security. Once they were grown and on their own, she'd return to New Orleans and find some way to repay Hugo what she owed him. Whatever she found to do, it could never be as bad as what he'd demanded of her. As for those merchants and the notes she supposedly signed, it was a problem she had no idea how to solve.

In his small apartment over the jailhouse, Justice lay on his bed fully dressed because it was his night to be on alert for any mischief in town. Esperanza never had such troubles, but Justice and his deputy still traded off nights to keep watch. Sean was probably sawing logs in his rented room over at Starlings. As for Justice, he couldn't sleep for thinking about Evangeline. Her beautiful face, which wily Susanna had arranged for him to observe over dinner, bore a haunted look. Was it grief over that scoundrel Benoit? Justice wondered how the man had died, and whether it was his death that had put a burr under the saddle of his sullen boy.

Justice was nineteen when his own father died. A godly, honest man, Father had been ruined by the shady dealings of his business partners, Evangeline's father and Lucius Benoit, who'd put all the blame for the business's losses on Benjamin Gareau to save their own necks. Having just returned from Europe, Justice had been too young, too inexperienced, too grief-stricken to investigate the particulars. The same day Father died, the day Justice needed Evangeline's support more than ever, she'd refused to see him, instead choosing to marry Benoit.

If he could have spoken to her back then, he would have promised he'd work hard to prepare a comfortable life for the two of them, but she didn't care enough even to bid him adieu. With Mother already long in her grave, he hadn't seen any reason to stay in New Orleans, so he'd sold the house and furnishings his father left him to pay off his debts, then lit out for Texas. After trying his hand as a cowboy and doing many foolish things in bad company, he'd signed on with the Texas Rangers. Jubal Tucker became his mentor and put him on a straight path and brought him back to the Lord.

He knew the Almighty had brought him to Esperanza, but why had He brought Evangeline here, too? Was this a test of some sort? Was he supposed to—

Gunshots and wild hollering erupted in the street below, followed immediately by the sound of shattering glass. Justice sprang from his bed and raced to the window. Across the street and down a half block, men on horseback were shooting up Mrs. Winsted's mercantile. Justice grabbed his guns and raced down the back stairs and through the jailhouse in time to see the gang ride off toward the west. No use chasing them. By the time he woke Sean and they saddled their horses, the varmints would be miles away in who knew what direction. He'd try to track them in the morning.

As Justice strode down the street to make sure Mrs. Winsted and her family were safe in their apartment over the store, he decided this was the worst day he'd endured since leaving New Orleans. Not only had Evangeline disrupted his life, but for the first time in his tenure as sheriff, outlaws had shot up a good citizen's business. What else could go wrong?

Oh. Right. Tomorrow was his birthday. Having his past come back and smack him in the face wasn't the way he'd planned to celebrate.

* * *

A slender beam of light shone through the window to brighten a patch of wall in Lizzie's bedroom, waking Evangeline. Despite bawling cattle outside and frigid temperatures seeping into the room, she'd slept hard and awoke rested and full of hope about beginning her new life. Even her dreams of Justice frowning at her from his physical and moral height couldn't subdue her excitement over her new job, because she'd also dreamed of the Christmas village and already had some ideas for how to decorate it. She looked forward to seeing its size and learning how she could help complete it. What fun that would be.

She rose from the cot and dressed quietly so Isabelle and Lizzie, both still blissfully asleep in the four-poster bed, wouldn't waken. She found Susanna in the kitchen. The aromas of coffee, bacon and freshly baked bread roused her appetite. "Mmm, smells wonderful."

"Thank you." Susanna gave her a quick peck on the cheek before turning back to the sizzling bacon in the cast-iron skillet. "Pour yourself a cup of coffee and have a seat. Nate should be back from his chores in a minute, and we can eat in peace before the children need tending. We let them sleep late on Saturdays."

Evangeline did as she was told. From her vantage point at the round kitchen table, she watched in awe as her cousin bustled about the room with the grace of a ballet dancer and the energy of a whirlwind. Having never learned to cook, in fact, having spent little time in her own kitchen except to hand weekly menus to the cook, she couldn't imagine how Susanna knew what to do. Yet the moment Nate entered the back door, his face and hands still damp from washing up on the back porch, everything was in place for him to sit down to breakfast.

After greetings and prayers, they began to eat while Nate told Susanna about his plans for the day. "I still have some work to do at the big house before I head up in the hills on Monday to join Rand, so I'll be around another day or two. I don't mind showing Gerard what we do around here while you ladies go to town."

Evangeline's face must have shown her alarm because Susanna patted her hand. "Don't you worry about a thing, Evie. Nate knows how to wrangle little cowboys."

"He'll be fine." Nate grinned, and his green eyes twinkled. "We're not breaking broncos or doing any other dangerous work. Does he know how to ride?"

"Forgive me." Evangeline laughed softly. "I'll try not to be overprotective. Yes, he rides." A bitter memory came to mind. "He had his own pony until…" When Lucius died and Evangeline learned about his staggering debts, everything had to be sold, including the pony.

"That's a good start." Nate appeared finished with the conversation and his breakfast. He stood and kissed Susanna. "Bring him out to the barn after he eats. I'll get the buggy ready for you." He strode from the room, whistling slightly off key.

Susanna watched him leave and exhaled a sweet sigh, clearly still in love with her kind, handsome husband. "Well, let's get the children up and fed." She stood and put feet to her words.

Following her, Evangeline felt a bitter pang. Susanna assumed she'd had a happy marriage, too, but that was far from true.

Evangeline didn't have time to ponder the matter. Awake and full of energy, five children demanded attention and food. After tending their needs, she and Susanna delivered Gerard to Nate and boarded the buggy with the other four. The instant friendship sprouting between Isabelle and Lizzie reminded Evangeline of her own closeness to Susanna when they were growing up. At least her daughter found a reason to be happy with the changes in her young life. Maybe Gerard would enjoy the challenges of learning about ranching.

Susanna drove the horse down a nearby lane leading to a house similar to her own. After introducing Evangeline to her sister-in-law Marybeth, a pretty Irish girl who'd married Rand, one of Nate's brothers, Susanna instructed her three children to mind their aunt.

"I'll bring you some penny candy, but if you haven't behaved, you won't get any."

All four, including Isabelle, nodded solemnly. "Yes, ma'am."

Evangeline smiled at her daughter, who never needed such a warning. The child strove to please almost to the point of perfectionism.

"I'm sure they'll do fine." Marybeth handed Susanna a shopping list. "Be sure to get the oatmeal. It's about the only thing I can eat these days." She patted her slightly rounded belly. "You'd think I'd be past this morning sickness by now. With Randy and Beth Anne, I felt better at four months." She gazed fondly at her own two offspring, who appeared to be about five and three years old.

"Oh, dear," Susanna said. "Shall I get something from Doc for you?"

"No, thanks. I'll be fine. You girls go have fun."

With her blessing and the children's enthusiastic farewell waves, Evangeline and Susanna were on their way. Evangeline hadn't noticed even a hint of envy in Marybeth's behavior over not going into town with them. Her own so-called friends in New Orleans had been far more exclusive regarding friendships. If Susanna's other acquaintances in Esperanza were as generous, perhaps this was a place where she could truly rest her heart instead of fighting on every side simply for survival. Keeping Justice from learning about her past as they worked side by side and providing for her children were enough to contend with.

The mid-October breeze cut through Evangeline's cloak, and she shivered. Her wardrobe and those of her children would never be sufficient in this cold climate. But Evangeline's rapidly dwindling money wouldn't be enough to buy material to make winter clothes. When she'd fled New Orleans, with its warmer weather, suitable clothing for Colorado winters had been the last thing on her mind.

As though hearing her thoughts and perhaps noticing her shiver, Susanna leaned into Evangeline's arm. "It's a good thing we're about the same size. I have some warmer clothes you can wear until we can make some for you."

"That would be lovely." Evangeline enjoyed sewing and always preferred to make her own clothes. Her society acquaintances scoffed at her refusal to patronize the fashionable *modistes* in New Orleans, but even they admitted she was every bit as talented as those seamstresses trained in Paris.

"We can get some fabric today and get started. Won't that be fun? I have a Singer, so it should go pretty fast. Just think. Sewing together as we used to." Susanna giggled, which warmed Evangeline's heart and reminded her of their merry girlhood adventures. "I'm sure Mrs. Winsted still has plenty of wool, heavy muslin and denim left, and she'll be receiving new shipments by train until the Pass closes."

"That sounds wonderful." Evangeline didn't know how she'd pay for the fabric, but perhaps Mrs. Winsted would give her a line of credit. She could pay her later from her earnings at the library.

They arrived in Esperanza shortly before nine o'clock along with many other people. Buggies, wagons, horses and pedestrians seemed to be streaming into town from all directions.

"It certainly is busy." Evangeline scanned the various businesses. "What's happening?"

"Ranchers and farmers come to town on Saturdays to do their shopping. And many people are stocking up for winter." Susanna reined the buggy horse to a stop in front of a store with a large sign on the roof reading Winsted's Mercantile. "Oh, my. Whatever happened here?"

Broken glass lay on the boardwalk in front of the door and was strewn over items displayed in the shattered window.

Susanna stepped down from the buggy and tied

the horse to a hitching rail. "Come on, Evie. We need to help Mrs. Winsted clean this up."

Evangeline followed her, carefully stepping over the shards. Inside the store, she stopped short. Near the counter, Justice stood talking to a woman perhaps in her late fifties, who wrung her hands. Every nuance of his posture and expression bespoke kindness and sympathy for the weeping woman. This was the Justice she recalled from long ago.

"We followed their tracks south beyond Cat Creek, but they mingled with too many others for us to sort them out." He set a hand on the woman's shoulder. "Don't worry, ma'am. We'll find the men who did this, and before I ship them off to Canon City Penitentiary—" his voice took on a hard edge "—I'll make them repay every penny it costs to replace your window and any ruined merchandise."

While the woman gave him a grateful smile, Evangeline's heart froze. No, this was not the young man she'd grown up with. True to his name, Justice would see punishment meted out to the vandals. He'd become an unbending lawman and would show her no pity if he learned about her flight from her debts, both real and false.

"Mrs. Winsted." Susanna hurried over to embrace the lady. "Let us help you clean up this mess." She beckoned to Evangeline. "This is my cousin I told you about. You give us a broom and a dustpan, and we'll make things right as rain in a jiffy." She looked up over her shoulder at Justice. "Hello, Justice. Are you going to help out or just make promises?"

He scowled at her and slid a brief glance in Evangeline's direction, never actually focusing on her face. "Well, of course, I'm going to help, Susanna." He pulled a pair of leather gloves from his belt and donned them. "You going to run this cleanup, or shall I?"

If Evangeline weren't so nervous in his presence, she would laugh. Despite her diminutive size, Susanna had always been bossy and obviously hadn't changed.

"Why, I am, of course." She led Mrs. Winsted to a chair. "Now you sit here and catch your breath, honey, and we'll take care of everything. Evie, honey, fetch us some of those work gloves." She pointed to a shelf. "We'll have Homer Bean—he's the store clerk—put them on my tab when he gets here. Now, you two get busy." She waved Evangeline and Justice to work.

"Guess we'd better do what she says." Justice's bemused expression didn't look entirely sheriff-like.

"I guess so." Evangeline's heart ached to enjoy working beside him, but how could she, when by simply doing his job, he might bring an end to everything she held dear?

When Evangeline sashayed into the mercantile, Justice's heart kicked up something fierce, and he almost walked out of the store. If not for poor Mrs. Winsted's dire circumstances, he'd leave bossy Susanna Northam and her cousin to restore order. But after her challenge, he couldn't shirk his duty. Besides, he might find some clues as to the identity of the vandals among rifle slugs found at the scene.

"Y'all be careful not to get cut." Susanna took a broom and began sweeping at the front door. "The glass seems to be sprayed mostly in that direction." She pointed toward the right side of the store where material, guns, lamps and other wares were displayed. "If we can make a path to the cash register, folks can still buy what they need. Good thing all the food is on this side." She nodded toward the shelves behind the counter.

She continued a running commentary about what she was doing and what sorry souls those vandals were and a host of other chatter. Preferring quiet, Justice wished she'd hush up and work quietly like Evangeline. Then he saw Mrs. Winsted stand and give herself a shake.

"You're right, Susanna. This isn't the worst thing ever to happen to me." The woman brushed away tears, grabbed a pair of gloves and joined the cleanup. "Thank you."

Justice cast a questioning glance at Evangeline, who was smiling at her cousin. What had he missed?

"She's amazing," she whispered. "I would have sat beside Mrs. Winsted and cried with her." She carefully picked up shards of glass from a bolt of material and dropped them into a china bowl.

Her smile did something odd to Justice's insides. She was still as beautiful as the young girl he'd fallen in love with. Even more beautiful now that she was a woman. To cover his admiration, he shrugged and went back to work. Women sure did communicate differently than men did.

He heard a soft intake of breath and jerked his attention back to Evangeline, an odd little fear crowding into him. "Did you cut yourself?"

"No." She stared at him, wide-eyed. "I just re-membered. Today's your birthday."

He scowled. "I suppose so. I don't really pay much attention anymore." And yet his chest expanded with foolish pleasure because she recalled it. To deflect her regard before she could say more and have the others notice, he added, "I seem to recall it's also your anniversary. Same day you got married back in '76?"

She winced. More than winced. More like cow-ered. Here she was trying to be nice, and he'd re-minded her of Lucius's death. "I'm sorry for your loss. I'm sure you miss your husband."

Now she actually shuddered. Justice supposed a year wasn't long enough to grieve such a significant loss. After all these years, he still grieved for his par-ents. If he were honest with himself, he still grieved over losing Evangeline's love.

Nonsense. All water under the bridge.

"Please accept my belated condolences for your father's death." She gazed at him, her blue eyes glis-tening. "I didn't know he'd died until—"

"Thanks." He cut her off, not wanting to hear her platitudes, even if they were accompanied by tears. Instead, he bent to lift a broken kerosene lamp with a delicate flowered glass shade. "Shame about this."

She stood silent for a moment. "Yes. A shame." Then she went back to work.

One by one, people began to enter the business, including Homer Bean, the clerk, and most dug in right away to help. Despite the busyness, Susanna managed to introduce Evangeline to everyone, all of whom welcomed her. Despite much conversation, in about an hour, they'd cleaned up the store, and Mrs. Winsted had assessed the damages to her inventory.

"They didn't steal anything," she told Justice. "But some items are beyond repair."

"You make me a list and include the cost of each one. I'll make sure you're compensated." Justice pocketed the slugs he'd found and fetched his hat from the front counter. "Thanks for your help, folks." He raised his voice so all the helpers could hear him. "If you hear anything that can help me catch the culprits, let me know. I'll arrange a reward."

He donned his hat and strode out the door. As usual, the good people of Esperanza had come together to help one of their own. Then why did he feel downright depressed?

Easy question to answer. The woman who'd abandoned him at the moment of his greatest grief was casually weaving her way into the fabric of *his* town, and he couldn't do anything to stop her.

"So you're going to be our librarian." Mrs. Winsted seemed nicely recovered from shock over her disaster. "Let me show you what we've been doing up to now." She led Evangeline to the back of the store, where numerous books rested on several shelves. "Keeping track of these has been both a privilege and a bother, too often the latter. I don't have time to chase people down when books are due back for the next person who wants to read them."

"Are you sure you don't mind my taking the books?" The last thing Evangeline wanted was to have one more person in Esperanza who held something against her. The hour working side by side with Justice nearly undid her.

"Not at all. It's a relief." Mrs. Winsted tilted her head toward the nearby barred window behind which were mail slots. "In addition to running my store, I'm also the postmistress, so I have plenty to do."

"Why, yes. You were the one who knew Susanna's maiden name and passed my letter along to her."

"That's right." The lady appeared pleased to have her clever work remembered. "She was delighted to hear from you."

They each spoke of their mutual affection for Susanna and for her father, who now lived in a small town in the southern part of the San Luis Valley with his second wife. Evangeline remembered Edward MacAndrews as a kind, loving father and uncle. What she didn't tell Mrs. Winsted was how differently Edward Junior turned out. Once he found out his widowed father married a Mexican lady, he told all of their relatives Susanna and their father died on their trip west. When Evangeline realized she needed to flee New Orleans, she wrote to Edward in Georgia for help. He forbade her to come to Marietta but said she might find Susanna in Esperanza, Colorado. Shocked at his rejection but overjoyed to learn Susanna was alive after all, Evangeline had written to her. She'd posted the letter in a small town outside of New Orleans to throw Hugo off in case he tried to track her. But with his equally dishonest friends hiding behind every bush, she couldn't be sure her ruse was successful.

"I'd best get back to work." Mrs. Winsted stepped

toward the counter where her clerk was busily serving customers. "Thank you for your help, everyone."

"We were glad to do it." Susanna approached from the other direction, her arms loaded with bolts of fabric. "Mrs. Winsted, I'll take these. Evie and I have a lot of sewing to do."

"But, my dear, some of them are damaged." The storekeeper fingered the torn material. "Let me cut off the ruined parts."

"Nonsense." Susanna tugged the bolts away from her. "We can use all of it, even the small pieces. Lizzie and Isabelle can make clothes for their dolls, and we can make ragdolls for children coming to the Christmas party." She winked at Evangeline, sending a private signal regarding other possible uses for the fabric. "Are you ready to see the library?"

"Yes, indeed. Mrs. Winsted, if it's all right with you, I'll come in on Monday and move these books to their new home."

With all in agreement, Susanna completed her purchases, and the clerk loaded them into the back of the buggy.

Across the street and down several doors from the mercantile sat the sheriff's office, which included the jail. As Susanna drove the buggy past it, Evangeline saw Justice through the large front window, seated at a desk and bent over his work. An involuntary shudder rippled through her.

Susanna gave her a curious glance, but nodded toward the next building, a pink stone edifice with two stories. "That's the bank. The library's around the corner."

They passed a charming stone fountain in the

middle of the intersection. Despite last night's freezing temperatures, artesian water streamed from a stone pitcher held by a sculpture of a fair lady in pioneer dress.

"Here we are." Susanna drove up to another pink stone building, this one narrow and deep, with a single story and a sign boasting Library in bold letters on the front of the flat roof.

Evangeline stepped down from the buggy and followed Susanna inside. The front room, about the size of her large front parlor back in New Orleans, was dimly lit by the two windows on either side of the front door. A wood stove stood sentinel in one back corner, with a small stack of wood beside it. A desk and chair sat near the front window, and five tables with four chairs each were placed in random fashion about the room. Wooden boxes of books were stacked in front of the shelves built into three of the room's walls.

"The books were donated by various folks in and around town," Susanna said. "Not many are new, but they're in good condition."

Evangeline gazed around at the site of her new occupation, and the depression she'd felt since seeing Justice lifted. She couldn't wait to get her hands on those books. Perusing the titles, she pulled a copy of *Pride and Prejudice* from one box.

"Remember those summer nights when we stayed up late reading this to each other?" What romantic girls they'd been. At least Susanna had found her Mr. Darcy.

"I do." Susanna smiled like a proud mother. "Isn't this a lovely room? The men managed to get the walls painted and the shelves stained before roundup began, but we ladies have been busy with putting up our gardens, so we haven't had time to make curtains for the windows." She tapped one cheek thoughtfully. "I planned to sew them, but since you and I need to make clothes and you'll also be working here, I should hire Mrs. Starling. She's a sweet widow lady with four children, so it's good to send work her way when we can."

Evangeline gave her cousin a wry smile. "You're good at helping widows."

Susanna blinked, then hurried over to give Evangeline a hug. "Oh, my dear, I'm so sorry. I'm sure you miss Lucius terribly." She waited expectantly for an answer.

The urge to tell the truth about her horrible marriage nearly overwhelmed Evangeline. But she merely sighed wistfully, hoping Susanna would take it for agreement.

"Well." Quickly changing her mood, Susanna released her and posted fists on her hips. "There's a great deal to be done here, but for now, I think we should return home and start our sewing."

Soon on their way, they fell into the girlish chatter of their childhood. Only this time, instead of romantic dreams, they shared the joys and difficulties of motherhood.

The sound of hoofbeats rapidly approaching from behind put a stop to their conversation. While Susanna reined the buggy closer to the side of the road, Evangeline looked over her shoulder.

Justice. Was he pursuing them? His tall, dapple-gray horse moved nearer, but at least he was now cantering rather than galloping as though chasing a criminal.

He pulled up beside them and slowed to match the moderate trot of the buggy horse. "Good morning, ladies." He tipped his hat.

"Hey, there, Sheriff." Susanna smiled brightly at him. "Didn't we see you a while ago? Don't tell me you just happened to be out for a ride." She turned to wink at Evangeline. "Why, I do believe you're following us."

Heat rushed to Evangeline's face. She should have warned her cousin not to try matchmaking her with the sheriff.

"Not at all, ma'am." Justice still hadn't looked directly at Evangeline. "I'm headed out to the various ranches down this way to see if I can find out who shot up the mercantile."

"Oh, yes. Of course." Susanna laughed as though she didn't believe him. "Well, carry on, then. And if you're hungry in an hour or so, stop by our place for dinner."

"Thank you, ma'am. I'll see what happens." He touched the brim of his hat. "Ladies." He kicked his horse into a gallop and soon became a speck in the distance.

Evangeline exhaled so forcefully, she nearly tumbled from the buggy in relief.

Misunderstanding, Susanna laughed. "Oh, my dear, do I have plans for you."

Justice's stomach was already growling because he'd missed breakfast, so the mention of dinner ignited his appetite. But the last thing he planned to do was accept Susanna's invitation, especially after seeing the look of horror on Evangeline's face. His presence must be distasteful to her. Too bad, since they'd have to work together starting on Monday. She might even have to put up with him for a few minutes when he stopped by Nate's house to ask about his temporary cowhands. He'd stop there last, and maybe they'd be finished eating. But otherwise, he'd stay as far away from her as possible.

He checked at the first ranch and learned from George Eberly that all of his seasonal cowhands were reliable men not given to troublemaking. Less than a mile down the road, he came to the main property of Four Stones Ranch. Foreman Seamus O'Brien, who'd been shot by outlaws a few years before and never recovered enough to participate in the roundups, told Justice he'd have to check with Nate to be sure about a few of the new men.

This warranted a quick change of plans. If he hurried, Justice could ride to the smaller house and speak to Nate before the ladies reached home. As tempted as he was to bypass the place, he needed to do his duty. He spurred Thunder to a gallop and raced over the fields instead of wasting time by going back to the main road. He rode into the small barnyard behind the house and heard unmistakable sounds of a ruckus coming from inside the barn.

He dismounted and unbuttoned the strap securing his gun to its holster. Edging up to the partially open door, he peered in. Dismayed but not surprised, he saw Nate hauling Gerard over his shoulder toward a stall, where he set the struggling, hollering boy down with a thump.

Towering over the youngster, Nate fisted his hands at his waist. "Now you stay in here and don't move."

The boy crossed his arms over his small chest and said, "Make me," as he had at the restaurant the day before.

"Need some help?" Justice stepped inside and towered over Gerard from the other side. Poor Evangeline, having to deal with a son who seemed determined to cause trouble. The boy needed a man's strong hand to guide him.

"Hello, Sheriff." Nate used his title, probably to intimidate Gerard.

While it wasn't the way Justice preferred to interact with children, in this case it was probably best.

"Howdy, Nate."

"Tell me, Sheriff, how do you deal with a boy who chases milk cows out of their stalls and shoots barn cats with a slingshot?" As he talked to Justice, he watched Gerard, whose eyes darted from one man to the other and back again. Still, his defiant expression remained unchanged.

"Well, Nate." Justice scratched the back of his head, causing his Stetson to tilt forward. "My father used to tan my hide when I did anything that rotten." It happened only once, which was enough for Justice to mend his ways. But then, his godly father had been easy to obey. Lucius might not have disciplined his son.

"Sounds like a good idea to me." Nate reached out, but Gerard ducked into a corner of the stall.

Justice managed to grab his shoulder. "You ever had your hide tanned, son?"

"I'm not your son," the boy screamed while trying to twist away.

"What's going on here?" Evangeline stood in the barn doorway, her face pale.

Gerard broke away, rushed to her and threw his arms around her waist. "Mother, save me. They're gonna kill me."

She hugged him close and glared at Justice, then Nate. "I'll repeat myself. What is going on here?"

To her credit, while Nate described the boy's mischief, her face went from angry defender to embarrassed parent.

"If those cows get scared," Nate said, "they'll stop giving milk, which puts us all in a bad spot. And we need those barn cats to keep down the mice population because mice eat the grain that the cows need to eat."

"I see." She brushed a hand down her son's face. "Now that you understand, will you promise not to do those things again?"

"Yes, ma'am," Gerard said in a sing-song voice. He turned to face Nate and Justice and gave them a triumphant smirk. "May I go play now?"

"Not right now. First we'll eat, and then we'll go over to Marybeth's to see the new foal. You'd like that, wouldn't you?"

A tiny hint of vulnerability streaked across Gerard's face. "Yes, ma'am." Something akin to eagerness colored his words.

"If you'll excuse us, gentlemen?" Evangeline ushered her son from the barn.

Nate exhaled a long breath and eyed Justice. "Don't know what I'm going to do with that boy. I have to leave on Monday, and if he's going to cause trouble for Susanna—"

Before he could stop himself, Justice blurted out, "Don't worry. I'll keep an eye on him."

"Thanks, Justice. That relieves my mind considerably."

And yet the idea of riding herd on a recalcitrant brat, especially Lucius Benoit's lookalike son, did anything but relieve Justice's mind.

Chapter Three

Evangeline studied her image in Susanna's long mirror and brushed a whisk broom down the length of her bombazine gown to smooth out wrinkles and remove lint. Although black wasn't her best color, she should have worn mourning while traveling instead of the light brown suit. Then perhaps Susanna wouldn't be trying to play matchmaker, a useless endeavor, especially with Justice. After one bad marriage, Evangeline would never again put herself under the power of a man. However, with all of the children around, she hadn't spoken to her cousin about the matter. To keep others from getting such ideas, she'd have to wear black whenever she went to town, both for church like today and for her work in the library.

Yesterday's incident in the barn was alarming, especially when she saw how angry Nate was at Gerard for his mischief, even to the point of threatening her son. Justice stood there adding his official presence, which made matters worse. Later, Susanna explained to Evangeline how important this time of year was for the whole ranch because their livelihood depended on getting the cattle safely down from the mountain and to the trains. Before leaving, Nate needed to be sure his home was secure, not endangered by a boy who didn't understand ranch life. Evangeline could accept that. She only hoped Gerard did, too.

She joined Susanna in the kitchen and donned the offered white apron.

"Will you beat the eggs, Evie?" Susanna stood at the blazing cast-iron stove and used a fork to turn bacon in her skillet. "The biscuits will be done soon."

Evangeline looked around for the implements to do as she asked. All she located was a basket of dirty eggs on the work counter.

Susanna must have noticed her mild revulsion. "Wipe them off with a damp cloth." She jutted her chin toward the sink where dishwater sat in a tin pan. "Then break them into a bowl and beat them with a fork." Another jut of her chin pointed to a crockery bowl on a shelf.

"Very well." Evangeline squeezed out a thin cloth and proceeded to clean the newly gathered eggs, trying to hide her disgust. A glance at Susanna revealed she was trying to hide a grin. *Very well, indeed.* If her cousin, who'd also been raised with cooks and servants, could overcome her squeamishness about henhouse soil, so could Evangeline.

After breaking the cleaned eggs into the bowl and removing the bothersome bits of shells, she took a fork and stirred them. While some yolks broke, the yellow refused to blend with the whites.

"Harder," Susanna encouraged.

Evangeline obeyed with enthusiasm, causing yellow slime to splash on the hand holding the bowl. With her cousin still chuckling under her breath, she figured out how to modify the action, and soon the eggs were a consistent creamy yellow. "There."

"Good." Susanna carried a plateful of cooked bacon to the table, where Lizzie was showing Isabelle how to set around the silverware and plates.

Feeling a bit more confident, Evangeline took the bowl to the stove and started to pour the eggs into the pan on top of the bacon grease.

"Wait." Susanna rushed to her side. "We have to drain it first."

Evangeline managed to pull the bowl upright before much of the liquid eggs slid into the sizzling pan. Susanna dumped the greasy, unappetizing mess into a bucket beside the sink.

"Never mind, honey. The pigs will be thrilled to have such a treat." She returned the hot skillet to the stove and finished cooking the scrambled eggs to perfection.

Soon the family had gathered around the table. After Nate offered a prayer, the food was served, and everyone seemed eager to clean their plates. Even Gerard appeared to be in a good mood. He winked at his male cousins and closed his eyes in bliss as he ate his raspberry preserve–covered biscuits, causing Natty and Frankie to giggle…and copy him. Evangeline's heart lifted at this glimpse of the boy he used to be. Perhaps things would improve now.

Yesterday, after unpacking their purchases and eating dinner, Susanna had driven Evangeline and her son over to Marybeth's to fetch the other children. As expected, Gerard was smitten with the two-day-old foal and stayed out of trouble the rest of the day. Even Nate was impressed. If only Justice could see Gerard at such times, he wouldn't be so hard on him.

Why did she care what Justice thought? Yes, he was the sheriff and had the power to arrest her if he ever learned why she'd fled New Orleans. But he couldn't arrest an energetic boy simply for being mischievous. Could he?

After breakfast, they all climbed into a surrey and drove to the church in town. Evangeline greeted some of the people she'd already met and was introduced to even more, including the charming pastor, Reverend Thomas. His Virginia accent differed from Susanna's Georgia drawl and Evangeline's broader Cajun intonations, but there was no mistaking his southern origins. She also met the rest of the vast Northam family, including Colonel and Mrs. Northam, their youngest son, Bartholomew, nicknamed Tolley, and Tolley's wife, Laurie.

Having played hostess for her father and husband, Evangeline put her keen memory skills to use and filed away something unique about each person so she could remember their names in the future.

"Justice." Susanna stood in the aisle by the pew and waved to him as he entered the church. "I saved you a spot." She indicated the space beside Evangeline.

If Evangeline weren't in church, she'd be tempted to smack her cousin's arm...*hard.* As it was, she saw Justice wince and look around like a scared mouse trying to escape a cat. The crowded sanctuary offered few remaining seats, so he had no choice but to obey the summons.

Justice brushed against Evangeline's shoulder and skirt as he sat. "Morning, Mrs. Benoit." His deep, rich voice caused a pleasant shiver to roll down her neck and arm. She eased the effects of her involuntary reaction by noting he'd lost some of his Cajun inflections in the past eleven years. She doubted he'd deliberately changed his speech to fit in. Justice was never one to follow the crowd.

"Good morning, Sheriff Gareau." She was rescued from having to make further conversation when the pastor took his place at the front of the congregation and announced the first hymn.

Sneaky Susanna had arranged for them to share a hymnal, but it wasn't entirely unpleasant. Justice's baritone voice had always been strong and sure, unlike poor Nate's. Even standing down the row from him, she could hear his off-key voice and she gave a quick shake of her head. At the end of the verse Evangeline glanced up when she heard Justice clear his throat, in time to see him smother an amused smile. She couldn't keep from responding with one of her own.

Dismissing such foolishness, she sang the alto line in the second stanza of "A Mighty Fortress Is Our God," and a tiny thrill wove its way through her heart. So often while growing up, they'd stood side by side in the church where their families had worshipped and harmonized as they now did, enjoying hymns of praise to the loving God they both believed in. The God Who dwelt among His children in this humble community church as surely as He did in the grand New Orleans cathedral. If only she could erase the past eleven years…

No. That would mean she wouldn't have her two precious children, whom she loved more than words could say. She must protect them at any cost, must protect all three of them from the strong, imposing lawman beside her, whose manly, orange-scented cologne made it difficult to concentrate on anything other than him.

Forcing such foolishness from her mind, she bowed her head and prayed, as she always did in church, for God to speak to her today. Then she settled back to enjoy the rest of the service.

After announcements, the offering and another hymn, Reverend Thomas began his sermon with Romans 13:8. "Paul tells us we should 'Owe no man anything…'"

Stuck on those words, Evangeline didn't hear the rest of the verse. Owe no man anything? And yet she owed thousands of dollars. Her guilt, compounded by the presence of the man beside her, routed out every good feeling she'd experienced that morning.

Justice always enjoyed the services in this homey little church, but today, Susanna's matchmaking caused him a great deal of discomfort. He couldn't avoid Evangeline's scent of gardenias, a fragrance he recalled from his early teen years when he'd plucked the snowy-white blossoms from his mother's bushes for the beautiful young girl he loved. When the two of them sang the familiar hymns, they fell into the natural harmonies they'd enjoyed so many years ago. Even their silent communication over poor Nate's legendary tone-deafness tugged on his heartstrings because he remembered the harmless laughter they'd shared as children over the foibles of being human. They'd never been cruel, only good-humored toward others, as youngsters tended to be when the future seemed bright and certain before them. Over the years, Justice often wondered how differently things might have turned out if he hadn't gone on his Grand Tour. Would his father have died so young after being swindled out of his money? Would Mr. LaPierre have given Justice permission to marry Evangeline instead of granting that privilege to Lucius Benoit? He'd never know.

The minister read from Romans 13:8, and Justice listened carefully, as his godly father taught him. "'Owe no man anything, but to love one another: for he that loveth another hath fulfilled the law.'" Father also taught him never to contradict the Word of God. But it was difficult with Evangeline seated next to him. How could he love her? Yes, he knew the verse referred to Christian love, not the romantic sort. And he knew the law to be fulfilled referred to the commandment Christ called the second most important, to love one's neighbor as oneself. Yet he would have a hard time being around Evangeline and loving her in Christ without thinking of the love they'd promised to one another so long ago. Thus, he should stay as far away from her as possible. Not easy when he'd be working on the Christmas village in the library's back room. And then he'd promised Nate to keep watch over Gerard. There was no way he could win in this situation.

After the final hymn, he nodded to his seatmates

and strode up the aisle, ignoring Susanna's call. She'd trapped him for the church service, but he wasn't about to get invited to dinner and have to spend Sunday afternoon in the same house as Evangeline.

He snagged his hat and winter jacket from the cloakroom and shook hands with the preacher before exiting into the churchyard. Nate's brother Tolley and his wife, Laurie, were walking toward their home three blocks away, so he caught up with them. Tolley carried their one-year-old son on his hip, and Laurie grasped his other arm.

"Nice day." Feeling more than a little foolish, Justice fell into step beside them.

"Yes, it is." Tolley looked at him expectantly.

Laurie, being the more perceptive of the two, elbowed her husband. "Sheriff, won't you come for dinner? We're having our usual pot roast and sure would enjoy your company."

"Sheriff." Susanna bustled after them, waving her hand in the air.

"Thank you, Laurie. I'd be pleased to accept." Relieved to have successfully escaped Susanna, Justice inhaled a deep breath of the fresh autumn air. *Safe. At least for today.*

"Sheriff, are you going deaf?" Susanna caught up with them and took a moment to chuck her young nephew under the chin. "Hello, sugar." She turned her attention back to Justice. "Don't you recall my inviting you to Sunday dinner?"

"Did you?" Justice recalled it well. He also recalled not exactly accepting. "I'm sorry, but Laurie here has invited me, too."

Susanna gave her sister-in-law one of those looks

women gave each other when they were put out. "Laurie, surely you knew I wanted him at my house today."

"Oh, dear." Laurie batted her dark red eyelashes. "Well…" She looked up at Justice.

"Tell you what," Tolley broke in. "He can eat with us today, and next week he can join all of us for our monthly gathering at the big house."

"That might work." Though he wanted to shake Tolley's hand in gratitude, Justice instead tipped his hat to Susanna. He'd probably be forced to attend next week, but at least he'd be among a larger group where he might be able to avoid Evangeline. "Thank you for thinking of me," he said to Susanna. "We poor bachelors depend on the kindness of our married friends to keep us fed."

She crossed her arms and tapped one foot on the hard-packed dirt road. "Very well. Next week, then. And I can count on you to keep an eye on Evangeline as she begins work at the library tomorrow?" Her expression held that private meaning she was so good at. Only a few people knew about the Christmas village, and this younger Northam couple was not among them.

"Yes, ma'am." He was sunk as surely as if he'd stepped into quicksand. He'd never be able to escape Susanna Northam's matchmaking. And now he couldn't avoid Evangeline, the woman who'd irreparably broken his heart and made him determined never to give it to another.

Early Monday morning, the little family waved goodbye to Nate as he rode off toward the hills to the south. While Wes, the trusted cowhand he'd left behind to tend chores, hitched up the buggy, Susanna and Evangeline prepared the children for school.

"Are you sure you don't want me to drive you into town?" Susanna finished washing the last breakfast dish and handed it to Lizzie to dry.

"I'd much rather you spend the time cutting out the children's new clothes so I can help you sew them this evening." Evangeline tugged on her leather driving gloves. After dropping off the children at school, she would be starting her first day as the town's new librarian.

"I'm sure you'll be glad to see a certain sheriff again." Susanna still hadn't let up on her matchmaking. She sniffed dramatically. "Your lovely gardenia perfume is sure to attract his attention. Why, it must have cost you a small fortune. Well worth it, I'd say."

"You know better than that. Don't you remember when our mothers taught us to make our own perfume one summer? It's much less expensive." She ignored her cousin's suggestion about wearing the perfume for Justice's sake. It was the fragrance she always wore, a reminder of the better parts of her old life, nothing more.

Their dinner pails packed with sandwiches and apples, the children donned their jackets and climbed into the buggy, all except two-year-old Frankie, who cried over being left behind with his mother.

The breeze blew brisk and chilly, but the sky was a rich blue shade. Evangeline gazed west across the San Luis Valley at the San Juan Mountains, then east to the Sangre de Cristo Range. If not for her fears of being dragged back to New Orleans, she could relax and enjoy this beautiful country.

"Let's sing." Isabelle didn't wait for agreement, but broke into "Boys and girls all sing this song, Hoo-rah, Hoo-rah. Girls grow pretty and boys grow strong. Oh, hoo-rah ray. Goin' to eat my peas, Goin' to eat my ham. Gonna eat biscuits with butter and jam. Oh, hoo-rah ray."

The others joined in, and Gerard and Natty tried to out "hoo-rah" each other in the silly folk song. They fell into giggles, bringing joy to Evangeline's heart. By the time they reached the one-story clapboard schoolhouse in town, they were making up their own verses, most of them nonsense.

She tied the lead rope to the hitching post and escorted the children inside. The school had three classes, two grades in each one. Natty and Isabelle scampered off to the first and second grade room, and Lizzie to her third and fourth grade room. Evangeline was left to escort Gerard to join the fifth and sixth graders. She recognized the teacher, Miss Prinn, from church, and the sturdy middle-aged woman welcomed Gerard.

"You may sit here." She indicated an empty seat in the second row.

All happy songs forgotten, Gerard looked around furtively, as though searching for a way to escape. The other children eyed him with friendly curiosity.

"He will be fine, Mrs. Benoit." Miss Prinn gave Evangeline a severe look, dismissing her.

"Yes, of course."

With a library to organize, she subdued her maternal worries and drove to the mercantile. There,

Mrs. Winsted helped her load four wooden boxes of books into the buggy.

"I'd send Homer over to help you, but he's unloading a new shipment of merchandise." The woman brushed gray hairs back from her face. "Can you manage?"

"Yes, thank you." At the least, she could carry a few books into the library at a time.

The short trip down the street and around the corner onto Center Avenue brought her to the library. Seeing the sign brought an unexpected thrill to her heart. She'd already planned how to organize the books.

After unlocking the door, she went to fetch the first box of books. She tried to lift it, but it proved too heavy. The wind whipped her lightweight skirt and petticoats around, adding a struggle for modesty to her concerns. Her black straw hat chose that moment to fly away, headed straight for the fountain.

"Oh, bother." Planning to give chase, she misjudged how far she'd slid the box off the back of the buggy and it teetered, spilling books onto the ground. Some fell open, and their pages fluttered wildly in the wind. She gasped. What a horrible way to begin her new job. Kneeling to check for damage, she shook grit from the precious tomes.

"Ma'am, I believe this is yours." Justice stood tall above her and handed her the wayward hat.

Her heart seemed to stop beating. Yet still she lived. "Thank you." She clutched the hat in one hand and continued picking up books with the other.

"Let me help you." He didn't wait for an answer

but knelt and joined her efforts. "You go on inside. I'll bring them in."

"Well—"

Again, he didn't wait for her, but stood and grasped her elbow, then gently pulled her to her feet. "Permit me to assist you, Mrs. Benoit." His formal address and tone did little to comfort her, and he looked down at her with a courteous but uninterested expression.

"Thank you." She grabbed her small dinner hamper and a pail of cleaning supplies and hurried inside the building. After setting the basket on her desk, she rubbed her arm where he'd touched her. Such a firm grip. And yet, what should have been a reassuring gesture only made her nervous. Surely no criminal could escape his grasp.

As she propped the door open so he could enter at will, she noticed how easily he lifted the first heavy box and gave herself permission to admire his strength. After all, she supposed a sheriff should be strong.

Such admiring ruminations would not get her work done, so she turned her attention to the shelves. If she organized the books as planned, they'd fill less than a fourth of the dark-stained pine planks. Too bad she must keep her location a secret or she might consider writing to potential benefactors for donations. In the meantime, she already knew she wanted her desk closer to the window so she could catch all possible daylight.

She shoved the heavy oak desk, or rather, shoved at it. The beautifully carved monstrosity refused to budge.

"I'll do that as soon as I bring in the last box." Justice set his load down and returned to the buggy for another.

The final remnants of the happy energy that had infused her earlier disappeared. She'd be foolish to turn down his help, but from his frown, she could see he disliked this forced contact as much as she did. Of course he would be a gentleman and help her. Yet his distant, austere demeanor was very different from the laughing, fun-loving manner of the young man with whom she'd grown up.

"That does it." He set the last box on a table beside the others and removed his hat and jacket. "I'll send Adam Starling over to take your horse and buggy to the livery stable. Can't have the little mare standing outside the library all day."

"Oh. Of course." Evangeline never considered such a thing. Servants had always taken care of the horses and conveyances for her. Then, after losing everything, she'd walked wherever she needed to go.

"Where do you want the desk?" Justice glanced about the room.

"About two feet from the front window."

"You sure?"

Suddenly annoyed by this uncomfortable meeting, she snapped, "If you don't approve, put it wherever you think is best." Shame filled her. She had no reason to be snippy, especially since he was being helpful.

He huffed out a sigh. "As the winter wears on, it gets mighty cold sitting so close to a window. You'd be better off doing your work closer to the stove."

"Oh—"

"Here." He took her by the hand. "Step over to the window and feel the glass."

His gentle touch sent shivers up her arm and down her back. He didn't seem to notice her response, but tugged her to the window and placed her hand on the glass. Even through her gloves, she could feel the cold.

"Oh, my. Not the best place to sit."

"Yep." He dropped her hand as though he realized how tightly he'd been holding it. Or maybe that he'd been holding it at all.

She decided to rescue them both. "Well, then, I'll take your advice. Can you move the desk by yourself? Or will you need help?"

He cast an amused glance her way. Then, with the strength of the biblical Samson, he easily shoved the heavy desk across the wooden floor without so much as taking an extra breath. "This all right?"

"Fine." Did her voice actually squeak? Oh, my. Justice might not have required a deep breath after moving the desk, but she needed one after being so close to his imposing presence.

He gazed down at her for a moment, and she stared up at him, unmoving.

"Where do you want the tables?" An odd softness flickered in his eyes.

"Um, well." She broke the visual contact and stared blindly around the room. "They're fine."

"Fine," he repeated. Even so, he began to move the tables and chairs into a more sensible configuration. "What do you think?"

"Fine." She couldn't think of a different word. "Thank you."

"You're welcome." He gave a firm nod before glancing at the door in the back wall. "You want to see the village?"

"Oh, yes." How could she be standing here talking with Justice Gareau as though eleven years didn't stand between this moment and all the good times they'd enjoyed so long ago?

Justice broke the mood by stepping over to the back door and pulling a key from his pocket. "We have to keep it locked so the youngsters won't get nosy."

"That makes sense." She followed him into the dark chamber.

After he lit the kerosene lantern on a table, the room filled with light, revealing a rough but exquisite array of four-by-five-inch buildings. Although unpainted, each had a clear identity. A church, numerous houses, a livery stable and more. He'd carved people, horses, trees, all with remarkable detail.

"They're beautiful, Justice." Again she looked up into his once-beloved face. "You're truly a gifted wood carver. I know the children will love their little village. I'll be happy to help in any way you need."

His eyes displayed a pleased expression. "I've been thinking about it. Could you paint everything?"

"I'd love to."

"Good." He ushered her toward the door. "I have some rounds to do this morning. I usually work on the village in the afternoon while my deputy is on duty at the office."

"Oh. Very well. But first, please sit down and have some coffee." Other than her sandwich, she had only Susanna's cookies and some cold coffee to offer, but her Southern manners demanded some form of gratitude for his help.

He grimaced and huffed out a sigh of obvious resignation. He sat at the table across from her desk.

They partook of the refreshments in silence until Evangeline's sense of etiquette took over. One simply did not sit quietly under these circumstances. She considered several topics of conversation. As unwise as it might be, she could think only of one.

"I've often wondered about your Grand Tour. Did you enjoy it?"

His deeply tanned face turned pale around the edges, and his lips formed a grim line.

Oh, yes, indeed. That was the wrong question to ask.

Stricken more than he wanted to admit, Justice could only stare at Evangeline, dumbfounded. Why would she ask about an event of so long ago, a trip he could barely remember because of the horrible home situation to which he returned? From the way her dark blond eyelashes fluttered, he could see she regretted asking about it.

"I'm so sorry." Her blue eyes filled with tears. "I shouldn't have—"

He waved a hand dismissively. "I suppose if we're going to live in the same community, we should address the past and, well, get past it."

She nodded and gave him a wobbly smile. "I suppose."

He swiped a hand down one cheek before remembering the informal gesture wasn't appropriate for a gentleman visiting with a lady. But then, so many of the elegant manners he'd been taught by his gentlemanly father had gone by the wayside as he'd adapted to the less formal West.

"Paris was beautiful. Rome was educational. Venice was breathtaking. London interesting, especially St. Paul's Cathedral and Westminster Abbey." In his own ears, he sounded like an uninspired tour guide, but she nodded politely as he spoke. Manners dictated it was his turn to try a polite inquiry. "Did you go to Europe after your marriage?" Somehow he managed not to choke on the words.

"N-no." She looked away, perhaps to hide the odd hurt in her eyes.

He should press her for details. Should ask why Lucius Benoit hadn't taken his beautiful young bride abroad to show her off. Instead, he cleared his throat. "I'd better go. I'm late to finish my rounds." He stood and picked up his hat and jacket.

"Yes, of course." She rose gracefully from her chair. "Thank you so much for your help."

She reached out to him, and he took her small hand in his larger one. Against all that was sane, he bent to brush a well-mannered kiss across her fingers. A tremor shot from his lips to his neck and down his back. Then he caught a whiff of her expensive gardenia perfume, saw her exquisitely styled widow's weeds and recalled she'd chosen to become a wealthy man's wife so she could have a lifetime of such luxuries. The memory cut like a knife through his chest. By the time he straightened, he'd managed to paste on his no-nonsense lawman face.

"I'll be back later to work on the village." He donned his hat and walked toward the door on wooden legs. Despite her betrayal, this woman still had a strong effect on him.

"Thank you." She closed the door behind him.

As he strode toward Main Street, a glance over his shoulder revealed she continued to watch him through one of the front windows. Oddly, it pleased him. He'd have to get over it, and fast.

Chapter Four

When Justice glanced back at her, Evangeline resisted the urge to step away from the window. She'd been caught, plain and simple. But then, he'd looked back and seemed to smile, so she'd caught him, too. Maybe it wasn't a smile, but a grimace over her ill-advised question about his European travels. Or maybe, like her, he was discombobulated over their strange situation. Did he also wonder why the Lord brought them together in this remote town? Instinctively, she lifted a hand to wave at him, but he'd already resumed his purposeful stride toward Main Street. Soon he was around the corner and out of sight.

She sighed. *My, he cuts a fine figure and—*

"Of all things, Evangeline. Stop it."

Mortified by her thoughts, she could only be thankful no one caught her admiring a man only a year after her husband died, especially since she'd never admired Lucius. From the moment he'd entered her mother's drawing room all those years ago and Evangeline had been forced to endure his inappropriate gazes, she'd felt queasy every time he'd come calling. After Mama died and Papa declared Evangeline must marry his new business partner, her life had been a torment. No matter how much she begged Papa to let her wait for Justice to return to New Orleans, he'd waved off her pleas, at last confining her to her room with no way to escape. Even the servants who'd known her since childhood refused to help her escape for fear of Papa's wrath. Certain of Justice's love, she'd prayed he would rescue her, but alas he never came.

She truly must stop such ruminations on the past. She had a library to organize.

She found the cleaning supplies Susanna sent with her and pulled out a dust cloth for the shelves and a feather duster for the books. It had taken only a weekend for her to realize that dusting was an ongoing chore in the San Luis Valley. Wind swept over the landscape almost every day, leaving fine grit on every surface. She must find a way to seal the windows to keep some of it out.

After she'd cleaned the shelves and swept the floor, she sorted through the books, placing them around the room according to type. She didn't find many children's books, but each one looked delightful; Mother Goose and Brothers Grimm, *Heidi*, *Five Little Peppers and How They Grew*, *Treasure Island*, *Hans Brinker or the Silver Skates*, along with several others. And of course *McGuffey Readers*. She imagined the children would get enough of those at school, but she still placed them on a lower shelf so smaller children could reach them.

As she shelved the books, she put two to the

side—*Rio Grande Sheriff* and *She Wore a Six-Gun*, both by A Cowboy Storyteller, whoever that might be. Those she set on her desk to read, hoping they would help her understand how people in the West lived.

Shortly after Justice left, the young groom, Adam Starling, came for the horse and buggy. He entered the library and removed his hat before introducing himself. Then he cast a longing look at the books.

"Do you like to read?" Evangeline noticed his shabby but clean clothes.

"Yes, ma'am." He touched the spine of Volume I of Edward Gibbon's *The History of the Decline and Fall of the Roman Empire*, which sat on an upper shelf. "Once you open, I'll be one of your first patrons." He looked at the children's bookshelf. "I'll bring my younger brother and sisters, too. They like to read, too."

As Adam drove her buggy away, Evangeline's heart went out to him. Obviously poor, the young man was well-spoken and hungered for knowledge. She could guide him, perhaps even help him improve his lot in life. Her growing sense of purpose filled her with excitement. More than a job, this was a true calling.

With so much work at hand, she found the morning passed quickly. When she began to feel some of the altitude dizziness Doc Henshaw mentioned, she sat at her desk to eat her sandwich. She hadn't finished her second bite when Justice thrust open the door, his large frame filling the doorway. With sunlight behind him, she couldn't see his face clearly, but from the hunch of his shoulders, his displeasure was evident. Evangeline's heart leaped to her throat, and she barely managed to swallow the bite in her mouth. Had he learned of her debts? Was he here to arrest her?

Trembling, she rose to face him as he strode toward her.

"Mrs. Benoit, you need to get your son under control, or he's going to be expelled from school before his first week is out."

She dropped back into her chair with relief. But the scowl on Justice's face as he approached her desk brought her up short.

"Wh-what did he do?" Surely it couldn't be too bad.

His visage shadowed by the broad-brimmed hat he hadn't removed, Justice sat on the corner of her desk and leaned over her. "When Miss Prinn's class was outside at recess, he and two other boys sneaked back inside and emptied the contents of her inkwell over the papers on her desk."

Still flushed with relief that he hadn't come about her debts, she waved a hand carelessly. She couldn't help but compare her son's misdeeds to her own. "Is that all?"

"Is that all?" Justice's eyes blazed, and he stood and fisted his hands at his waist. "The papers were essays the children wrote this morning. Now they're illegible."

Feeling flustered, she stammered, "B-but surely they can rewrite them."

Justice huffed out a cross breath. "It was a test essay. The children had done their best work only to see it destroyed."

"Well…but…" Suddenly she turned cross. She stood and returned his glare. "Who are these boys who dragged my son into this? Or maybe they did it all themselves and put the blame on the new boy in class."

His eyes didn't so much as flicker. "Gerard was rather proud of his leadership in the gang."

"Gang? Little boys involved in mischief?"

"Little boys? Mischief?" Justice snorted in a decidedly ungentlemanly way. "It's hardly mischief when it's that destructive. Miss Prinn tried to clean up the mess, and the ink stained her white shirtwaist. I suppose you have an answer for that."

Evangeline opened her mouth to speak, but Justice held up his hand to stop her. "Do you have any idea how much, or should I say, how *little* a school-teacher is paid? Miss Prinn can't afford to buy new clothes anytime she wants, unlike some people." He eyed her dress.

Shame overshadowed Evangeline's indignation. He seemed to assume she had plenty of money and could buy new clothes whenever she wished, probably because he'd seen her buying fabric at Winsted's on Saturday. The least she could do was make the teacher a new blouse with the material she'd bought for herself. "I'll see that Miss Prinn's shirtwaist is replaced."

Justice crossed his arms over his broad chest. "What are you going to do about your son?"

Evangeline met his gray-eyed glare with one of her own. "I will speak to Gerard."

He snorted again. "You do that. In the meantime, he'll have to stay after school the rest of this week to clean the blackboards and erasers and sweep the classroom."

"And the other boys?"

He'd turned toward the door and now stopped midstride. "You leave them to me," he said as he exited the building.

This time, she didn't bother to watch him. Instead, she sat there wondering whether she should remove Gerard from school and teach him herself.

Justice hated the days when he didn't finish his rounds before noon because it caused a disturbance in his well-ordered world. Sometimes it took days to restore balance. Today, his extended stop at the school and subsequent return to the library meant he still needed to check in with several businesses. He also needed to visit his new house being built next door to Tolley and Laurie Northam's.

After speaking with Mayor Edgar Jones at his barber shop, Justice walked a few yards away to Mrs. Winsted's mercantile, where he observed the workmen installing the new front window.

"Keep up the good work, men." It never hurt to remind these workers Mrs. Winsted had someone watching out for her. Justice felt a responsibility to see she was treated right, as he did for all widows with no man to protect them.

Does that include Evangeline?

He huffed out a harsh breath. Evangeline had her cousin-in-law Nate Northam to look out for her once he returned from his roundup.

Justice made a stop at Miss Pam's café to purchase

a ham sandwich and then headed over to his property, consuming the food as he walked.

Oddly, for the first time in many years, he recalled how his mother would have been appalled by his lack of manners. Not only had he failed to sit down at a proper table to eat, but he'd failed to remove his hat at the library. Nothing warranted such ill-mannered neglect, not even Evangeline's ridiculous defense of her troublesome boy. She was still a lady. Justice was still a gentleman. Years of living in the less formal West shouldn't change him for the worse. Even amid tragedy and loss, Father never lost faith or failed to treat others with respect. Nor had Justice's Texas Ranger mentor, Jubal Tucker. He needed to remember these godly examples and try to emulate them, no matter what was happening around him. Or to him.

An unexpected, unwanted thread of admiration for Evangeline wove through him. She'd stood up to him like a mama bear defending her cubs. Because of his size and profession, not many people in Esperanza would have likewise faced him. But then, she'd known him in his softer days, back when life was filled with hope and promise. She probably thought she could wind him around her little finger as she had back then. Too bad she'd chosen to marry another man. Despite admiring her courage, he'd never let her bend him to her will again.

As for Gerard, well, the apple didn't fall far from the tree. He was turning out to be every inch his crooked father's son. As Justice feared, the boy had already fallen in with those troublemakers Deely and Cart. Justice had warned all three boys they'd face dire consequences if they disrupted the class again or destroyed any more property.

After leaving the school, he'd considered visiting Reverend Thomas for advice on how to deal with the boys. But the minister was a bit too perceptive. He might ask questions about Evangeline that Justice wouldn't want to answer. The only way to get past the hurt of her reappearance in his life was to keep all the pain inside.

As always when he approached his house, satisfaction flooded his chest...until unbidden dreams of coming home to Evangeline resurfaced from his youth. Perhaps it would be nice to have a beautiful, loving wife waiting for him at the end of the day. No. He must dismiss all such disturbing thoughts. He'd never let her hurt him again, not her nor any other woman. With what self-control he could muster, he banished the vision and focused again on the house.

The east-facing, two-story structure boasted a covered porch that crossed the front and wrapped around to the south side. The architect had talked Justice into much more house than he'd ever need, saying it must match the other fine houses on the street. He'd been comfortable enough living in the two rooms over the jail this past year, so he didn't feel the need for more living space. However, for his neighbors' sakes, he'd agreed. With his mine up near Creede continuing to produce, he could certainly afford it. Besides, now used to the idea, he liked the house more each day.

The builders had laid the foundation early last spring and recently finished the red brick exterior. Now they perched on the roof nailing shingles in place. Justice climbed the three steps to the front porch and entered the portal where the door would soon hang. The interior showed progress as well. Rising from the center of the wide entryway to the second story, the curved staircase would soon have mahogany bannisters and turned spindles. Finished oak floors awaited polishing. Walls were framed in, and in most rooms, lath strips were nailed in place, ready for plastering. Justice still hadn't decided whether to have the walls painted or papered.

What would Evangeline like?

Not that he should care. In fact, he needed to stop these annoying thoughts. After she'd been in town for a while, he'd get used to her presence and his hard-won self-control would return.

Except he had to work in the library's back room every afternoon, where he'd hear her musical voice as she spoke to patrons, smell her expensive garde-nia perfume filling the air around her, see her still breathtakingly beautiful face…and dream of what might have been.

Tumbleweed! The mild interjection Jubal taught him came to mind. He must not let these maudlin thoughts about Evangeline take root. Dreams never got a man anyplace. Action did. If she and her trou-blesome son were going to live in this community, Justice could either move someplace else or learn to deal with them.

He remembered she was skilled at drawing and painting, so she'd be a big help with his Christmas village. While he could create the tiny buildings, he didn't have as much confidence in his ability to paint them with a steady hand. The attention to detail had attracted him to the displays in Europe, and the children of Esperanza deserved no less than the finest village Justice could put together.

Only thing to do was swallow his pride and ask if she still wanted to help. Or was willing to help. Or—

"Anything need changin', boss?" The building foreman interrupted Justice's thoughts.

"Nope. Everything's looking mighty fine, Joe. Keep up the good work."

He left the men to their labors and headed back to the center of town. His deputy now tended the office, so he headed toward the library. Contrary to what he'd told Joe, something did need changing: his attitude toward Evangeline and her children. And he needed to start right now.

After some consideration, Evangeline decided not to remove Gerard from school. No matter what the other boys had influenced him to do, he must accept his punishment. He must learn to be a leader, not a follower. As for poor Miss Prinn and her ruined shirtwaist, Evangeline must begin work on a new one this evening.

And she would visit the school and take a book to read to the class while Miss Prinn ate her dinner. She'd read *Treasure Island* to them, perhaps organize a treasure hunt. No, Long John Silver's antics might inspire pirate-like misdeeds. She sighed. Best to stick with *Hans Brinker*.

All such thoughts ceased when Justice entered the library, this time with a considerably less hostile posture than before. He even removed his hat and hung it on the hat stand. Still, she stiffened, wondering whether he would continue his criticism of Gerard.

"Afternoon, Evangeline." He ambled past her desk, pulled a key from his pocket and unlocked the door to the back room.

Afternoon, Evangeline? So casually spoken as though they hadn't parted a mere hour ago with a decidedly hostile air hanging between them? Well, two could play that game.

"Good afternoon, Justice." She kept her tone only a degree above frosty as she focused on the list on her desk, determined not to give him any further attention. After all, she had work to do. She must make a list of all the books entrusted to her care, along with the authors' names, publishing information and brief descriptions of the contents. Marybeth Northam offered to borrow the typewriting machine at the bank where she used to work, and make a neat reference card for each book. She would also make cards for borrowers to sign when they wanted to take a book home.

"Got a minute?" Justice leaned against the doorjamb. Although he wasn't smiling, his expression appeared almost friendly.

Evangeline's heart skipped. Why did he have to be so handsome? She tamped down her emotions and embraced the austere persona of her boarding school headmistress. "Of course." She rested her pen on the inkwell and followed him into the storage room, leaving the door open for propriety's sake.

At the back of the deep, narrow room, the solid exterior door was bolted from within. Small windows high on the north and south walls provided a minimum of light. Justice lit a kerosene lamp, which provided enough additional illumination for the work to be done.

As she had when she saw the tiny carvings earlier, Evangeline marveled at the detail Justice included. The houses, businesses and church weren't solid blocks. Each roofed structure had four individual walls and a hinged door. Carved lines on the exterior gave the appearance of unpainted clapboard siding. For the church, tiny colored glass squares gave the illusion of stained glass windows like those in the cathedral back home.

"I can take the windows out if it will make it easier for you to paint." In spite of his words, Justice's eyes held a question, as though he wasn't sure she still intended to help.

"Please do." She gently lifted an evergreen tree. "Oh, my. I can see the pine needles. Carving such fine detail must be challenging. It looks exactly like a tree."

His expression lightened with a hint of boyish pride in his work. "Needs a coat of paint."

"Yes." She mustn't keep him wondering about her helping. "The paints?"

He gave her an almost-smile and indicated a shelf against the wall, where paints and brushes stood ready for use. "There's everything you need."

"Ah." She perused the assembled supplies. "You really did get everything."

"You can thank Susanna for that." He settled on a stool beside the workbench, picked up a carving knife and a piece of wood and began to cut.

"Was the village Susanna's idea?"

Now bent over his work, he shrugged. "It was a group plan." The hint of red coloring his ears betrayed him.

"It was your idea."

He shrugged again, this time adding a little smile as though pleased she'd uncovered the truth.

"How clever, Justice. And so thoughtful to do something like this for the children." *Especially since you have none of your own.* The thought made her heart ache. Despite her wretched marriage, the Lord had blessed her with two precious children.

"It's not something I came up with on my own." He cleared his throat. "I saw villages like this one in Germany the Christmas I spent in Europe." A frown replaced his smile, and he hunched over the bench as though finished with the conversation.

She longed to touch his shoulder, to give it a reassuring squeeze as she did Gerard's or Isabelle's when they needed encouragement. But this was no child, however boyish his eagerness to please the children of Esperanza. This was the man who could arrest her and send her back to her debtors if she couldn't convince him she intended to pay back her actual debts, if she couldn't prove at least some of those debts were not her responsibility. Instead of reaching out to him, she sorted through the painting supplies and planned which colors to use on each figure. Her decision made, she addressed Justice's hunched back.

"I should get back to my own work. Once the library is organized, I'll begin painting."

After a long pause, he said, "Yep."

First hot, then cold. Oh, how she ached to know what this once familiar, but now mysterious man was thinking. Yet if she drew him out to confide in her, he might turn the tables and persuade her to tell her own secrets. Which could only lead to her destruction.

Once Evangeline left the room, Justice set down his carving tool and flexed his hands to stop their shaking. It wouldn't do to ruin this prime piece of apple wood from the stock he'd ordered from a company back East.

What was wrong with him? He'd often faced outlaws with a steady hand on his gun and a stern expression on his face. Even the admirable Northam brothers praised his cool head in dealing with troublemakers. And yet Evangeline's presence sent him into spasms of uncertainty.

He hadn't meant to bring up his trip to Europe. The tour itself had indeed been grand, but coming home to family tragedies had put an end to both his happiness and his youthful innocence. Although bitterness over his losses diminished over the years, he rarely mentioned his Grand Tour to anyone. Last spring, when Susanna had noticed his carving skill, he'd told her about the toy villages he'd seen in Germany, and between the two of them, they'd come up with the idea for the Christmas village. Other than her, only Evangeline knew about it, and she was the last person he'd ever discuss it with, because then they'd have to discuss what happened when he returned. And yet, in her presence, he felt vulnerable, and even his sternest admonitions to himself produced no defenses for his heart.

Now he must work side by side with her on this project. While his unforgetting mind kept returning to the pain she'd caused him, his traitorous heart felt a curious sort of well-being he refused to examine. One thing was sure. The war raging within him chased away all peace.

Yes, he needed help to finish the village before Christmas. But why couldn't Susanna have enlisted someone else to assist him?

Chapter Five

On Tuesday, without telling anyone her plan, Evangeline ate her sandwich early and then walked to the school with *Hans Brinker* in hand. She arrived at the white clapboard building with her thoughts wavering between confidence in her new project and concern over whether Miss Prinn would reject her idea out of hand. She reached for the schoolhouse door only to have it open inward with a whoosh and reveal an unexpected sight. Justice stood there, his imposing presence seeming even taller because of the threshold's three-inch elevation.

"Justice!" With a gasp, she stepped back, and her foot slipped down to the lower tread, throwing her off balance. "Eeep!" She grasped for a nonexistent bannister, one hand grabbing air, the other clutching the book as if it could save her.

"Whoa." He clasped her flailing hand and pulled her up, rescuing her from a painful tumble. He then gripped her upper arms to steady her. "Are you all right?" Concern filled those probing gray eyes, making him more like the young man she once knew than a threatening lawman.

Shivers running down her arms and pulse racing, she struggled to breathe normally, but instead gasped in air. Heat rushed from her neck up to her cheeks. "Thank you."

"Altitude still bothering you?" His sympathetic look and question offered an excuse for her lack of breath. She didn't have to tell him it was really her reaction to him.

She nodded. "No doubt."

He glanced at the book. "Planning to learn how to ice skate?"

Still struggling to calm down, she emitted a girlish giggle. "Not at all. I'd be as graceful at skating as I was just now." Wanting to prolong this moment of camaraderie, she gave him a little smirk. "Living in this cold climate, I suppose you skate?"

"More or less." He chuckled, a deep, throaty sound, and her pulse raced again. "I've been working on it for a few years. The Wakefields flood an area behind the hotel and freeze it. Come December, the rink's a favorite gathering place for the community. Everyone's welcome."

"How lovely. I know Gerard and Isabelle will enjoy learning to skate."

At the mention of her son's name, Justice's "sheriff face," as she'd come to think of it, returned. Evangeline's heart fell to her stomach.

"I looked in on Miss Prinn's class," he said. "So far today, Gerard and his friends have put a snake down another boy's shirt and blown spit wads at the other students...and their teacher." He crossed his arms over his chest. "That's worth another week of detention. Miss Prinn says their disruptions are making it hard for the serious students to learn. If they don't settle down, we're looking at suspension." His stare bored into her accusingly. Or so it seemed.

Sighing, Evangeline looked away. "I'm sure if Miss Prinn could get to know Gerard, she'd see he does want to learn." She held up her book. "I thought I'd offer to read to the class while she eats her dinner."

His eyebrows rose in surprise. After a moment, he uncrossed his arms and lowered his hands. "You do that." He proceeded down the schoolhouse's four steps, then turned back. "I'll be at the library around one o'clock."

"Yes." She hurried inside the schoolhouse, where she took a minute to reorder her emotions. Those few precious moments of polite conversation felt so good, only to be shattered by harsh reality.

Why couldn't Justice give Gerard the opportunity to prove himself? Was it because of his close resemblance to Lucius? Her son couldn't help inheriting his father's face. In truth, Lucius had been quite handsome in his day, although by the time they married, his dissolute lifestyle had diminished his aristocratic appearance. But Justice wasn't being fair to punish the son because he resembled his father.

She could well imagine he thought ill of Lucius. Her husband had made many enemies over the years, but she knew few specifics. Neither Papa nor Lucius had ever said much to her about their business partnership. She only knew Justice's father had also been a partner and Mr. Gareau's personal finances had failed shortly before he died. Then Papa and Lucius had worked together to save the business Mr. Gareau damaged. Although it seemed unlike the godly man she'd known all her life, Evangeline often wondered whether Justice's father had embezzled money from the other two. Lucius had certainly never said anything good about him.

Her thoughts stalled. Were her memories correct? Or had Lucius poisoned her thinking? Since he was dead and Papa had died six years ago, perhaps she'd never know the truth about Mr. Gareau *or* Lucius. But Justice had no cause to blame Gerard for anything her husband might have done.

She shook herself. Standing in this hallway ruminating on the past wouldn't help her son. She walked to the classroom and peered through the window in the door. Gerard was seated with his hands folded politely on his desk, his full attention on Miss Prinn, who was writing on the blackboard. Two tiny white balls of paper clung to the bun at the back of her head. The boy next to Gerard nudged him, and with a mischievous look they both threw more wads of paper at their teacher.

Not bothering to knock, Evangeline opened the door, her eyes on her son's. Gerard dropped his hand and slumped in his seat, returning a scowl.

"Good morning, Miss Prinn. I do hope you'll excuse me, but may I speak to you for a moment?"

The startled lady recovered quickly and addressed her students. "Write your answers to these arithmetic problems on your slates. Be sure to show your work." She joined Evangeline in the hallway. "What can I do for you, Mrs. Benoit?" Her disapproving frown proclaimed her displeasure over the interruption.

"I thought perhaps I could read to the children while they eat dinner." She held up her book. "Then you could have a few minutes to yourself."

The lady blinked, and her jaw dropped slightly. "Why, that would be lovely. As soon as the children finish their arithmetic, I will take up their slates and grade them while you read."

Not what Evangeline expected. "Wouldn't you prefer to go outside and enjoy this lovely day?"

Miss Prinn looked through the window into the classroom. Before she turned back, Evangeline snatched the two spit wads from her thin, graying hair and slipped them into her pocket. What a cruel thing to do. Somehow she'd failed to teach her son to respect his elders.

"Very well." The teacher led the way back into the room. "Class, we have a surprise for you. Our new town librarian, Mrs. Benoit, will be reading to you while you eat your dinner."

Exclamations of delight were mixed with a few groans, one of which probably came from Gerard. Evangeline smiled at her son, but his attention was on the boy beside him, who was rolling his eyes.

"Write your names on your slates and pass them in." Miss Prinn stood at the head of the first row to collect them. "Be careful not to smudge your work." After she stacked the slates on her desk, she gave Evangeline a tight smile. "I shall return in a half hour." She picked up her satchel and left the room.

With some twenty-five pairs of eyes now focused on her, Evangeline experienced a moment of unease.

Then she remembered that while she and Lucius were still in society's favor, she'd conducted meetings of the ladies' aid alliance. This couldn't be too much more difficult.

"You may fetch your dinner pails—" she waved a hand toward the shelves on the inner wall "—but go quietly and then quickly return to your seats."

The children lined up politely to obey. Only Gerard and two other boys started to push ahead of the others. Evangeline snatched up a wooden ruler and slapped it on the desktop. The loud snap caused every child to stop and look her way.

She leveled her gaze on her son. "I would not wish to use this on rude children."

Of course she'd never strike a child, but they didn't know that. Wide-eyed stares met her. Even Gerard's face, tanned from the sun, grew white around the edges.

Back in their seats, the children opened their pails and Evangeline began to read.

"'On a bright December morning long ago, two thinly clad children were kneeling upon the bank of a frozen canal in Holland.'" The children seemed as caught up in the story as she was, except for Gerard. He nudged the boy next to him and glared. Then the child took on a scowl to mirror her son's. No doubt Gerard was embarrassed to have his mother conducting class. Yet the further she read, the more she could see the Lord had directed her to this particular story. The young boy, Hans, was poor but heroic, a good example for children. If she could persuade Gerard and his friends to emulate this fictional lad, she could consider this endeavor a success.

* * *

By Friday of that week, work on the Christmas village had progressed significantly due to Evangeline's help. Seated at his bench, Justice shaved away the last nub from the tiny wall and slid it into place, creating the last of the stalls for the livery stable. Still, he wouldn't glue any of the pieces into place until they were painted. From the corner of his eye, he watched Evangeline dip the small brush into the bottle of green paint and then dab it on the tree he'd made. She seemed to immerse herself in the task.

She probably didn't realize she was humming as she worked. Yesterday he'd caught himself humming along with her. Despite his determination not to care for her, he did give himself permission to admire her artistic talent and her eagerness to help with the toy village. Yet as they spent these hours every day working side by side, his resolve began to slip. No more humming. Instead, he'd use the natural wedge between them to maintain his distance.

"You probably know Miss Prinn moved the boys so they're not seated together anymore." Justice sharpened his blade on his whetstone, then picked up an uncompleted piece to work on. "She says most of their mischief stays on the schoolyard during recess. So far they haven't done anything too destructive."

"Yes, I know. And Miss Prinn invited me to come back to read to the class anytime." She smirked. "Gerard has no idea when I'll show up, so I think he's decided to behave himself."

"At least in the classroom."

She set the painted tree on the drying stand and swished the brush in the jar of turpentine, causing its pungent odor to mix with her ever-present gardenia fragrance. "That will have to do for today. I need to finish my list of novels so Marybeth can typewrite the reference cards for them." She cleaned her hands on a cotton cloth and rose from her chair.

"Novels first? Why not the history or science books?" He should have let her go, but against all reason, he didn't want their time together to end.

She lifted one shoulder in a ladylike shrug. "I think most people read for diversion from their daily lives, so, yes, the novels come first. Reading uplifting stories is a harmless escape and may even inspire a person to better things."

He grunted. Escape? That explained why she couldn't face the reality of her son's bad behavior.

As she moved toward the door, her elegant bearing stirred his reluctant admiration. Evangeline had grown more beautiful and graceful with time, and he couldn't take his eyes from her. Too bad she turned and caught him staring. She gave him a questioning look, then a smile.

"I'll have the library open by Thanksgiving. Then I'll have less time to work on the village with people coming and going."

Justice cleared his throat. "I'm sure Susanna and the other ladies of the library board will be pleased." He forced his gaze back to the wood in his hand. As she moved beyond the doorway and out of his sight, he exhaled a long sigh. Before she came to town, he knew who he was, knew what he wanted. He'd honed his reputation as a tough, no-nonsense lawman. Good people respected him, counted on him. Troublemakers feared him and stayed out of his town. Then, in one single week, Evangeline turned his world upside down. He hardly knew himself anymore. But at least now he had until Monday afternoon before he'd have to endure the torture of her presence again. Maybe he could reclaim his former self by then. Of course he'd see her in church on Sunday, but with careful planning, he could avoid Susanna's manipulations and sit on the other side of the sanctuary. Knowing Nate's wife, however, he could only hope to succeed.

Saturday dawned, and Gerard roused his sister and cousins for the anticipated excursion. They dressed and played quietly in the parlor awaiting breakfast. Evangeline, who still found the kitchen workings a mystery, stumbled through helping Susanna get the food on the table. While she could break and scramble the eggs, her one attempt at making biscuits had produced hard, thoroughly inedible round pellets.

"Children, time for breakfast," dainty Susanna called out rather piercingly. "Be sure you're washed up."

Evangeline hid a smile. When she and her cousin were growing up, they were taught never to raise their voices. At mealtimes, a buffet breakfast was served in the morning room, and a butler quietly announced when dinner and supper were served. She supposed Susanna needed to use a piercing tone to break through the children's noisy chatter in the other room. In any event, it worked. The five youngsters scrambled to take their places around the kitchen table. As before, Natty and Frankie looked to Gerard for their example, and they all giggled over his elaborate way of shaking out his napkin and tucking it into his shirt collar.

"Humph." Looking like a miniature of her mother, Lizzie daintily unfolded her napkin and laid it across her lap, with Isabelle following suit. Then they all giggled again.

This moment of playfulness warmed Evangeline's heart. Gerard was a good boy. Somehow she must prove it to Justice.

But why did she care what Justice thought? Although he was pleasant enough to work beside at the library—enjoyable actually—his changing demeanor at the mention of her son could not be overlooked. Given time, if he was as fair as Susanna seemed to think he was, he'd see Gerard had the best of intentions. But Susanna never missed an opportunity to praise Justice or to bring his name into the conversation, no matter what the topic, so Evangeline didn't dare tell her about his unreasonable dislike of her son. She'd probably say Evangeline was misreading him.

After breakfast, they all took the buggy to Marybeth and Rand's ranch house down the road. In the barnyard, they were greeted by Seamus O'Brien, Marybeth's brother, the ranch foreman who was keeping watch on her while Rand was away, and little Randy, who held his uncle's hand. With the family connections being so close, all of the children called the Northam foreman Uncle Seamus.

"Is Marybeth ready for us?" Susanna asked.

"Yes, ma'am. She's inside baking up something fine, you can be sure." Seamus's Irish accent colored his western slang. "If the boys'd like to help me with the chores, I'd be glad to have 'em." He nodded to Gerard and Natty.

"Yes, of course." Susanna lifted little Frankie onto her hip. The two-year-old stuck his thumb in his mouth and stared longingly after his brother and cousin. "We'll go inside and help Marybeth."

"Have fun." Evangeline gave Gerard a stern look intended as a warning, but he'd already headed toward the barn where the new foal resided. Surely his love for horses would keep him out of mischief.

Seeing Isabelle take to baking with enthusiasm, Evangeline could forget her worries for a while and watch her daughter learn to become a good cook. She herself stuck to helpful tasks such as washing and drying the used bowls and utensils. With help from the girls, she also made sandwiches. When the meal was ready, Isabelle asked to ring the dinner bell hanging from the back porch. Evangeline lifted her so she could reach the triangular chime with the iron ringer. The clang rang out across the property, and in seconds, Seamus and the three boys emerged from the barn. The boys raced across the barnyard, stirring up dust. Before they could dart through the back door, Evangeline stopped them.

"Hey!" In her own ears, she sounded as piercing as Susanna. "You boys need to wash up."

"Yes, ma'am," Natty and Randy chorused as they hurried to the washbowls on the stands outside the back door.

Gerard rolled his eyes but followed their good example.

Once they were all seated around the kitchen

table, Seamus offered a lovely prayer in his lilting Irish accent, and they began to eat.

Evangeline focused on her son. "Tell me about the foal. How tall has he grown since last week?"

Gerard's eyes lit up as they hadn't in months. "His withers are already at my waist." He stood and held out his hand to indicate the comparison. "Seamus says he's going to make a fine cowpony."

Little Randy announced, "My pa says if his temper'ment turns out good, he'll be my first horse."

Perhaps only Evangeline noticed Gerard grew sullen. Was he thinking of his own pony, sold to help pay off his father's debts? His cross demeanor continued as the children were dismissed to play in the parlor.

"Well, now that I'm done riding herd on those little rascals, maybe I'll get some work done." Seamus's grin revealed he hadn't minded "riding herd" at all. "Sister, me darlin', I'll be working over at the big house until this evening." He grabbed his hat from a peg by the back door and made his exit.

"Thanks, Seamus." Marybeth called as she gave him a fond wave.

Evangeline always longed for a brother, especially one as thoughtful as Seamus. Susanna once told her Marybeth's brother went missing for many years. She came to Esperanza looking for him. They'd had a grand reunion and never wanted to be separated again.

As the ladies cleaned up the dinner dishes, Evangeline enjoyed a half hour of pleasant fellowship with her cousin and her new friend.

Until a child's scream of terror pierced the calm.

"That's Randy!" Marybeth raced toward the parlor. Evangeline trailed after them, fearing and yet knowing what trouble lay ahead. Sure enough, Gerard stood halfway up the staircase dangling Randy by his ankles over the bannister. At ten years old, he wasn't really strong enough to hold onto a five-year-old, and his hands slipped on the younger boy's ankles.

"Gerard." Her shout of dismay was drowned out by Marybeth's horrified cry.

Marybeth hurried to catch her son, but Evangeline beat her to him. "Gerard, you will lower Randy carefully into my hands. Now."

Gerard did as he was told. She gripped Randy's shoulders and rolled him to an upright position, holding on for all she was worth. Once he was safely standing on his own two feet and Gerard came back downstairs, he whined, "Aw, Mother, we're just playing. Aren't we, Randy?" He glared at the boy as though daring him to disagree.

Marybeth collapsed into a chair, one hand on her rounded belly and the other holding her son. She fumbled for a handkerchief in her pocket and wiped Randy's tear-streaked face. He gave Gerard a doubtful look, but mumbled, "Yes."

Marybeth's struggle with her emotions was evident in her stricken face. She looked at Evangeline. "Please go."

"Marybeth—" Susanna began.

"No." Evangeline raised a hand to silence her. "She's right."

"Gerard will not be welcome here until Rand comes home from the roundup."

"I understand." Heartsick, Evangeline could think of no reason her son would be so cruel to little Randy, who appeared to adore him as much as Natty and Frankie did.

As expected, Justice knew he was in trouble the minute he entered the church on Sunday morning and saw Susanna standing at the end of a pew and waving at him. Last Sunday, he'd agreed to have dinner with the larger Northam family, but in the busyness of the past week, he'd forgotten. Wanting to get out of it, he searched for another empty seat, but the pretty little matchmaker approached him, oozing Southern charm.

"Good morning, Sheriff. We saved you a place." She gripped his arm and tugged. "Come sit with us."

"Well, I need to—" He couldn't think of how to finish the sentence. Nor could he resist too stridently or he'd make a scene.

Her delicate eyebrows bent in a frown, Susanna stood on tiptoes to whisper in his ear. "You promised Nate you'd help with Gerard. And my, oh, my, do we need your help." She stepped back, her sunny self again. "Come along now."

Justice looked beyond her to see Evangeline staring at him, her face flushed with embarrassment. Beside his mother, Gerard sat with face forward and his shoulders bunched up in a defiant posture. A sudden, strong resolve gripped Justice, a determination he'd felt when pursuing outlaws as a Texas Ranger. But while it was one thing to take down an outlaw and put him in jail, it was another thing entirely to corral a wayward boy and show him the error of his ways. Justice didn't know exactly how to deal with Gerard, but he'd never shirked his duty, and he wasn't about to start now.

With some clever maneuvering, Susanna placed Justice on the aisle next to Gerard, with Evangeline on the other side of her son. Gerard shifted close to his mother and scowled. He pretended to sleep when the minister read the story of the prodigal son from the Gospel of Luke and preached his sermon about the Lord always welcoming sinners home. The story always reminded Justice of his own few years of rebellion. With his father gone, he hadn't had an earthly father to return home to in repentance, but he'd returned to the Lord. Maybe Gerard would do the same.

Several times, Justice traded a look with Evangeline over her son's head. He hated seeing the shame in her eyes. Whatever her faults were, whatever wrong choices she'd made, she was still a mother suffering because of her son's recalcitrant ways. And at the end of the service, the boy was as petulant as ever.

A sharp autumn wind blew in from the west as Justice followed the caravan of buggies traveling to Four Stones Ranch after church. In addition to Susanna's rig, Colonel and Mrs. Northam, Tolley and Laurie Northam, Garrick and Rosamond Wakefield, and Marybeth Northam rode in separate conveyances, with sundry children dispersed throughout. Led by the Colonel's buggy, which Seamus O'Brien drove, they turned down the lane leading to the main house on the Northam property.

The party entered the white, two-story edifice through the back door and kitchen, as was the custom in these parts. The house seemed built for entertaining large parties, and Mrs. Northam was in her element directing everyone to various tasks to get dinner on the table. The ladies brought their best cooking, and a huge roast had cooked in Mrs. Northam's fine new stove overnight, so mouthwatering aromas filled the house. Justice had seen the stove weeks ago and, at Mrs. Winsted's insistence, ordered one for his new house. Would Evangeline like to cook on such a fancy appliance? And why was he thinking about her and his new home in the same sentence…again?

He'd lost count of the children scampering around the house. He did notice Marybeth kept her two youngsters close by and her eyes on Gerard. He'd yet to learn the rest of the story, but Seamus had hinted there'd been trouble.

"Let's get out of the way, gentlemen." The Colonel beckoned to Tolley, Garrick, Seamus and Justice. "Join me in the parlor while the ladies finish their preparations," he said, hesitating a bit as a result of his stroke two years ago. He rolled his wheelchair in that direction.

For a half hour, Justice let himself relax in the presence of these good men as they discussed the expansion of the railroad, the cattle industry and last year's severe winter, during which many herds had died and numerous cattle fortunes had been lost. They asked Justice if he had any suspicions about the men who'd shot up Mrs. Winsted's Mercantile. He opined that they were probably seasonal cowboys who were on the roundup, and he planned to interview them all when they returned to town.

Dinner was called, and everyone gathered in the large dining room, where the ladies had laid out the food on the elegant mahogany buffet and two side tables. Once Colonel Northam asked the blessing, the children were served and sent to eat in the kitchen, while the adults sat around the long mahogany dining table. In this homey setting, Justice could well imagine the happiness of having his own family gathered this way in his new house.

Of course Susanna placed him beside Evangeline, and wisps of her familiar gardenia perfume reached his senses. If not for her son, he might consider... No, he'd never give her his heart again. Years ago, she'd made it clear she cared only for wealth, and he hadn't seen anything to indicate she'd changed, as evidenced by her expensive perfume. He wasn't about to let her know he owned a productive gold mine and had considerable funds in the Esperanza bank for fear she'd become a willing participant in Susanna's matchmaking schemes. No, if he ever decided to marry, he wouldn't let the lady know about his wealth until he'd won her heart.

Still, against all that made sense, he felt drawn to her, undoubtedly because she represented the best parts of his happy youth. Why did his daydreams keep wandering to images of a future with her? And how could he divert his thoughts when he needed to spend weekday afternoons with her in order to finish the Christmas village in time for the Christmas party?

Chapter Six

After a hearty meal, Justice thanked his hostess and took his leave of the party. He walked toward the barn, where he'd left his horse. The wind still blew briskly, covering the sound of his footfalls on the hard-packed barnyard, its whistle through the cracks in the barn wall blending with the squeak of the massive door as he opened it.

Inside, in the dim light of a lantern that shouldn't be burning with no adult to watch it, he saw Gerard holding one of the Northams' black-and-white puppies as he stared wistfully at a young horse in its stall. He'd probably lit the lantern so he could see the animals in the dark barn. Justice thought about scolding him, but decided this was a good opening for friendship.

"Afternoon, Gerard." He kept his tone friendly as though talking to another man.

The boy looked up, startled, and wiped one hand down his cheek. So he'd been crying. Justice would allow him his dignity by ignoring it.

"You interested in learning how to ride?"

Gerard glared at him. "I know how to ride." He set the puppy down in the straw and stalked away toward the back of the barn.

Justice rested one hand on the top rail of a stall and bent his head. *Lord, please help me to reach the boy. Help me not to blame him for his father's—*

The shattering of glass beside him interrupted his prayer. It was followed by a burst of flame near his feet. Down the center aisle of the barn, Gerard held his slingshot, hatred shooting from his eyes.

"You—" The flames quickly reached hay and straw, so Justice halted his scolding and grabbed a bucket and scooped water from the trough. "Go get help!" He yelled at Gerard, but the boy stood stock still, transfixed by the fire.

Seamus entered the barn whistling. Seeing the fire, he grabbed a blanket and soaked it in water to beat the flames. Justice grabbed a pitchfork and separated the burning straw from the untouched. With considerable effort, they managed to avert disaster.

"What happened?" His face covered with soot, Seamus continued to kick dirt over the remnants of hot straw.

So angry he couldn't speak, Justice nodded toward a defiant Gerard, who'd watched them fight the fire.

Seamus snorted. "First he tries to break my nephew's neck. Now he tries to burn down Colonel Northam's barn." He started toward the boy, who ran out the back door.

Justice gripped Seamus's arm. "I'll get him."

He ran out the front door in time to catch Gerard. As he'd suspected, the boy was headed for the house and his mama. Justice gave him a good shaking.

"What's the matter with you, boy?"

"Let me go!" Gerard kicked at his shins, but Justice avoided his thrashing feet.

Justice lifted him up, tucked him under his arm and hauled him toward the house, where Evangeline and the others were preparing to leave.

Evangeline ran toward them, her face pale with alarm. "What happened?" She tugged her son from Justice's arms and ran her hands over his face. "Are you all right, my darling?" She sent an accusing glare in Justice's direction. "What did you do to him?"

"Your son tried to burn down the barn."

She started to respond, but Justice held out a hand to stop her.

"Listen to me, boy." He poked a finger at Gerard. "You start any more trouble like this, and you'll wish you'd never seen—"

"That's enough, Sheriff." Glaring at Justice, Evangeline tucked her son behind her back.

"Oh, my." Susanna stepped between the warring factions. "Evie, let's take the children home. They're tired." She cast an apologetic look in Justice's direction.

Gerard peered around his mother and scowled. In Justice's brief acquaintance with the boy, he'd never looked more like his father. Unable to quiet the rage inside, he gave the elder Mrs. Northam an apologetic nod and returned to the barn to saddle his horse. He rode back to town at a gallop, but the usually calming exercise failed him this time. With Evangeline protecting her son and refusing to see his wicked deeds for what they were, he had no idea how to protect his town from Gerard. Despite his prayers to be able to separate the son from the father, he could only see Lucius in the boy. A feeling he feared was too close to hatred filled his chest, and all of his Ranger training wasn't helping him at all. To make matters worse, he must deal with his own exasperating attraction to Evangeline.

"Lord, You're going to have to fix this situation because I sure can't."

During the drive to Susanna's house, neither she nor Evangeline said a word. Even the younger children were quiet, no doubt sensing something was amiss. For some reason, Gerard didn't give Evangeline any trouble for the rest of the evening. In fact, he acted as though nothing happened at the ranch's main house.

At bedtime, Evangeline sat on the edge of his bed and brushed damp hair back from his face. He smiled up at her.

"What happened in the barn?"

His open expression closed, and he turned on his side with his face to the wall. "I'm sleepy." He tugged the covers up over his head.

Evangeline sighed. If she forced him to answer her, he'd probably throw a tantrum and wake Natty and Frankie. With school and work tomorrow, they all needed a good night of rest. She patted his shoulder and whispered a prayer he'd find a way to be happy. When he stiffened, she knew he'd heard her. Lately he hadn't wanted her to pray for him. But didn't he want to be happy? With a sigh, she left the bedroom.

"There you are." Susanna greeted Evangeline

from her seat at the kitchen table. "Have some coffee."

She wasn't alone. Wes, the middle-aged cowhand, gave Evangeline a skeptical look and then hid his expression behind his coffee cup.

"May I have tea? Coffee will keep me awake." She'd prefer to escape a possible confrontation with Susanna, but maybe her cousin could help her in some way once Wes left. While she took a seat, her cousin fetched her teapot and added tea and hot water.

"Mrs. Benoit." Wes set down his cup. "Seamus rode over a while ago and told me about the trouble up at the big house today. I'm gonna barge right in here because it's my business as much as everybody else's on the ranch. You gotta git that boy under control, or there's gonna be bad trouble. He took his slingshot and shot out a burning lamp, and the flames hit a pile of straw and took off from there. If Seamus and the sheriff hadn't put it out right quick, the whole place could've burnt down, maybe even the house, what with the wind blowing so hard today. Fire ain't no game out here, ma'am. If a barn burns down, horses and milk cows die, and a year's worth of hay for the cattle is lost."

"Thank you for stating the obvious." His story shocked Evangeline, but she wouldn't let him or Susanna see her chagrin. She stood and walked to the door. "I'm sure if all the details were known, my son would be found innocent of any wrongdoing." She marched down the hallway to the girls' room and prepared for bed.

The very idea of a rustic cowhand scolding her

about an incident he hadn't witnessed… Scolding her about the way she was rearing her son—

But he's right.

The thought brought her up short. She *was* having trouble with Gerard. He *did* start a fire. He wasn't innocent at all. But she couldn't help him when he wouldn't even talk to her.

Maybe when Nate returned, he could help her figure it out. At the least he would provide a good male example for Gerard. Too bad Justice couldn't fill the role, but his obvious dislike for her son made it impossible. That realization brought on a deep sadness and a hint of resentment. If Justice had rescued her from her forced marriage to Lucius, none of this would have happened. As always, such thinking reminded her that if she hadn't married Lucius, she wouldn't have her two beloved children. As she fell into an uneasy slumber, she couldn't stop the dreams. In her dreams it wasn't Lucius but rather Justice as their father.

After his night of bad dreams and little sleep, Justice dreaded returning to the library to work on the Christmas village. Earlier that day he'd visited the school, and while most of the children gave him their usual friendly smiles, Gerard refused to look in his direction. The boy didn't have to like him, but he did have to respect the badge. Justice would make sure Gerard learned the lesson or died trying.

Approaching the library, he felt himself taking slower, smaller steps. He dreaded a confrontation with Evangeline, but he'd have to stand firm about her son. He stepped up on the boardwalk and glanced through the window. She sat at her desk with a pile of books beside her. He knew once he opened the door and the scent of her gardenia perfume reached him, he'd lose all perspective. If he didn't need the little bit of daylight shining through the high windows and illuminating the back room, he'd work on the village at night after she went home so he wouldn't have to deal with her. Or rather, what her presence did to him.

Inhaling a bracing breath, he opened the door. "Afternoon, Evangeline."

She didn't look up. "Good afternoon, Sheriff." Few people spoke as dismissively to a lawman of his reputation as she did.

He walked past her desk. Instead of gardenias, he smelled paint and turpentine. In the back room, he found she'd already painted everything he'd carved so far. With her part of the work completed, they wouldn't be working side by side, at least not today. Perhaps never again. Contrary to his earlier thoughts, disappointment filled him. Two kinds of disappointment, in fact. He regretted her choosing to let her son run amok rather than asking him to help her discipline the boy. But most of all, he regretted not being near her. He missed the scent of gardenias, his favorite flower, which could never grow in Colorado's cold mountain climate.

He set to work on his carving, trying to envision the scene he would set up in the church's reception hall on the day of the pageant. When the children completed their performance, they'd be greeted by a delightful surprise. Justice thought about adding a toy train to the tiny village, but with so much to finish, he'd have to wait for another year.

Building this surprise for the children would help them understand that their sheriff cared for them, that he wasn't some stern presence sent to monitor their behavior and scold them for every minor infraction. While he deserved their respect, he never wanted them to be afraid of him.

The sound of humming wafted into the back room. Evangeline. Against all reason, his heart swelled with...what? He tried to name the pleasant emotion, but the perfect word eluded him. So he quit trying and let peace, however momentary, invade his heart.

After the near disaster at the Northams' main house, Evangeline expected to be shunned. Yet, the following Sunday, everyone at church remained warm and friendly, unlike her acquaintances in New Orleans after Lucius's fall from their good opinion. They asked about her progress at the library and expressed their appreciation for her work there. One older woman, after glancing at Justice across the sanctuary, suggested Evangeline might add a little color to her wardrobe since she'd been a widow for over a year. Perhaps softened by the new shirtwaist Evangeline made for her, Miss Prinn already welcomed her back to the classroom without hesitation. The Northam family—Justice, too—must not have mentioned the incident to anyone. How thankful she was for their discretion, their kindness in giving Gerard another chance to prove himself a good boy. The only change she noticed among those people she knew was in Susanna, who'd ceased her attempts at matchmaking.

For her own part, keeping her distance from Justice was proving harder than she'd expected. The smell of his orange-scented cologne as he passed her desk each day brought back memories of pleasanter times both recent and long past. But other than courtesies he showed toward everyone, he'd never hinted at any interest in her beyond her ability to paint the Christmas village. Her only recourse was to finish her work on it in the mornings so she wouldn't have to work beside him in the afternoons. And try to stifle her longings for what might have been had her father not forced her to marry Lucius.

If only Justice had rescued her instead of ignoring her plight when he returned from Europe. After such thoughts, she chided herself. After all, his father died and his inheritance was in shambles. How awful for the young man he'd been. But then, perhaps during his year and a half in Europe, he'd forgotten his promises to her. She'd likely never know the truth.

The first week in November, Nate and Rand returned briefly with the cattle they'd brought down from mountain grazing. Evangeline expected Susanna to report Gerard's behavior to her husband, but this year's roundup had been late and slow. Thus, Nate barely had time to kiss his wife and children before loading the cattle onto the train and embarking for the Denver stockyards before the snows blocked La Veta Pass. From Denver, the cattle would be sold or shipped eastward to Kansas City or Chicago. The brothers expected to be gone for a few more weeks as they bargained for the best prices for their prime beef. At first Evangeline considered Nate's extended absence to be a reprieve. Then she wished it could all be over, even though Nate might ask her to move out once he knew about Gerard's missteps. If he did, where would she go?

As always, the town was thrown into turmoil while the herds of cattle were driven to the train yard. While everyone else stayed out of the way, Justice waited on the platform to question the seasonal cowhands about the shootings at Mrs. Winsted's mercantile. Before he located them, Nate brought two young men to him.

"These fellas have something to tell you." Nate patted each one's shoulder, then touched the brim of his hat. "See you in a couple of weeks, Sheriff."

"Good trip, Nate." Justice waved to his friend, then put on his severest face. "All right, boys, what do you have to say for yourselves?"

Not even out of their teens, the short, stocky duo shuffled their feet and looked as guilty as two five-year-olds who'd stolen some cookies.

The blond took off his hat and rolled it in his hands. "We're the ones who shot up that store."

The redhead nodded. "Ain't got no excuse, Sheriff. We come to town for a drink before the roundup, and we was mad y'all don't have no saloon."

"Weren't no reason to shoot up the nice lady's store," his friend added.

"I see." Justice tipped his hat back on his head and crossed his arms over his chest. "What inspired you to confess?"

They traded a look before the blond said, "You ever hung out with Nate and Rand Northam?"

"Ain't never heard such preaching, not even from a preacher man." The redhead guffawed. "Ever' night round the campfire, same thing. Repent your sins. Come to Jesus."

"Ain't nothin' we could do but—" the blond's expression softened "—but—" He looked at his friend.

"Repent our sins and come to Jesus," they chorused.

Justice swallowed a laugh. The godly Northam brothers had done his work for him. And in light of these cowboys' repentance, he knew the best way to keep them on a straight path was to apply grace instead of prison, where they might fall in with some truly evil men and choose a life of crime.

"All right, boys, here's what we're going to do. I know you just got paid, but you'll need your money to make it through the winter. So you're going to work off your debt to Mrs. Winsted until her new window and ruined merchandise are paid off. Whatever she tells you to do, you'll do it."

"Yessir."

"Starting today, you'll clean up the streets where the cattle were driven through, and for the next month, you'll keep the streets clean of horse leavings. I won't lock you up, but you'll sleep at the jail where my deputy and I can keep an eye on you."

"Yessir."

"And if you try to leave Esperanza before you've paid off your debt, I'll chase you down like a hungry cougar chasing a fat jackrabbit."

"Yessir."

Justice escorted them to the jailhouse so they could get acquainted with their temporary home.

As they passed the intersection of Main Street and Center Avenue, he involuntarily glanced toward the library. Evangeline stood outside the door watching him, her expression unreadable at this distance. He didn't expect her to know what he'd done for these young men or even to admire his peacekeeping methods. But he sure did wish she and her son understood he could be fair to any miscreant who admitted wrongdoing and tried to reform. While Gerard had behaved for the past few weeks, Justice often saw him hanging out with Deely and Cart after school. A bad combination that would surely cause trouble one of these days. Justice would have to be vigilant and tell his deputy to keep an eye on them, too.

By the second week of November, Evangeline had completed the organization of the library, which meant the Thanksgiving week opening was right on schedule. She'd also painted the figures Justice had carved so far. The village was coming together beautifully, and she was thrilled to be part of its creation. Gerard hadn't caused any more trouble at school, probably because she continued her biweekly surprise trips to his class. Life seemed to be settling into a pleasant, if lonely, pattern.

While gossip didn't seem to be a problem in Esperanza, general news did spread quickly, helped by the charming little newspaper, the *Esperanza Journal*. Knowing how the townspeople worried about the mercantile shooting, the owner and editor, Fred Brody, wrote a fine article about Justice's even-handed way of dealing with the guilty young men. Fred quoted Mrs. Winsted, who expressed her appreciation for the extra workers. On Sunday morning, Reverend Thomas commended the sheriff's decision from the pulpit.

This was the person Evangeline remembered from her childhood. Kind, thoughtful, prudent. If she sensed he would treat her as well as those cowboys, she might consider telling him everything about her painful marriage and the debts she'd left behind. But from the way he reacted to Gerard's boyish mischief, she feared he would lock her up and send word to her creditors. One moment, fear kept her silent. The next, she ached to rekindle their long ago friendship.

The yearning wore on her, and, finally, after weeks of essentially ignoring him when he came to the library, she relented and spared him a friendly smile.

"Good afternoon, Justice." She spoke before he could.

He blinked, and his jaw slackened. Vulnerability crossed his face. He paused at her desk and she felt a little ping near her heart.

Oh, no. Such feelings wouldn't do.

"Good afternoon, Evangeline." He cleared his throat. "How are you today?"

She set down her pen and folded her hands on the desk. "Well, thank you. And you?"

"Fine. Fine." He didn't move on. "Your painting is bringing our little village to life. I couldn't have done half so well as you."

"Thank you. I never cease to be amazed at your carving skill."

He grinned, then chuckled. "I'd say we work well together."

"Yes. We do." She couldn't take her gaze from those piercing gray eyes. Nor did he seem eager to break this moment of truce.

"Well, I'd better get busy. That is, if you don't need anything."

She scrambled mentally to think of something, anything to hold on to their connection. Nothing came to mind. "No, not right now. I'll let you know if I think of something."

"You do that." He nodded. "Well, I'd better get busy." He didn't seem to realize he'd repeated himself.

"Me, too." With desperate determination, she forced her eyes to the list of tasks on her desk, a list she knew by heart and didn't need to review.

As his footsteps moved away from her desk, she looked up. What a fine figure of a man he was. Tall, broad-shouldered, strong. Then he turned back and caught her watching. And grinned.

"You think of something I can do for you?"

Heat rushed to her cheeks. "No. Thank you." Again she forced her eyes to the desk.

This really must stop. But then, she'd never been able to subdue her reactions to him.

"Mama, how did you know where all the books should go?" Isabelle gazed around the library with the wonder of an eager student.

Evangeline stood beside her daughter and brushed a hand down her silky golden curls. "I put similar books together so people could easily find what they were interested in." She picked up a volume from her desk. "This book describes a Mr. Melvil Dewey's system of library organization, which I plan to study. Perhaps I can rearrange the books by his system." She surveyed her shelves, satisfied with what she'd done. "For now, though, I wanted to open the library this Friday after Thanksgiving Day, so I just used my best instincts."

Isabelle blinked her blue eyes and gazed up at her. "What are instincts?"

Evangeline's heart welled up with love for her bright, sweet child. How she did love to learn new things. "It's a way of thinking or feeling about something that you know without learning it."

Her daughter blinked again. "Like Gerard feels mad all the time?"

Evangeline turned away to hide her sudden tears. "Oh, I don't think he's angry all the time, my darling. He's happy when he's playing with you and your cousins at Susanna's house." She set down *Dewey Decimal Classification and Relative Index* and gathered the stack of reference cards Marybeth had completed. "Now, I want you to sit at my desk and arrange these in alphabetical order by the authors' last names. See them at the top of each card? Do you think you can do that?"

Isabelle beamed. "Yes, ma'am."

"When you finish these—"

The door opened with a whoosh, and Justice ushered in Gerard, one hand gripping the back of her son's plaid coat collar.

"Mrs. Benoit, we have a problem." He wore his severest "sheriff face."

Gerard's defiant look and blazing eyes proclaimed his usual response to Justice.

Evangeline's heart jumped to her throat, and her knees threatened to buckle. "Wh-what..." She choked on her words.

"Tell your mother what you've been up to." Justice released the boy's collar but kept a hand on his shoulder.

As much as she longed to reach out for her son, she forced her hands to remain at her side. Behind her she heard Isabelle sniffling. Her sensitive, loving daughter doted on her big brother and suffered terribly when he got into trouble. "What do you have to say for yourself, Gerard?"

"It wasn't my fault." His expression quickly went soft, innocent, appealing.

Evangeline looked at Justice, who crossed his arms over his chest. "Perhaps you'd better tell me what happened."

He snorted in disgust. "Gerard and his friends let the chickens out of Laurie Northam's coop and killed some of them with their slingshots."

Evangeline gasped. "Gerard?" She took his face in her hands so he couldn't avoid her stare. This time she wouldn't let him sway her. "Why would you do such a thing?"

He broke away, stared at his feet and shrugged.

"And who are these supposed friends who led you into this mischief?" Even as she spoke, Evangeline knew she'd said the wrong thing, and not only because of Justice's growl.

"Deely and Cart claimed it was Gerard's idea."

Gerard's eyes blazed again, but he said nothing.

"I made them clean up the mess, but they're going to have to repay Laurie for the dead chickens."

Evangeline gulped down a protest. After all, this was the sort of punishment he'd doled out to the cowboys who'd shot out Mrs. Winsted's window, and everyone agreed it was more than fair. But those young men earned a salary. Gerard had no way of making money.

"Do you have anything in mind?" She could pay Laurie out of her salary, but perhaps it would be better for Gerard to pay for his mistake.

"They can clean the streets from now until Christmas. Storekeepers have been responsible for the areas in front of their stores, but after those cowboys were assigned the task, the town council decided to make it a paying job. The boys can do it until they earn enough money to pay Laurie for her losses."

Evangeline studied Gerard, whose glare copied Lucius's worst scowl. Anger flooded her mind and heart. Not directed at her son. Nor at Justice. At Lucius. The man who'd never had time to be a father because of his wastrel habits. With all the self-control she could muster, she gripped Gerard's shoulders and forced him to look at Justice.

"Very well, Sheriff. Do you want him to begin now?"

Justice's expression lightened with surprise, and his posture relaxed at least a little. "No time like the present."

Gerard bristled. "I want my slingshot back." He pointed to the three Y-shaped toys sticking out from the pocket of Justice's leather jacket.

Justice shook his head. "Nope. I'm going to burn these…and any you might make in the future."

"Oh, Sheriff." Evangeline couldn't bear to see her son lose his favorite toy. "Couldn't I keep it until his punishment is over?"

Justice's face closed again. "No, ma'am. He can't be trusted with a weapon like this. Come with me, boy." He reached out for Gerard, but her son broke away and flung himself into Evangeline's arms.

"Mother, don't let him take me."

Pity for him sent another shard of ire through her. As before, she wondered whether Justice was being harder on Gerard because he was Lucius's son. That simply wasn't fair. "Where are the other boys? What are they doing? Are they going to be working, too?"

Justice narrowed his eyes. "The other boys are none of your business."

Evangeline held Gerard securely. "Until I know they're being punished every bit as much as my son, I will not permit you to force him to bear the punishment alone."

"Fine. I'll arrest him and put him jail." Again he reached for Gerard. This time he grabbed his shoulder and removed him from her embrace. "What will it be, son? Jail or cleaning the streets?"

After an almost interminable pause, Gerard swiped his nose across his coat sleeve. "The streets."

As he and Justice exited the library, Evangeline slumped against her desk. Coming to Esperanza had been a terrible mistake. Now she was trapped with no way of escape, no way to protect her children.

She walked to the window and saw Justice directing not one but three boys in how to use shovels to clean the street and dump the horse leavings into a wheelbarrow. So he hadn't singled her son out. She shouldn't have misjudged him. She should have realized he'd require the other two to work alongside Gerard. Maybe she and her children were in the right place after all.

Glancing beyond the little work crew, she saw a familiar form walking along Main Street, a carpetbag in hand.

Hugo Giles. Her husband's cousin had found her.

Chapter Seven

Against his better judgment, Justice accepted the Northams' invitation to spend Thanksgiving Day at Four Stones Ranch. Since Monday's incident with the boys, Evangeline had been unusually skittish when he'd come to the library to work on the Christmas village, so she might not be happy to see him. Further, throughout the first three days of street sweeping, Gerard remained hostile, which should have put an end to Justice's annoying but persistent imaginings of seeing Evangeline in his future. Being in her company for an entire day couldn't produce anything good. The last thing a lawman needed was to be involved with a woman whose son took after his father and seemed bent on lawlessness.

Which didn't mean he wouldn't keep trying to straighten the boy out, along with the other two boys. At least Deely and Cart each had what some might call excuses for their waywardness. Deely's father was hanged for stealing horses, and Cart's widowed father abandoned him to the care of an aunt who was less than kind. Nate and Rand did their best to get the boys to their Sunday school classes, but neither would attend. While Evangeline coddled and defended her son, at least she brought her children to church.

Nate and Rand had returned from Denver, so Justice could offer no credible reason to decline their Thanksgiving invitation. He left his deputy in charge of the town and fetched his horse from the livery stable. Adam Starling had already saddled the gelding for him. Adam tried to refuse the offered tip, but Justice reminded him Christmas was coming, and children needed to receive something special. After his father's death the previous spring, Adam had become the man of the family, helping his mother rear his younger brother and two sisters. Too bad Gerard, Deely and Cart didn't follow Adam's example of honesty and hard work.

A light snow lay sprinkled over the landscape as Justice rode south toward Four Stones. He passed the Eberly ranch on the west side of the road just as George and Mabel Eberly, along with their youngest daughter, Georgia, came driving up the lane toward the highway on their way to the Northam celebration. Justice reined his horse to a stop and waited for them.

"Howdy, Sheriff." George Eberly waved a gloved hand.

"Morning, George, Mabel, Georgia."

The ladies chorused their greetings in their usual friendly fashion as he nudged his mount into a walk beside their buggy.

"We got sweet potato pie, Sheriff." Mabel hooked a thumb over her shoulder to indicate the box of food in the back of the buggy.

"And pecan pie," Georgia added. "I made it myself."

"That a fact?" Justice clicked his tongue in appreciation. "Haven't eaten pecan pie since I left New Orleans. You be sure I get a slice." He could tease the eighteen-year-old because she took it with a grain of salt, unlike some of the more flirtatious girls in town.

They continued to chat about the anticipated feast, with Justice growing hungrier by the minute. Mabel was a fine cook, and she'd passed her skills on to her five daughters. He always enjoyed his meals at their house.

Along with the Northams, the Eberlys and a few other families founded Esperanza, and most still lived in the surrounding community. The four older girls were married, Maisie to Doc Henshaw, Beryl to an Englishman with whom she now resided in England, Grace to Reverend Thomas and Laurie to Tolley Northam. With the older generation of their families getting on in years and the younger generation producing numerous offspring, they frequently held large gatherings at Four Stones Ranch because the house was big as a mansion. Until Evangeline came to town and disrupted his well-ordered world, Justice felt honored to be included in the Northam-Eberly celebrations, even though the happily married couples often made him long to have a family of his own.

There he went again, thinking of Evangeline and family in the same sentence, a useless idea if ever he had one. Unless... Perhaps in the informal setting of the ranch, he could try again to befriend Gerard. He knew the boy liked dogs and horses. What else did he like? He lifted a silent prayer for a breakthrough, some way to reach his heart, turn his thinking.

In his own life, Justice had quickly tired of his rebellious ways, no doubt because his father lived an exemplary life and he didn't want to besmirch his memory. Then Jubal Tucker had come along and become a second father to Justice. Gerard didn't have those same advantages. Lucius had been a scoundrel, plain and simple. And the boy was following in his footsteps. Justice needed to figure out how to gain the boy's esteem, how to become his friend, how to be an example of what a man should be.

As they turned down Four Stones Lane and approached the house, Justice found himself in a state of nervous anticipation. Was it because of the challenge Gerard presented? Or because, against all reason, he couldn't wait to see Evangeline again?

Riding in the wagon with the five children and Susanna and Nate to their Thanksgiving feast, Evangeline couldn't seem to settle her nerves. Nor could she stop her eyes from scanning the areas they passed, ever on the lookout for Hugo Giles. Although she'd been certain that was he she'd seen on Monday, perhaps she'd been mistaken. Over the last few days, he hadn't come to the library for her, and when she'd visited the mercantile and the bank, no one had made mention of a stranger looking for her. Still, she must be on alert. While she didn't have the resources to flee Esperanza, she might be able to hide behind the reputation of Nate's family. No, such a ploy wasn't right or fair. They had no part in her debts, and she wouldn't expect them to rescue her no matter how successful their cattle sales were.

They drove into the barnyard behind the big house, aptly named, she thought, even though the main Northam residence was only about three quarters the size of her home in New Orleans. She was greeted by the aromas of roast beef, baked ham and apple pie wafting from the house. Evangeline still wasn't used to the custom of guests entering the house through the back door, although she'd begun to see how useful it was when one brought hot food to add to the feast. She helped carry in the turkeys that Nate had shot and Susanna had roasted to perfection.

With so many women bustling about the kitchen, all knowing exactly what to do, Evangeline offered her only skill: organizing the buffet. The food would be served from the mahogany sideboard and two side tables. The desserts already covered one table, and a variety of breads and condiments another.

She was searching inside the buffet's side doors for trivets when Justice swung open the kitchen door and entered the dining room. Evangeline gasped when she saw the determined look on his face, and her heart sank. Had he come to arrest her? Was Hugo right behind him? Her hands shook, and she dropped a cast-iron trivet on the floor.

"Good morning, Evangeline." His face creased in a smile of surprise. "My, that's a lot of desserts. I'd better keep moving, or I'll start eating them before the main course." He picked up the trivet and handed it to her. "Do you know if the Colonel is in the front parlor?"

"Y-yes." Her knees threatened to buckle with relief, but she managed a shaky smile and a wave in that direction.

Before she could think of something else to say, Nate barged through the kitchen door. "Say, Justice, Tolley's gathering the youngsters for a game of baseball. You want to play?"

He paused. "Let me pay my respects to the Colonel first."

"Sure thing. Come on out back when you're done."

"Exercise will sharpen our appetites, as if they needed it." Justice spoke conversationally, not as a lawman bent on arresting someone. "You think Gerard will want to play?"

Evangeline's heart tripped over itself. How kind of him to think of her son. "Why, yes. He loves baseball." From his twinkling gray eyes, she could tell he was pleased, but she couldn't guess why.

"Good. I'll make sure he's invited to join us." He continued his journey to the front of the house.

She breathed deeply to slow her racing pulse and hide the warmth creeping up her neck from Marybeth, who'd entered the dining room with a tray of desserts to add to the already full side table.

So Justice wasn't all about punishment. Maybe he'd seen some promise in Gerard's behavior during their afternoons of street cleaning, some inkling he could reach her son.

"Please, Lord." She whispered her prayer, hoping Marybeth didn't hear her.

"Hmm. What could you possibly be asking the Lord for, Evangeline?" Marybeth giggled. "I mean, didn't a tall, handsome sheriff just walk through here? Was that a prayer he'll notice you? Seems to me he already has."

"Oh, nonsense." Now Evangeline's face burned. "If the boys are going to play baseball, I only—"

"Uh-huh." Marybeth giggled again and returned to the kitchen.

Evangeline sighed with relief. Not only did she have a reprieve from being arrested, but Marybeth seemed to have forgiven and forgotten the incident with Gerard and Randy.

"Thank You, Lord." This time, no one heard her prayer except the One to whom it was addressed.

Justice helped Rand bring the Colonel outside in his wheelchair so he could watch the game. The old man might not be able to get around too well, but his green eyes were bright with interest in everything happening on the ranch he'd built on a rocky field he and his family had cleared. When Justice first came to Esperanza, he'd learned that Four Stones Ranch was named for the four stones Colonel and Mrs. Northam's four children laid out as they planned the footprint of the house. Now each one owned a part of the vast enterprise.

Despite the powdery snow covering the barnyard, both boys and girls eagerly joined the game. In addition to Lizzie and Natty Northam and Evangeline's son and daughter, several children of Four Stones ranch hands also came out to play. Most of them were pretty small, so an adult shadowed each child. Tolley divided the players into equally balanced teams, assigning to Justice Rand's firstborn, five-year-old

Randy. For some reason, the boy shied away from Gerard. Yet they ended up on the same team.

Justice planned to "help" team captain Randy pitch, but after giving everyone on the team a try-out, Gerard turned out to be the most talented pitcher. Justice suggested to Randy they should take charge of first base. Georgia Eberly assisted Seamus's youngest boy at both second and third, due to insufficient players and their two other teammates covering the outfield.

Isabelle was first up to bat. Gerard moved close and tossed a slow, underhand pitch to his sister. She swung and missed. On the second pitch, with Nate's help, the girl connected with the ball and sent it rolling several yards.

"Run!" Nate pointed toward first base, and Isabelle dashed from home plate in that direction.

Gerard pretended not to find the ball until she reached first base, a brotherly kindness no one on either team seemed to mind. The gesture surprised and impressed Justice. So the boy wasn't entirely a rapscallion.

Lizzie was next to bat. The dainty little blonde, almost a twin to Isabelle, held the bat above her right shoulder like a professional and narrowed her eyes at her cousin. Gerard tossed another easy underhand pitch. Lizzie swung and missed.

"Strike one," umpire Doc Henshaw called.

"Come on, Gerry berry." Lizzie stood with one hand on her hip in a cute imitation of Susanna. "Pitch like you mean it so I can hit it."

"You asked for it." Gerard grinned like any rascally ten-year-old might. Justice was surprised to see the affection in his eyes for his sister, and his play-fulness with his female cousin was equally impressive. In fact, he was protective of Natty and Frankie, too. Justice must look for ways to break through his shield and find that tender place.

Justice's ruminations almost caused him to miss what happened next. Gerard threw overhand, the ball landing right in catcher Tolley's leather glove.

"Strike two," Doc called.

"You sure you don't want an easy pitch, sissy Lizzie?" Gerard mocked.

"Give me your best pitch, cousin."

Lizzie's blue eyes sparkled like Evangeline's, a family trait. Justice shook off the thought and tried to concentrate on the game.

Gerard threw overhand again. Lizzie swung hard. Her bat connected with the ball and sent it bouncing across the ground. Gerard snatched it up and shot it to Randy. With only a little help from Justice, Randy caught the ball and stood triumphant on first base. Lizzie ran for all she was worth, but Randy held the ball up and grinned.

"You're out," Doc called. "Sorry, Lizzie."

She shrugged. "That's all right, Doctor John." She skipped back to her team full of giggled apologies, her earlier competitiveness giving way to simple enjoyment of the game.

After Natty also struck out, the teams traded places, with Gerard praising his side as they went. "Good job, team." He shook every player's hand.

Justice took a chance and reached out to him. Before he could catch himself, Gerard responded with a firm grip and a grin. Then, as if realizing he'd made a mistake, he yanked his hand back and abruptly stomped away toward the barn, his usual sullen mask firmly back in place.

"Hey, Gerard, you're up to bat first," Georgia called.

The boy continued his journey without responding.

Watching from the mudroom window, Evangeline held her breath as Justice reached out to Gerard. Because of his kind gesture, she permitted herself a moment of joy, perhaps even a renewed affection for the man. But when Gerard pulled away from him, her heart sank. Why couldn't her son respond to Justice's kindness? The answer was simple, and especially so since she'd seen Hugo walking the streets of Esperanza last Monday. One day Justice would find out she'd left behind Lucius's unpaid debts. He would arrest her and send her back to face her creditors. If what Hugo told her was true, she could be imprisoned, and her children would become wards of the state. He would take them in, of course, and treat them as his own. That was, until golden-haired Isabelle was old enough to—

Stop it. Evangeline couldn't do anything about Hugo's threats right now, but she could do something about Gerard. She hurried from the house and caught Justice as he followed Gerard toward the barn.

She touched his arm. "I'll speak to him."

Justice stopped and stared down at her. Pain filled his eyes, but he quickly masked it with his sheriff face. "Good." He turned back to the game.

Heart aching, Evangeline searched for Gerard and

found him seated on the floor of a stall in the barn. He was giggling as he hadn't in a long time because of the half dozen black-and-white puppies crawling all over him, licking his face, tugging at his clothes, biting his ears. Their mother watched nearby with no indication she was concerned for her offspring. That was a good sign. A mother dog could tell if someone meant harm to her children, just like a human mother. In that fact lay Evangeline's dilemma in regard to Justice. One moment he was a stern disciplinarian who intimidated her almost as much as he intimidated Gerard, the next he was a friendly baseball teammate making sure her son was included in the game.

Gerard looked up as she came near the stall. "May I have a puppy, Mother?" His dark eyes sparkled in the light beaming through the barn door. "For Christmas, I mean?"

She knelt and picked up one of the wiggling creatures, holding it away as it tried to lick her face. "For Christmas?" She had other gifts in mind for her children. "I'll have to ask Susanna and Nate if they want another dog at their place. They already have the two to help herd the cattle and Lady, the watchdog." Another thought occurred to her. "I would imagine Nate might be more likely to consider it if he knew he could count on you to help with chores…and show a good attitude while you're doing it."

Gerard blinked innocently. "Sure, I'll help." He petted the puppy in his arms. "I like Cousin Nate."

This was new. And yet, maybe not. Recently, Gerard's attitude had improved at home. He'd even spoken respectfully to Nate since his return from Denver.

"I'm glad you do." She set the puppy down and petted the mother dog. The presence of these sweet, playful animals seemed to have opened a door for Gerard, for he appeared willing to talk about serious matters for the first time since Lucius died.

"I don't like that sheriff," he blurted out.

Evangeline smothered a gasp over his sudden change of mood...and his vehemence. "Why not, my dear? He has a job to do, and—"

"I don't like the way he looks at you."

Sometimes I don't either. But she didn't think they were talking about the same manner of looking. "Why not?"

He shrugged.

"Well, you must have a reason. What bothers you about the way he looks at me?" She wouldn't even think about her own way of viewing Justice when she thought he didn't notice...and yet he always seemed to catch her.

Gerard shrugged again. "I don't know." His face clouded. "I don't want you to get married again."

She laughed without meaning to. "Oh, my dear, you needn't worry, especially where Sheriff Gareau is concerned. If you see any kindness in his expression when he looks at me, it's only because we were friends when we were children." And beyond childhood into their teen years, when young love blossomed only to die on the vine. "I have many fond memories of our families going to church together, having suppers together. We were neighbors. I've told you this." She wouldn't tell him Justice had known his father and disliked him exceedingly.

His forehead wrinkled thoughtfully. "I still don't like him."

"I'm sorry you don't, but no matter how you feel, you must behave so he doesn't have any cause to correct you. It's that way with all of the adults we know. They all want the best for you, as I do."

As if someone had rung the dinner bell, the puppies suddenly swarmed their mother for dinner, abandoning their human friends.

"Let's go back to the house. Or you can play some more while we ladies get dinner on the table."

"All right." He smoothed the furry head of the mother dog, stood and brushed straw from his clothes.

The barnyard was deserted, so they washed their hands in the mudroom and hurried inside to find everyone gathered in the dining room. After Reverend Thomas offered a Thanksgiving prayer, the adults helped the children fill their plates and find a place at the dining room table. Then the adults followed suit, proceeding to the ballroom, where two long damask-covered tables were set with crystal, silverware and linen napkins.

To Evangeline's relief, Susanna didn't try to seat her beside Justice. In fact, they found places across the room from each other. She slid a surreptitious glance in his direction and found him looking at her, too. But his eyes held more sadness than admiration for her, probably because he'd failed to reach Gerard. She gave him what she hoped was an encouraging smile. His face lightened, and he gave her a smile she could only describe as tender.

Her heart skipped. If that was the look Gerard noticed, Justice's feelings for her might be more than nostalgia. But it wouldn't do any good to encourage him, even if she wanted to, when Gerard disliked him so much. Not when Hugo Giles had come to town to collect money she didn't have and would demand her arrest.

As planned, Evangeline left the children at the ranch and drove into town to open the library on Friday. Susanna dearly wanted to come, too, but little Frankie had a cold, so she stayed home to nurse him. Ever the generous cousin, she cheerfully sent Evangeline off with a box of cookies for the patrons who would no doubt flock to the opening.

The event was a grand success. Several ladies had set up a refreshment table with lemonade and cookies, to which Evangeline added Susanna's offering. It seemed the entire community came to inspect the place, giving Evangeline a chance to meet more of her neighbors. Justice had locked the back room door, and when anyone asked what was in there, Evangeline could answer truthfully it was cluttered with unfinished work. The children were out of school, and mothers eagerly showed them around, encouraging them to find something to read.

In the busyness of the morning, she forgot her fears about Hugo. Then, at noon, they came rushing back when Georgia Eberly took her place and sent her off to eat dinner, and she found herself looking at every man who passed Williams's Café. If Hugo was indeed the person she'd seen the previous Monday, he certainly was taking his time making himself known to her. Of course, he didn't know she'd seen him. He'd been walking west at a brisk pace and didn't turn to stare down Center Avenue, and she'd been out of sight inside the library at the time.

But then, he'd always been a sneaky sort. Which meant he was probably busy making plans to worm his way into the fabric of the town, to earn everyone's respect so they'd have no trouble believing his claims about her being a fugitive from the law. Unfortunately for her, she was.

Dismissing her woeful thoughts, she paid Miss Pam for her ham sandwich and stepped back outside into the brisk breeze to return to the library. After all, until Hugo made himself known, she must carry on as though he didn't exist.

"Ah, there you are." An unmistakable, silky smooth male voice came from behind her, startling her all the more because of what she'd been thinking. "Dear Cousin Evangeline, how good to see you at last."

A violent shiver swept down her back. Calling on her many years of hiding her emotions from Lucius, she drew in a long breath, straightened to her full stature and turned to meet her doom. As a frightening chuckle erupted from her adversary, her dinner threatened to come back up. Somehow she managed to speak in a cool, aristocratic tone that would have made her mother proud.

"Why, Hugo Giles, imagine meeting you here."

Chapter Eight

Justice couldn't be more pleased over the way the building of his house was proceeding. With all of the outside work completed, the workmen only needed to finish the inside, and Justice could move in a few days before Christmas. Some of his furniture had arrived from Denver and waited in the storage shed behind the house. He hadn't decided on other furnishings, such as drapes and rugs. Such decisions would need a woman's touch. Evangeline's face, as always, floated across his mind's eye. He quickly dismissed the images.

He'd also need kitchen supplies. His battered blue coffee pot would look out of place on the new cast-iron range Mrs. Winsted insisted he must purchase. She seemed to think he wanted to keep up with the Northams, but he certainly couldn't cook for himself, no matter how grand the appliance.

"After all, with such a fine new house," she'd said, "you must furnish it with fine new appliances."

This was the same lady who'd insisted—shortly after Evangeline arrived—he also needed the bergamot cologne he now used. If he didn't wear it, she'd scold him. After Susanna, she was the most persistent matchmaker in town. He'd only humored her because he'd still felt bad for not preventing those foolish young cowboys from shooting out her front window.

He rounded the corner onto Main Street in time to see Evangeline disappear around the far corner onto Center Avenue. He quickened his pace to catch her so he could ask about the library opening, but before he walked three paces, he spied a dandy entering the jailhouse. He'd seen the man at a distance the other day but left him alone, assuming he'd soon be traveling farther west to Del Norte or Creede in search of gambling halls or gold mines. If the visitor needed something from him, duty must come first. The trip to the library would have to wait.

Striding along the boardwalk, he felt a pinch of annoyance. He'd looked forward to seeing Evangeline's success, wanted to hear firsthand the compliments folks would no doubt pour out on her. She was too modest to repeat such praises. He might not plan to attempt a renewal of their long-lost courtship, but he did want her to do well. After all, she'd worked hard to organize those books.

Opening the door to his office, he set aside his annoyance and pasted on his professional face. The young dandy of perhaps twenty-five years was chatting amiably with Deputy Sean. Both men looked up as he entered.

"Sheriff, this is Hugo Giles." Sean nodded toward the man.

"How do you do, Sheriff?" A mild Cajun inflection colored the stranger's words as he reached out to Justice. His firm, friendly handshake revealed surprising confidence for someone his age. Or was it bravado?

"Doing well, thank you." Justice rounded his tones. No need to give the man a hint of his own background, at least not yet. He could see the awareness in Sean's eyes over his pronunciation, a sign the deputy would follow his silent lead in this situation, as he always did.

Justice casually measured the other man's appearance for clues to his character. Of medium height, perhaps five feet ten inches, he had dark hair and eyes, was clean-shaven, wore a mild, sweet cologne that came just short of being too feminine. He sported a handsome new black wool suit, a pristine white shirt, a modest black cravat, a dark gray jacquard waistcoat, a black bowler hat and black city shoes shined to a military brilliance. Something about his well-formed face seemed familiar, but at the moment Justice couldn't say why. Perhaps it was because his visage was so thoroughly Cajun, with features Justice had observed while growing up and bore a bit of himself.

"What brings you to our little town, Mr. Giles?"

"Simply traveling the country." Giles offered a pleasant smile that seemed sincere.

"At the start of winter?" Justice kept his tone good-humored.

"What can I say?" Giles chuckled and shrugged. "Probably not the best idea I've ever had."

A vague answer, but not enough to unduly raise suspicions. Yet he hadn't offered a solid reason for choosing the stop in Esperanza, a town with no saloons or gambling halls, which he probably knew by now. Could be he wasn't a gambler, despite his slick, dandified appearance.

"You're welcome to town. Folks here are pretty friendly. A tight community. Everybody looks out for everybody else." Again, he kept his tone light so the warning didn't sound ominous but still made his point.

Oddly, Giles's face brightened even more. "Sounds like a fine place to settle down."

"You looking to settle down?"

"Well, no." He shrugged and chuckled again. "Well, maybe."

Justice acknowledged his remark with a nod, taking note of Giles's self-contradiction. "You let me know if you need anything." He hoped the man would take the hint and leave so he could get over to the library.

"Thank you, Sheriff. I shall." Giles donned his hat and gave Sean a friendly nod. "Deputy." Then he left.

"Huh." Sean stared after him. "Wonder what that was all about."

"Same here."

Justice had learned from Jubal Tucker not to judge a man too quickly but also not to ignore his instincts. Giles seemed to be a fine fellow, almost to the point of perfection, but something about him made the hairs on the back of Justice's neck stand up. After all these years lived among cowboys who were mostly rough around the edges, he had a hard time in the company of someone who represented all he himself might have been, had his father not lost his fortune and died. Still, despite the emotional pain he'd endured, he wouldn't trade these past eleven years for anything, except to have his father back, because his trials had made a man of him.

He should have remarked about Giles's Cajun accent. Should have mentioned he'd come from New Orleans and was part Cajun himself. The quickest way to dispel those nagging feelings of unease concerning the man was to learn more about him, which was often accomplished by finding common ground. But Justice wanted to get over to the library before Evangeline closed it for the day, so he'd deal with Giles later. After telling Sean he'd return shortly, he left the office. A glance westward revealed Giles had crossed the street and now ambled down the boardwalk toward the hotel, twirling his ebony walking stick as he went. He was a dandy, all right. But that didn't mean he was harmless.

As Justice headed east toward the library, annoying anticipation arose in his chest, probably because of the smile Evangeline had given him over Thanksgiving dinner the day before. He tried to ignore the urge to seek her advice about those drapes and other furnishings for his house. If he were to ask any woman for help, it would be Mrs. Winsted, a middle-aged widow with excellent taste who would sell him quality merchandise at a reasonable price without entangling his heart. Or perhaps Mrs. Jones, the mayor's wife, or...well, anyone but Evangeline.

"There you are, Adam." Evangeline's hands shook as she finished checking out Michael Faraday's *Experimental Researches in Electricity—Volume I* to

Adam Starling. On another day, one when she wasn't worried beyond distraction, she might try to engage the young man in conversation about his interests. She hoped her smiles would catch people's attention rather than her trembling fingers and frame.

"Thank you, ma'am." Adam gazed at the book with excitement, so at least he didn't notice her nervous twitching. "If you can find some similar books, I'd greatly appreciate it."

"I'll see what I can do. The library association has given me a budget for new acquisitions, so I'll make certain to look for books about the latest scientific advancements."

Adam thanked her, and she turned to the next patron, Mrs. Trujillo, whose husband owned a large ranch north of town, according to Susanna. "Did you find anything to your liking?"

"I did." The dark-haired woman held out the final copy of *Jane Eyre* for Evangeline to record. "I'm surprised I snatched this up before Georgia." She glanced at Georgia Eberly, who stood nearby watching the proceedings. "We all know how she loves a good romance."

"Yes, I do." Georgia laughed. "I'm happy to say we own a copy of Miss Charlotte Brontë's fine novel, among others, and I've read all of them over and over. When you finish reading *Jane Eyre*, we should get together to discuss it."

Mrs. Trujillo raised her delicate black eyebrows. "What a grand idea. Mrs. Benoit, what would you think of starting a book club right here at the library?"

Evangeline gulped down a sob, changing it to a

strangled laugh. "A book club is indeed a grand idea, especially in the winter when fewer outdoor activities are available. And a library is the perfect place to hold such meetings. You must spread the word and find out the best evening for everyone who wants to take part."

Everyone but her. Only the Lord knew where she'd be in the coming days, but it certainly wouldn't be in this town she'd come to love.

After Hugo accosted her in front of Williams's Café, offering outwardly polite greetings infused with intrusive inquiries about the children that sent more chills down her spine, he'd stepped into the street and headed for the jailhouse...and Justice. Evangeline fled to the library, planning to close it and hurry home so she could explain everything to Susanna and Nate before Justice apprehended her. She must beg her cousins to protect Isabelle and Gerard from Hugo, to take care of and perhaps even adopt them, once she was arrested. Would they do it? After all, Gerard had been minding Nate recently, and everyone adored Isabelle.

When she arrived back at the library, however, it was crowded with too many eager patrons for her to chase out or trust to Georgia. The young lady still had much to learn about Evangeline's procedures. Unable to leave, she did her best to work as though nothing were wrong, praying no one would notice her fearful trembling.

Moments after she'd talked herself into a dismal resignation regarding her future, Justice walked into the building. As always, the outdoor light behind him hid his expression, but from his posture, she could see he was staring in her direction.

He approached, and she nearly reached out in supplication to plead for her children's safety. Yet when he stopped in front of her desk, she could see his pleasant smile. His relaxed smile. She tried to return the same, but every muscle in her body shook with fright.

"Are you ill?" Compassion and kindness now shone from his eyes. "Do you need a glass of water?"

"Mrs. Benoit?" Georgia leaned down to grip Evangeline's shoulders and study her face. "Are you all right?"

"Yes." The word came out as a croak. "Just…a bit overwhelmed. It's been a busy day."

Justice fetched her a glass of lemonade from the refreshment table. "Maybe this will help." He set it on the desk.

"Sheriff." Georgia huffed playfully. "Never put a damp glass on wood." She lifted the vessel and placed a thick woolen coaster under it. "There."

"Yes, ma'am." Justice chuckled and gave the feisty girl one of his casual grins.

In those few seconds, Evangeline frantically tried to evaluate her circumstances. She could see Justice hadn't come to arrest her…unless he planned to wait until all the patrons left the library. But surely he wouldn't be so cruel as to banter with someone he planned to put in jail, unless it was his way of throwing off her suspicions so she wouldn't try to escape. She sipped the sugary lemonade to give herself even more time to think, but no sensible thoughts came to mind.

"Mrs. Benoit." Georgia leaned close again and studied Evangeline's face, concern filling her blue eyes. "Why don't you let the sheriff take you home. I've been watching you work, and I can manage the library. Truly I can. I haven't mentioned it yet, but I think you should take Saturdays off and let me take over for you so you can stay home with Gerard and Isabelle."

"That would be lovely." Before Hugo's alarming arrival, Evangeline wondered what to do with the children when she needed to work and they weren't in school. Now, as she was about to lose everything, her children's future care was her greatest worry. This put everything else in perspective. Perhaps she'd been too possessive of the library. Georgia was a responsible girl, and now it would be in good hands once Justice took her into custody. "Thank you."

"That settles it." Justice beckoned to Adam Starling. "Would you fetch Mrs. Benoit's buggy and my horse?"

"Yessir." Adam dashed from the building at his usual running pace and headed toward the livery stable.

Justice wended his way through the crowd of library patrons to the coatrack at the back of the room, returning to the desk with Evangeline's hat and coat. "Permit me."

Filled with trepidation, she stood and permitted him to help her into the wrap. Was it madness to go with Justice, to be alone with him? Would he question her about her debts, about Hugo? As his large, strong hands rested briefly on her shoulders, warmth beyond what the coat provided swept down her being.

How easy it would be to lean into his broad chest and feel his strength supporting her. To tell him everything and beg for his help, praying he retained a remnant of his long ago love for her.

But she had no such claim on him, and he was a lawman with the power to destroy all she held dear.

Against all reason, Justice felt an overwhelming desire to protect Evangeline. He told himself those feelings were due to her widowhood and his own protective nature toward those who were helpless, the trait that had drawn him into law enforcement. For those few seconds he'd let his hands rest on her shoulders, he'd been tempted to turn her around and pull her into a comforting embrace. What frightened her so badly that she still shook as he helped her into the buggy Adam fetched?

Once seated, Evangeline sat as far from him as she could on the driver's bench. Her gloved hands were tightly clasped in her lap, and her blue eyes stared straight ahead. Even her lips formed a tense line. This was more than anxiety over the library's opening. If anything, from what Justice had seen in his few minutes there, the event was a huge success. As much as he intended to remain aloof from her, he couldn't keep quiet.

"Look, I'm not trying to intrude into your affairs, but—"

Evangeline's delicate jaw dropped, and she stared at him. She gave her head a little shake. "No, I'm sure you're not. I do appreciate your taking me home, but I really could have driven myself."

He could see she was trying to redirect the conversation, which made him all the more curious about her distress.

"Evangeline, what upset you back there? Did something happen at the library? Was someone rude to you?" The thought stirred his temper despite his efforts to distance himself from her, as she'd distanced herself from him on this bench.

"No. Everyone was wonderful. They love having a special place to find good books at a leisurely pace instead of having to crowd into the corner of Mrs. Winsted's store." She sent him a quick smile, then looked away again. "Speaking of books and readers, I think Adam Starling should have the opportunity to further his education. He's interested in science, specifically electricity. If he can't attend college, perhaps the library can acquire more science books, and he can teach himself."

She was avoiding Justice's questions. All right, then. He would follow her lead, since she didn't want to confide in him. At least he was taking her home to rest. He'd make sure Susanna knew why Evangeline had come home early. Perhaps she could ferret out the cause of her cousin's distress.

He considered asking Evangeline's advice about the furnishings for his house—merely to have something to talk about, of course—but with her refusing to discuss her problem with him, he certainly wouldn't share that part of himself with her. He doubted she even knew or cared he was building himself a house. So they rode in silence for the thirty or so minutes it took to drive from town to the farthest house on Four Stones Ranch.

They drove onto the property to find the children

playing tag in the barnyard. Spying his mother, Gerard dashed to the buggy the moment Justice stopped by the back door hitching post. When the boy saw Justice, his bright face and open smile clouded up like a sudden rainstorm.

"What's he doing here?" For a ten-year-old, he sure did have a grown-up growl to his voice.

"And hello to you, too, Gerard." Evangeline smiled at her son as she hurried to climb down before Justice could offer his assistance. "I see you're playing nicely, so run back to your game."

"Is he staying?" The boy jutted his chin toward Justice.

She didn't answer him. Instead, she turned back and offered a grateful, if tight, smile. "Thank you for bringing me home. Would you like to come inside for coffee?" Everything about her expression and posture conveyed hope he wouldn't accept.

"It was my pleasure to bring you home, but I'll pass on the coffee." He touched the brim of his hat and turned the horse toward the barn.

Wes met him by the corral and took over tending the horse and buggy. Justice untied Thunder from the rear of the conveyance, mounted up and kicked his horse into a brisk canter. Only when he reached the main road did he remember he'd planned to tell Susanna about Evangeline's distress. He dismissed his worries about the failure. After all, Nate's wife was caring and perceptive, especially toward her loved ones. She and Nate would see to her cousin's needs.

Yet Justice experienced a lingering, bitter regret that he couldn't be the one to solve Evangeline's problem, whatever it was.

* * *

At Sunday morning services, Evangeline kept her eyes on the minister as long as she could before involuntarily turning to survey the congregation. Would Hugo be there among the decent Christians gathered to worship the Lord? Would he torment her with those Lucius-like eyes and wily smiles that hid his threats from all except his victim? After the service ended, would he tell the minister and Justice of her debts, both real and false, in front of her new friends?

But he hadn't come to church. And if Justice's friendly nod in her direction was any indication, Hugo hadn't told him about her crime. Like a snake waiting to strike, he'd hide himself until his revelations could inflict a fatal bite.

Reverend Thomas read the passage from the second chapter of Matthew's Gospel, which told about the flight of Joseph, Mary and Baby Jesus to Egypt to escape Herod's wrath. Then he set aside his sermon notes and stepped to the side of the lectern. "With Christmas approaching, you all will realize this is a bit out of order for the happenings in scripture, but the Lord impressed upon me early this morning that I should address this passage." He continued with his exposition in his usual conversational fashion.

Without meaning to, Evangeline found her thoughts wandering. Her flight might not have been righteous, as the biblical family's had been, but she knew the desperation Joseph surely must have felt as he fled an evil king to save God's infant Son. Like him, she'd run from an evil man to protect her own son and daughter after Hugo revealed his plans to have her declared incompetent so he could seize custody of her children. They would become his minions, trained in his wicked ways. With his proclivity toward mischief, her son might easily slide into true wickedness. Isabelle's sweet innocence would be destroyed. Even now, Evangeline shuddered with fear and ached with shame for calling to mind such thoughts while she sat in church. Beside her, Gerard questioned her with an innocent gaze. She gave him a sideways hug and tried again to listen to the sermon. And again failed.

During the flight to Egypt, did Joseph employ any diversions as she had done? Evangeline had traveled east by train from New Orleans, hoping if Hugo tried to track her, he'd assume she'd traveled to Marietta, Georgia, where Susanna's brother lived. She wouldn't think about her disappointment in Edward Junior's refusal to offer her a safe haven, only of his news that Susanna still lived and might give her a home. After she and the children reached Memphis, she'd changed their tickets to a westbound train and eventually reached Esperanza. The town's name was Spanish for *hope*, and she'd hoped it was a sign the Lord would give her safety with Susanna. But Hugo had found her. What hope did she have now? And yet, until Hugo struck, she had no choice but to continue on as before.

"Dear friends," Reverend Thomas said, "perhaps you are fleeing from some sort of danger, real or imagined, physical or spiritual. Be assured of this: just as the Lord led Joseph on the right path of protection for His Son, He will guide you in your time of need if only you call upon Him."

Of course God would protect and guide His perfect Son. But what about a desperate mother whom some would call a thief who was fleeing debts she could never repay?

The minister concluded the service with an invitation to anyone who might want to accept Jesus Christ as their Savior. After the closing prayer and hymn, several people approached Evangeline and complimented her work at the library. Justice wasn't among them, but he did send her another friendly smile across the room. He'd never know how much those smiles meant to her.

Evangeline delivered the children to school the next morning, then proceeded to the library. Before opening it to the public at ten o'clock, she spent almost two hours working on the Christmas village despite doubting she'd see it completed and unveiled after the Christmas pageant. For Hugo undoubtedly would persuade Justice to take her away in handcuffs before then.

She finished painting the last of the wooden pieces, then opened the back room's high windows to let in a breeze to dispel the smell of turpentine as she cleaned her brushes and hands. A glance at her pin watch revealed it was time to open the library. As she set her supplies on an upper shelf, a knock sounded on the glass front door.

"Oh, Justice, use your key. You don't need to knock," she told herself, even as her pulse quickened at the thought of seeing him. Emerging from the room, she saw not the sheriff, but Hugo, a cheerful smile making the most of his handsome face. Too bad such cruelty lay behind his perfectly formed visage.

Heart dropping, she crossed the room and unlocked the door. "Yes? You wanted something?"

He laughed, a sound far too reminiscent of his cousin Lucius. "Good morning, my dear. You're looking beautiful, as always. Why don't you quit this ridiculous menial job and come to work for me? You and Isabelle will make such lovely additions to my…shall we say, harem?"

Her stomach did a violent turn, and she almost threw up in his face.

"There, there, my dear." Twirling that ridiculous walking stick, Hugo strutted into the library. "No need to make yourself ill. Like all of my girls, you'll get used to the profession after proper instruction."

Evangeline swallowed hard and repeated her question. "What do you want, Hugo?" She knew, of course, but she would make him say it.

"Why, I simply want to get familiar with your quaint little cow town. It's always interesting to observe how the rabble lives." He sauntered to the bookshelves and appeared to study the titles. "Not much of a library, is it? So few books."

"Of course there aren't many books. People have borrowed many of them." She shouldn't have answered him. He deserved no such information. She sat at her desk and busied herself with paperwork, happy to find Georgia had kept everything organized.

Hugo continued his perusal, taking down one book at a time to inspect its contents before replacing it on the shelf. "Tsk, tsk. Too bad you didn't bring

Cousin Lucius's books with you. They'd make this pathetic little hovel into a true library. Oh, wait. I forgot. The books were sold." He slid one of his sly looks her way, flattening his handsome face into a snake-like appearance. "Fortunately for me, I was able to buy them."

Evangeline gasped softly, but Hugo didn't seem to notice. So he was the one who'd purchased all of those lovely books at the auction. Some of them were first editions of classic novels. While Lucius was alive, she'd spent many a lonely day reading such great literature as Shakespeare's plays from an early printing and poetry by Milton or Donne. That vast library would indeed be a marvelous addition to this one.

"Tell you what."

She gasped again at his sudden appearance beside her desk, and he emitted a chilling laugh.

"There, there. Don't be frightened. I simply want to make you an offer. I'll ship my cousin's entire library to this dirty little hamlet. What do you think?"

She huffed out a laugh of disbelief. "I hardly think you'd give away such a treasure."

His laugh was now light, and he waved a dismissive hand in the air. "Of course not. All I want is for you and your lovely children to return with me to New Orleans, and—"

Evangeline jumped to her feet. "Get out." She pointed toward the door. Through the window, she saw Justice entering the bank across the street. Would he come here next? Would the two men confront her together?

"Very well." Hugo strolled toward the door. "We're not finished, you know."

After he left, she slumped down in her chair, fighting tears. So he and Justice wouldn't confront her, at least not now. But Hugo gave no reason for coming here today, nor had he mentioned the promissory notes Lucius signed, for which she was responsible. He hadn't reminded her of his friend Judge Grable, who would gladly declare her an unfit mother and seize her children. He probably came simply to torment her, to make her life miserable until she did what he demanded.

And she had no one to turn to now that her world was about to come crashing down around her.

Chapter Nine

Through the bank window, Justice observed Hugo Giles as he ambled up Main Street. It appeared he'd been to the library, yet he didn't carry a book.

"Hello, Sheriff." Nolan Means joined him by the front window. "Did you need to see me?"

"Nope. Just made a deposit." He nodded toward Reuben Brandt, who stood inside the teller's cage recording figures in a ledger. Earlier, Justice's foreman delivered his mine's latest haul and gave him a report on a new vein. With no place to keep the gold safe in his rooms over the jail, he always brought it next door to the bank right away.

"You see that fella?" He indicated Giles, who was almost out of sight.

Nolan followed his gaze. "Yes. Hugo Giles. He came in a short while ago. Hails from New Orleans."

"Did he open an account?" Or perhaps he was scouting out the place to see if it would be easy to rob.

The banker shook his head. "He wanted to introduce himself. Said he's thinking of settling down and wants to get the lay of the land."

"Hmm. Sounds harmless enough." And not exactly what he'd said to Justice.

Giles could still be considering a move to Esperanza. First he visited Justice, then the town banker. Friendly visits, the kind to demonstrate he was an upstanding citizen. He hadn't attended church yesterday, but maybe no one invited him. Justice could invite him, or he could ask Reverend Thomas to visit the man at the hotel. Having the minister call on a new man in town instead of the sheriff would be less threatening.

"Say, how's your house coming?" Nolan had been the first one to encourage Justice to build his own place.

"Should be finished by Christmas."

"Are you planning a housewarming?" Nolan asked the question as if it were a reasonable expectation, but Justice grimaced.

"Not likely."

The banker chuckled. "You let me know if you change your mind. My wife would be glad to help you with entertaining. She's not happy unless she throws a party every other week." He clapped Justice on the shoulder. "Our annual Christmas ball will take place on December 22. You'll receive our invitation in the next few days."

"Thank you. I'll keep the evening open." He bade Nolan goodbye and headed over to the library.

The moment he stepped into the cozy room, he knew Evangeline hadn't recovered from last Friday's distress, despite her peaceful countenance in church yesterday. Her eyes were rimmed with red, and her cheeks appeared pinched with anxiety.

"Morning, Evangeline." He kept his tone light.

"Good morning, Sheriff." She buried her head in the book on her desk.

"How are you today?"

"Well. And you?"

This wasn't solving anything. He brought a chair from one of the reading tables and set it beside her desk. "I don't think you're well. I think something's troubling you and—"

"Good morning, Evangeline, Sheriff." Laurie Northam entered the library with her year-old son on her hip. "Evangeline, Georgia tells me you had quite a rush on Friday and Saturday. I hope you still have some good books available. Little Bart here only takes one long nap these days, and since I can't practice piano while he's sleeping, I need something to read." She walked to the shelves holding novels and histories.

"Good morning, Laurie." Justice stood and moved his chair back in place. Two more ladies appeared in the doorway, and soon the women had turned the place into a hen party, gushing in their female way over the baby, the library, clothes and who knew what else. Disappointed at the interruption, Justice stared at Evangeline, hoping to catch her eye. She avoided his gaze and instead focused on the other ladies. He had no choice but to leave and hope for another opportunity to talk with her alone.

Back at the office, he considered how he was going to finish the Christmas village in less than four weeks if he couldn't work in the library during the day. More important, he needed to break through the wall Evangeline had built around herself. The moment he'd observed her anguished expression, he'd given up all pretense about remaining aloof. Something was wrong, and he planned to find out what it was.

Yesterday, when the pastor preached about fleeing troubles, Justice realized he'd been trying to run away from his past, at least the part involving Evangeline. She might have chosen to marry Lucius Benoit rather than him, but that didn't mean he shouldn't help her with whatever problem was tormenting her now. He wasn't certain he could help her without endangering his heart again, but he had to try.

"Lord, please help me figure this out." The prayer wasn't out of his mouth before a vision of Hugo Giles came to mind. "Huh. And I call myself a lawman. This Cajun man comes to town and I don't link him to Evangeline? Where has my brain gone?" On the other hand, the man's youth and gambler-like appearance made him an unlikely acquaintance of a decent society lady.

After his midday meal at Williams's Café, he would visit the man at the hotel. To invite him to church, of course. And to discuss their common background in Louisiana.

More ladies entered the library, and Evangeline indulged herself in some pleasant feelings regarding her successful enterprise. At least when she left town, citizens of Esperanza would have a library they could be proud of. Perhaps even the book club would proceed. Laurie Northam was Georgia Eberly's older sister and, like Georgia, had a knack for pulling people together, especially women. The sisters could lead the endeavor. Right now, Laurie basked in the praise the others were heaping on chubby little Bart, who, she explained, was named after his father.

"When my husband was born," Laurie said, "his sister couldn't say his name, so he was nicknamed Tolley. As in Bar-tolley-mew."

All of the ladies laughed at this revelation. Evangeline permitted herself a moment of restorative laughter, knowing full well she would have to address her problems once she returned home after work. Susanna and Nate had a right to know of Hugo's presence in town *and* her flight from justice.

"Mrs. Benoit, I understand you're starting a book club," Mrs. Stanley said. "You must tell me when it takes place and what book we'll be discussing so I can attend."

"Oh, tell me, too," Mrs. Brice chimed in. "Do you think we should include our husbands?"

"Humph. Not mine." Mrs. Stanley shook her head. "He'll take over the conversation. Let's limit it to us ladies."

The others laughed because Mrs. Stanley appeared to be joking. But not Evangeline. Lucius frequently told her to shut up if she dared to express an opinion while they were socializing. That bitter memory spoiled her current enjoyment and caused her to doubt her plans to tell Susanna and Nate about Hugo. She couldn't explain the debts without breaking down in tears and telling them how Lucius had controlled and abused her so cruelly. It would sound like an excuse for running away from her responsibilities. The memories themselves brought a rush of heat to her cheeks and shame to her heart.

Justice finished his dinner and stepped out onto the boardwalk to head for the hotel. A half block away, he saw Hugo Giles headed his way. This was good. He'd invite the man over to his office where Justice would have the upper hand.

"Hello, Sheriff." Giles lifted a hand in greeting. In his other hand, he held a brown leather portfolio. "I was on my way to see you."

"Come on over."

All the better for Giles to take the initiative, because the man wouldn't be as defensive as if a lawman approached him. They shook hands and proceeded across the street. Once seated across the desk from Justice, Giles studied his hands and cleared his throat.

"Sheriff, this isn't going to be easy for me. I don't like to cause trouble for anyone, especially a widow with children." He grimaced. "My late cousin's widow."

"Hmm." Justice offered a sympathetic frown while struggling to quell the sudden turmoil in his belly. So this man was related to Lucius Benoit... and, by marriage, to Evangeline. He hadn't known Lucius well, but now it began to make sense. "Your consideration is commendable."

Giles smiled modestly at the compliment and shrugged. "Have you met Mrs. Benoit, the town librarian? Yes, of course you have. You're obviously a man who takes his responsibilities seriously and knows everyone who lives in his community."

His ingratiating comment caused another turn of Justice's stomach. "Go on."

"Before Evangeline…Mrs. Benoit came here, she and my late cousin lived in New Orleans. I'm sad to say she left considerable debts behind. Slipped out of town, actually, as though she didn't mean to repay the hardworking dressmakers, milliners and other merchants with whom she ran up large bills. She also owes my own bank four thousand dollars, plus interest." Another grimace. "Unfortunately, it's my responsibility to collect those debts." He held out the portfolio. "I have all of the documentation here, if you'd like to see it."

So this man was a banker. Yet he hadn't told Nolan of their common occupation.

Justice took the portfolio in hand, released the latch and removed two dozen or so pages. With all the self-control he could muster, he studied the official looking papers. The first was a promissory note signed by Lucius to his cousin for unspecified debts owed for a total of four thousand dollars, with interest to accrue as long as any of the balance remained unpaid. The second page was a power of attorney assigned to Giles by seven merchants. The following pages were bills for hats, gowns, shoes and a myriad of female fripperies. A feminine hand had signed *Evangeline L. Benoit* on each one. Justice hadn't seen her handwriting in many years, but these elegant signatures appeared authentic.

"When she left New Orleans," Giles said, "she and the children traveled east by train. I assume she meant us to think she was going to her relatives in Georgia. But halfway to their supposed destination, they disembarked and boarded a train heading west. My investigators tracked her here."

A mask of sorrow covered the young man's face, down to the red rims around his eyes. Nonetheless, Justice felt deep in his bones something wasn't right. He could easily believe Evangeline had bought clothes and hats from the best New Orleans merchants. From what he'd seen, she still possessed them. Still wore them. But then, she'd always loved fine things. Loved them more than she'd loved him and had married the man who could provide them for her.

He tried without success to dismiss the pain. After all these years, the wound remained raw.

"It was difficult enough to lose my cousin," Giles continued, "but to have his widow abscond with his children, whom he asked me to rear…well, you can imagine my grief. It's my responsibility to see everything is set to right both for the debts and for the children's care."

Another alarm sounded in Justice's head, and he leaned toward Giles in an aggressive manner. "Did he know he was going to die? Is that why he asked you to take care of the children? Did he leave a will to that effect?"

Giles blinked, and he sat back defensively at the hammering questions. "Uh, no. It came up in casual conversation, and of course I agreed. He said Evangeline was neglectful, that the servants were rearing the children while she socialized, and the little ones suffered because of it. Unfortunately, he didn't have time to add this directive to his will." He lifted his chin with a determined look. "But of course we know a judge can declare a mother unfit and assign a caring guardian for the little ones." He placed a hand on his chest, maybe to enhance the appearance of sincerity. "Not that I would want to call for that unless it was absolutely necessary."

Justice resumed a more relaxed posture and toyed with a pencil on his desk. "Of course, since Mrs. Benoit lives in Colorado now, she'll be under the jurisdiction of our courts, should worse come to worst."

"Of course." Giles coughed artificially. "But one can assume Colorado law is similar to Louisiana law. I would think all courts would consider the needs of the children before anything or anyone else."

"I'll check into it." Despite his churning insides, Justice managed to keep his expression interested but neutral. "Then we'll see what we can do."

"Thank you." Giles sighed with apparent relief. "May I count on your help in convincing my cousin to return to New Orleans with me so we can avoid going to court both here and there? Please understand. I don't want to destroy her. I merely want to collect what is owed and make sure the children are well taken care of. I know she has the money because she sold my cousin's house and all its furnishings."

Justice didn't answer his request for help. "Have you spoken to Mrs. Benoit?" He gathered the papers and returned them to the portfolio.

"Yes, at the library this morning." Giles reclaimed his sorrowful look. "She was quite alarmed at seeing me, so I didn't linger. I didn't want to upset her while she was at work. I don't even know the best way to confront her so we can solve our problems in a way to benefit us all." He lifted his hands in a supplicating gesture. "Will you help me, Sheriff?"

Employing an old device used by his mentor, Justice stared out the window thoughtfully and tapped his chin as if considering the matter. At last, he spoke. "As I said, I'll look into the matter and see what I can do. In the meantime, I'll ask you not to confront the lady about these debts." He patted the portfolio.

Giles reached for it, but Justice pulled it back. Real alarm showed in the younger man's eyes.

"Relax. Let me show these to our town lawyer. He can help us build a case."

Giles hesitated, then nodded. "Very well." He stood and extended his hand, but worry still clouded his eyes. "Thank you, Sheriff."

"Giles." Justice rose and accepted his handshake.

"By the way, I never did get your name." He chuckled. "Other than Sheriff."

Justice held on to a laugh. "Gareau. Justice Gareau." He infused his last name with his thickest Cajun inflection.

Giles's jaw dropped, and he stared at him for a full five seconds. "You're from Louisiana?"

"Yep." He anticipated the other man's next question, which might cause problems, so he hurried on to say, "Left over eleven years ago. You know any Gareaus?"

"Well—"

"Yes, you're right. It's a common name. I've met a number of folks named Giles, too." He walked to the door and opened it. "I'll investigate this situation and get back to you. In the meantime, remember what we agreed. Don't confront Mrs. Benoit with your—for lack of a better word—demands."

"Yes. Yes, of course." Giles exited the office. He glanced east toward the library, but then turned west toward the hotel. He'd apparently taken the advice not to confront Evangeline.

As much as Justice doubted all of the man's accusations were true, he still could see Evangeline spending herself into debt. Even so, to his own hurt, he longed to protect her. Yet too many questions remained for him to take one side or the other. Her accuser might be a slick dandy, but that didn't discount the evidence.

He slumped back in the desk chair and put his head in his hands. If she did owe the money, should he send her back to her creditors? Didn't she still have the money from the sale of the house and its contents? If not, should he pay off her debts? He could see she was trying to make a good life for her children, but that didn't erase the past. Had she been part of her father's crooked dealings in the business their fathers shared? That would account for her character flaw of fleeing her debts. Before his father died, he tried to tell Justice something about her, but could not finish before he expired.

Justice examined the documents again. Along with other clothes, the dressmaker listed a red velvet evening gown and a red satin cape to go with it, but no widow's weeds. He couldn't imagine Evangeline in red. And who had sewed the two black bombazine dresses she wore? The milliner claimed a fee for hats with ostrich feathers and delicate evening slippers, but not the practical high-top leather shoes she wore every day. The stylish brown traveling suit and matching hat she'd worn upon arrival in Esperanza weren't listed. Nor did any of the bills mention the expensive gardenia perfume she wore. Perhaps she'd managed to pay for some of the items outright.

"Lord, please help me to figure this out because I surely cannot do it by myself." Nor could he dismiss the longing in his heart to fix everything for her.

After the ladies left the library, Evangeline reshelved the books they'd perused but didn't check out. Then she ate her sandwich. Now she had nothing to do but think, and all of her thoughts depressed her. If winter weren't almost upon them, if she had money for travel and a place to go, she would once again take her children and run. She tried to pray, but guilt held her captive. Finally, she managed to lift a petition for God's mercy…and Justice's, not for herself but for her children. A gentle peace stole into her heart, along with the odd feeling that Justice could be trusted despite the way he'd abandoned her all those years ago. But feelings had failed her before, so she wouldn't depend on them now.

The afternoon wore on, and a light snow began to fall. The fluffy flakes piled up and covered the streets, hiding the partially frozen wagon wheel ruts. Evangeline wished the ruts in her life could be so easily covered.

Around three thirty, small groups of children began to walk past the library on their way home from school. She watched for her own and Susanna's to join her, as they did every afternoon. Finally, Lizzie and Natty arrived a half hour late, but Isabelle and Gerard were not with them.

"I don't know where they are, Cousin Evie." Lizzie had adopted her mother's nickname for Evangeline. "A man was waiting for them after school, and Gerry knew him, so they went with him. We waited for them to come back, but Natty was getting cold, so we came here."

Terror struck her. Had Hugo kidnapped her babies, as he'd threatened to do before she fled with them from New Orleans? She grabbed her coat and put it on as she walked toward the door. Whatever the cost, she must go to Justice and beg his help to rescue them.

She hadn't yet put on her hat when they burst through the front door—with Hugo right behind them, a malicious smirk on his face.

"Mother," cried Gerard. "Look who's here. Cousin Hugo." He rushed across the room and flung himself into her arms. "Did you know he was coming to visit us?"

Evangeline hadn't seen her son this happy since before Lucius died. She hugged him tightly with one arm and held out the other to welcome Isabelle, who didn't look happy at all. In fact, her daughter buried her face in Evangeline's side.

"Good afternoon, Evangeline." Hugo removed his overcoat and laid it across the back of a chair. "I hope you're having a good day."

Her heart racing with relief and fear, she eyed him. His expression transformed into that of an indulgent older relative. She would not speak to him unless forced to.

"Come, my darlings." She ushered the children to a table, removed their coats and her own, and brought out the cookies and milk Susanna had sent, as she did each day. Lizzie and Natty welcomed the treat, but Hugo and her own children refused it.

"No, thank you, my dear." Hugo's smirk returned. "I've recently enjoyed a small repast."

"Cousin Hugo took us to the hotel for hot chocolate," Gerard announced with an air of importance. Then he relented. "Well, I will take a cookie."

Isabelle didn't speak, but stuck close to Evangeline while the others ate. She couldn't help but think that Hugo had done something to frighten her.

"Gerry," Lizzie called, her blue eyes twinkling, "tell your mother about our tryouts for the Christmas pageant."

He shrugged. "Who cares about that stupid play."

"It's not a stupid play." Lizzie scowled at him briefly, then gave Evangeline one of her sweet smiles. "We have the play every year, but it's always fun to do it again. Aunt Marybeth and Mrs. Means are our directors. We're having tryouts after school tomorrow."

At last Isabelle relaxed and smiled up at Evangeline. "I want to be in the play."

"Yes, you should be." Hugo winked across the table at her. "You'll be the most beautiful girl on the stage. I have no doubt you could be a great actress."

A sick feeling arose inside Evangeline as her daughter leaned against her again. But she still must not say anything to upset the children.

"We'll talk about it this evening," she told them.

Hugo stood and made a pretense of searching for

a book, clicking his tongue and shaking his head from time to time. "Such a paltry offering. Too bad my cousin's library—"

"You must excuse us, Hugo." Evangeline rose and started cleaning up the refreshments. "Children, put on your coats. It's time to go home." She'd noticed Adam approaching with her buggy.

"Good afternoon, Mrs. Benoit." Adam took off his hat as he entered the library. "Your buggy's ready. I thought with the snow you might want an early start going home." As he spoke, he looked at Hugo with polite curiosity.

Evangeline had no choice but to introduce them. "Adam, this is Mr. Giles." She refused to credit him as a relation. Nor would she present Adam to Hugo, as manners dictated when introducing a younger person to an older one, however small the gap in their ages.

"How do you do, sir?" Adam reached out to him.

Hugo sniffed and looked down his nose at Adam's hand. "Really, Evangeline, have you come to this? Presenting the help to their betters?"

Evangeline moved between the two young men. "Adam, here are some of Susanna's delicious cookies. Please take them to your sisters and brother."

"Thank you, ma'am." Adam, always humble, hadn't reacted to Hugo's inexcusable rudeness.

She, however, couldn't let the matter rest. Her back still to Hugo, she continued to address Adam. "I understand the tryouts for the Christmas pageant will take place tomorrow after school. I will be happy to see Molly and Jack get home safely afterward." She'd met Adam's well-behaved younger siblings at church.

He smiled. "Thank you, ma'am. That's mighty kind of you. I'll see what Ma says." He waved to the children and made his exit.

Evangeline held the door and stared at Hugo. "You may leave now."

He chuckled in his evil way. "As you wish. But I look forward to seeing you again soon. Very soon."

Her stomach twisted in knots at the warning, but she tried her best to keep her distress from the children. She must have succeeded, because on the way home, the little ones chattered and sang, as always. Even Isabelle perked up and joined the conversation. At supper, Gerard was still in good spirits, eager to tell Susanna and Nate about his "very important" cousin, who'd come to town solely to visit Evangeline, Isabelle and him.

"Cousin?" Susanna questioned her with raised eyebrows. "Have you mentioned him before?"

Before answering, Evangeline glanced at Nate, who watched with a shuttered expression. "No, I haven't. It never occurred to me to talk about my late husband's cousin. We weren't close, and I certainly didn't expect him to follow me here." Not quite a lie. She'd prayed Hugo wouldn't find her. Maybe Susanna's disagreeable brother had told him where to search.

"What do you suppose he wants?" Nate's tone was light, but his eyes asked more than his words.

Evangeline offered a smile and a ladylike shrug. "I can't imagine. He has yet to tell me."

Susanna gave her husband a meaningful look. He returned a nod.

"Well, of course we must have him out to supper."

Susanna busied herself serving Gerard more mashed potatoes and gravy. "Why not bring him out tomorrow after the tryouts?"

Isabelle stopped eating and leaned close to Evangeline. If she had a lick of sense, she would tell Susanna and Nate everything this very evening. Instead, after Susanna put her little ones to bed, Evangeline lingered at each of her own children's bedsides to learn all she could about their time with Hugo.

"Mommy, I don't like him." Isabelle whispered so Lizzie couldn't hear her, but her cousin had already fallen asleep.

"Why not, my darling?" Evangeline brushed her daughter's hair back from her sweet, innocent face.

"He looks at me funny." She studied Evangeline's face to see her reaction. "I don't like it."

"I see." She kept a mild expression in place.

"You told me to be polite to grown-ups." Tears appeared in Isabelle's eyes and glistened in the lamplight. "But I don't want to be polite to him."

Evangeline swallowed hard, trying to keep her supper down. "You don't have to be polite to anyone who makes you uncomfortable. Stay away from Hugo. If I'm not around, go to an adult you trust and ask him or her to bring you to me."

"I will." Isabelle smiled, satisfied with the answer.

Evangeline kissed her good-night and proceeded to the room Gerard shared with his boy cousins. Gerard was wide-awake and eager to talk.

"Mother, I like Cousin Hugo. He's real smart, and he talked to me about Father. Even though they were cousins, they were like father and son, he said. He said Father was a good man." He paused and gave her an accusing look. "He said the reason Father didn't spend more time with us was because you didn't want him to. Is that true?"

Tears burned her eyes, and she brushed a hand down Gerard's tortured face. He wasn't old enough to learn the truth about his father's evil activities.

"My darling, your father was a businessman with many responsibilities. He needed to spend a great deal of time away from home." She scrambled to think of a way to diminish Hugo's false accusation. "Your Cousin Hugo is an unmarried man without children—" at least none that she knew of "—so he doesn't understand family life."

Her response seemed to satisfy Gerard, for he nodded against his pillow. "I can't wait to see him after school tomorrow."

"You have tryouts for the play tomorrow." She would make him go, no matter how much he resisted.

"Ugh." He scowled at her and rolled on his side, pulling the covers over his head. "At least he's coming to supper tomorrow night," he muttered through the woolen blanket.

If the situation weren't so distressing, she would laugh at his boyish antics. Instead, she kissed him where his cheek should be under the blanket and left the room.

Although tempted to retire for the night, she walked down the short hallway to the parlor. With every step, she prayed for courage to tell her cousins why Hugo had come after her. To her relief, Nate wasn't there, but Susanna sat in her usual rocking chair, a basket of mending in her lap. She looked up and smiled at Evangeline.

"Nate's out at the barn seeing about a mare who's about to drop her foal."

"How wonderful. Another foal for Gerard to enjoy." She longed for the day when her son could have his own horse again.

"I know he was disappointed over not getting to see the colt at Rand and Marybeth's anymore." Susanna kept her eyes on the sock she was darning.

"Jealous, you mean." It wouldn't help to deny the truth about her son's volatile emotions. "I'm still mortified over the way he treated little Randy."

"Water under the bridge." Susanna removed the glass darning egg from the sock and picked up another one. "Speaking of Marybeth, she asked me to ask you to attend the rehearsals. That is, if Gerard is going to be in the play."

Evangeline sighed. "I don't blame her. Yes, I can close the library early or ask Georgia to come in for two hours each day until Christmas Eve."

The matter settled, she excused herself and went to bed. Upset about having to watch over her son's behavior, she no longer had the emotional strength to wait for Nate and begin a long, complicated discussion about her tragic life in New Orleans. All of that would come out soon enough.

Chapter Ten

After a night of agonizing prayer, Justice started his day at Tolley Northam's law office, next door to the jailhouse. The young lawyer studied the promissory note, the power of attorney and the merchant invoices.

"This is quite a stack of debts." Tolley shook his head. "I can't see Mrs. Benoit being so dishonest as to refuse to pay them. She appears to be a sincere Christian lady."

"That's the problem. She appears to be." Justice heard the sorrow in his own voice.

Tolley stared at him. "You sound personally disappointed. Were you and the lady more than acquaintances in New Orleans?"

The question startled him. During these two months Evangeline had been in Esperanza, no one asked it, despite their obviously common background. Glad to speak of it at last, he unfolded to Tolley the story of their youthful romance, including the promises to wait for each other while he traveled to Europe on his Grand Tour for close to nineteen months.

"Then I came home to find out she was about to marry Lucius Benoit, one of my father's partners and a crook if I ever met one. She refused to see me." He released a long sigh. "My father died the next day, the same day she married and...my nineteenth birthday."

"Ouch." Tolley grimaced in sympathy.

"I should have known something was wrong when she didn't answer my letters."

"I don't blame you for being disappointed, though sometimes letters do go astray, especially overseas." Tolley glanced at the documents again. "Here's what we'll do. Let me check into Louisiana laws regarding debts. Of course she'll have to pay the merchants."

"How about the note with Giles's bank? If memory serves, I think a widow can be held responsible for her husband's debts under Louisiana Civil Law, even if she didn't sign the note, but what about Colorado law?"

"Sounds like you want to protect her." Tolley gave him a questioning grin Justice chose to ignore. "You know, of course, most states agree to return felons to the state where the crime took place, even if their laws differ."

"Yes, I know." Justice shrugged helplessly. "I've never in my life as a lawman been in more of a quandary. I'm still not sure about the matter of the children. It's obvious Evangeline tries to be a good mother, so I'm suspicious of Giles in regard to wanting the guardianship."

"Let me check into Colorado law regarding custody of children whose father has died. In some states, a judge must grant a widow the right to rear her own children. Of course, if the mother is competent and can support them, as Evangeline seems able to do, I can't see any reasonable judge taking them from her."

"I can't figure out why her husband wanted Giles to rear the children."

Tolley gave him a long look. "Maybe he didn't."

"Ah." The question appeared as a lifeline, and Justice grabbed it. "So we should find out why a young, unmarried and probably busy banker wants to adopt two children who could end up penniless."

"Maybe they're not penniless. We need to discover whether or not Evangeline has the money from the sale of Lucius's property." Tolley took a lined tablet from his desk. "You know the quickest way to find out is for you to spend more time with her."

"I suppose." Justice wouldn't tell him about the secret Christmas village, but he must find a way to work alongside Evangeline on the project again. Then he'd casually ask questions about her marriage, even though the idea of revisiting the painful past turned his stomach.

"Do you mind if I bring Nate in on this?" Tolley often spoke of his oldest brother's wisdom, so Justice considered it.

"Since Evangeline is his houseguest, he has a right to know if he is harboring a lawbreaker." He hated the sound of his own words. "Tell you what. I'll invite myself to supper tonight and have a talk with him."

"Sounds good. I'll wire some folks in New Orleans and Denver to find out about these laws. Let's pray a winter storm doesn't bring down the telegraph wires before we get some answers." Tolley jotted down a few notes, then patted the portfolio, to which he'd returned the documents. "If it's all right with you, I'll keep these."

"Certainly."

"By the by, I've been wanting to commend you for the way you've dealt with Evangeline's son and his friends. They certainly did a good job keeping the streets clean as they worked off their sentence."

"Only because either my deputy or I watched over them."

"Still, you could have put them in jail. You know, when I was their age, I was a troublemaker myself. Probably should have been locked up for some of the things I did, but we didn't have a jail back then."

Justice nodded. "I've heard. Knowing what a stickler for the law you are now, it's hard to believe."

Tolley sat back and studied Justice. "Go easy on Gerard. If his father was as crooked as you remember, the boy needs strong, godly men in his life to show him a better path."

"I'll try." In fact, he already had tried, everything from kindness to quiet firmness, even joking. Yet every day when he visited the boy's classroom, Gerard's belligerent attitude remained the same. He traded looks with Cart and Deely, and they all sneered at Justice.

Contending with this troubled—and troublesome—boy was turning out to be as difficult as learning the truth about his mother.

"Children, I'm so proud of you." Marybeth Northam stood beside Electra Means at the front of the sanctuary, while some thirty children sat in the front four pews. "You're all such good little actors and actresses."

"It's always hard to decide how to assign the parts." Electra held up a small tablet where she and Marybeth had written notes during the tryouts.

Seated beside Evangeline, Isabelle wiggled with excitement. Beyond her, Lizzie sat still, but her eyes twinkled in anticipation. On Evangeline's other side, Gerard sat back against the pew with his arms crossed. To her surprise, he'd actually performed his forced tryout quite well, reading several parts, if not with enthusiasm, at least without rebellion.

"Now, if you aren't assigned the part you wanted," Marybeth went on, "don't be sad. Every part is important whether small or large, and we need each of you to do your best."

"Quit yapping and tell us who gets what." Gerard had the good sense to mutter the words quietly. Nevertheless, Evangeline nudged him with her elbow and softly shushed him.

"Our angel choir who sing to the shepherds will be Molly Starling, Lizzie Northam, Isabelle Benoit—"

While Marybeth announced several more children's names, Isabelle emitted a soft squeal of delight and hugged Lizzie. Evangeline couldn't be more pleased for the girls. She would happily sew their costumes, if they weren't already made.

"Our shepherds are Jack Starling, Natty Northam, Randy Northam…" Electra named several more children Evangeline didn't know as both shepherds and wise men. At the end of the list, only three parts remained.

Evangeline held her breath. Would Gerard be left out?

"Our innkeeper—" Marybeth sent a tight smile in her direction "—will be Gerard Benoit."

To her surprise, he sat up and grinned. Evangeline's heart skipped a beat. Perhaps this Christmas play would be just the thing to change her son's life.

Finally, Mary and Joseph were announced, children whom she didn't know. Then the directors dismissed them, and the sanctuary erupted in gaiety before the little ones dashed outside into the falling snow.

While Evangeline helped Isabelle and Lizzie into their wraps, Gerard started up the aisle toward the door.

"Wait, son—" She started after him, but stopped abruptly.

Hugo stood at the back of the room wearing a scowl. Beside him, Justice leaned against the wall, arms crossed, a lazy grin on his face that set her heart to racing. Both men now walked toward her. Would they bring her world crashing down around her right here in the church?

Justice reached her first. "Afternoon, Evangeline. Nate asked me to make sure you and the children got home safely. I brought a sleigh so we won't get stuck in the snow."

"No need, Sheriff." Hugo elbowed his way to Justice's side, blocking the aisle. "I can manage to get them safely home, wherever home might be."

Evangeline scrambled mentally to sort things out, as she'd often done with Lucius. Turning to the four children, hers and Susanna's, she forced a laugh. "My, my, imagine that. Two fine gentlemen both want to take us through the falling snow." She gave Hugo a little smirk. "Of course you realize, if Nate sent the sheriff to fetch us home, I must do as my cousin advised. You may follow along, if you wish." She choked on the idea of repeating Susanna's supper invitation.

"I'm going to ride with Cousin Hugo." Gerard stepped over to him as though taking sides in a baseball game.

"I don't know—" Evangeline looked to Justice, not really expecting him to help her.

"Cousin Susanna said to invite you to supper." Gerard gazed up at Hugo as if he were his hero.

"Did she? Excellent. It's settled then." Hugo put an arm around Gerard. "I shall rent a horse for the two of us, and we can follow the sleigh."

Gerard beamed at the mention of riding a horse. Evangeline regretted that Nate hadn't had time to let him ride one of the Northam horses. Now he admired Hugo all the more.

"Shall we go?" Justice spoke to Hugo, taking the situation out of Evangeline's hands.

If not for their earlier moment of apparent rancor, she would think the two men planned this.

While Hugo and Gerard went to the livery stable, Evangeline and the children, including the Starlings, were tucked under the blanket in the sleigh. Justice took the driver's seat and drove across town to deliver Molly and Jack Starling to their mother.

They met the others at the corner. Gerard rode proudly behind Hugo on a brown horse whose coat had grown long and shaggy for the winter. Natty and the girls sat between Justice and Evangeline, giggling and wiggling underneath the blanket as Justice urged the two sleigh horses forward. His own dappled gray mount was tied to the sleigh for his ride home. They made their way along the darkening streets of Esperanza to the highway leading south.

"Did you ever ride in a sleigh before?" Justice's question, asked over the heads of the still-giggling children, surprised Evangeline because of his jolly tone.

"No." She couldn't permit herself to imagine he truly meant to be her friend. She felt a shiver shake her body, not knowing whether it was the temperature or the fact that she was sharing a sleigh with Justice. "How long did it take for you to adjust to this cold climate?" The breeze nipped at her nose and froze her lips, making it difficult to form words properly.

"A few years." He gave her an open smile, which did nothing to soften her trepidation about heading toward an evening with evil Hugo Giles and the sheriff. She felt as if she were headed toward her doom. "Even in the worst blizzards, I never consider going South again."

"Why not?" And why, oh, why, was she making inane conversation about the weather with the man who would soon arrest her?

"I've found it's not where I live but who my neighbors are that makes a place home."

She could only nod in agreement. The people of Esperanza were good, decent folk who had welcomed and accepted her and her children. If not for her coming doom, she could be so happy here.

She knew that no matter how much it would sicken

her to speak of such things, she must tell Nate and Susanna of Hugo's plans. Surely they wouldn't permit Gerard and Isabelle to face such a dreadful future.

They arrived at the ranch in about a half hour. As always, Wes met them in the barnyard and helped Justice tend the horses. Obviously regarding himself above such labors, Hugo followed Evangeline and the children into the toasty warm house.

"Entering through the back door, Evangeline? How quaint." His sneer hadn't left his face by the time Susanna and Nate met them in the kitchen.

She could see Nate assessing Hugo and not liking what he saw. Susanna, though, bubbled over with hospitality, welcoming her own children first and then her guests.

"Come on in and get warm." Amidst all the hubbub, she took a moment to accept Hugo's overdone kiss on her hand. "My, such a gentleman. Now, you and Nate go on into the parlor. I'll have hot coffee for you in no time."

Justice came through the kitchen and joined the men in the other room. While Evangeline helped Susanna finish supper preparations, she ached to listen to their conversation. Surely they wouldn't confront her with the children present. Perhaps after supper. She trembled as she removed biscuits from the baking pan, a simple kitchen task she'd managed to master without breakage.

Soon everyone gathered around the dining table for Susanna's rich beef stew, the perfect meal to warm a body on a cold, snowy day.

Despite Susanna's flawless hostess skill at including everyone in the conversation, the adults all appeared to be watching each other. Nate kept an eye on Hugo, who answered polite questions vaguely. Justice reported on Esperanza's continuing peacefulness, emphasizing how folks looked out for one another. As she listened and observed, Evangeline's throat tightened and, though hungry, she couldn't seem to swallow. Finally, Susanna addressed the children one by one.

"We haven't heard from you, Gerard. How was your day?"

Grinning, Gerard glanced around the table, with a brief, requisite scowl at Justice. "I got the best part in the whole Christmas play."

Evangeline smiled with maternal pride.

"What part is it, dear?" Susanna asked.

"I'm the innkeeper."

"The innkeeper?" Nate played along, asking with artificial shock, "Why is that the best part?"

Gerard smirked. "I get to be mean to Mary and Joseph."

The room fell silent. The adults exchanged looks of shock. All except Hugo, who mirrored Gerard's smirk. He opened his mouth to speak, but Evangeline rushed to speak first.

"Why, yes, it's an important part of the story. When Mary and Joseph came to Bethlehem, there was no room at the inn, so the innkeeper sent them to the stable. But he wasn't mean to them, my darling."

Before any further comments could be made, Lizzie piped up. "Izzy and I get to be in the angel choir to sing to the shepherds."

"I get to be a shepherd," Natty added. "Dad, can I take a lamb to give to Baby Jesus?"

The innocent, round-eyed question caused everyone to laugh. Again, everyone except Hugo, who rolled his eyes and sneered…again.

"I don't know about that, son." Nate continued to laugh. "We'll see."

"Well, one thing's for sure," Susanna said. "Evie and I will need to purchase material and begin sewing the costumes as soon as possible."

"You like to sew?" Justice stared at Evangeline with apparent surprise.

"What a question, Sheriff." Susanna clicked her tongue. "Haven't you noticed her lovely clothes? No, of course not. You're a man, so why would you? Evie makes all of her clothes and those of the children. She always has. And her hats, as well. Why pay other people to do what she does so well? And she enjoys it, too, don't you, Evie?"

"Yes, very much so." With every eye on her, Evangeline's face warmed with embarrassment. Hugo seemed more annoyed than impressed by her cousin's revelation. Yet it was the probing expression on Justice's face that caused her the most chagrin. Why should he be surprised to learn of her sewing skill? Why should he even care about such a mundane thing?

After supper, Evangeline and Susanna put the children to bed. When they returned to the kitchen, they found Nate and Justice cleaning up the kitchen. Hugo sat at the kitchen table nursing a cup of coffee and a sour disposition.

"I must say, Mrs. Northam—" he gave Susanna

a puzzled look "—you certainly have your husband well trained." He waved a hand toward the sink, where Nate was scrubbing the cast-iron Dutch oven. "Thank you for your charming hospitality, but I must be going." He stood and shuddered slightly. "Sheriff, are you returning to town now? I'm not entirely certain I can find my way back to the hotel." His remark seemed aimed more at getting Justice out of the house than possibly needing a guide through the snow.

"As soon as I finish drying these dishes." Justice didn't appear to be in any hurry. "Evangeline, in case the snow keeps you from coming to town tomorrow, why don't you make a list of what you need from Mrs. Winsted's, and I'll bring it out so you ladies can get started on those costumes."

An emotion she couldn't name wound through her. If he planned to arrest her, surely he wouldn't offer this help. Nor would he speak of her making the costumes…unless he planned to trick her, as Lucius often had.

"Of course. I'll get some paper." She fetched scrap paper and a pencil from the parlor desk and returned to the kitchen. With Susanna's help, she composed a list of supplies.

"And to save my manly pride," Justice said, "would you sign the note so Mrs. Winsted won't think I've taken up sewing?"

Everyone laughed except Hugo. Again, he appeared inordinately displeased.

"I think it's a bit late for your manly pride," he muttered. "What real man washes dishes?"

Evangeline glared at him briefly before signing

the list with a flourish. "There. I'll humor you, Sheriff. We appreciate your consideration. But surely this light snow won't keep us home tomorrow."

"You never know. We could have a blizzard at any time." He finished his work and took the paper in hand. As he read it, an odd, and perhaps happy expression crossed his face. "This will come in handy." After that odd remark, he folded the page and stuffed it in his shirt pocket. "You ready to go, Giles?"

"Yes." Hugo shuddered again.

"Say, Giles," Nate said, "you want to borrow a poncho? Your coat's more suited to the Gulf Coast weather than Colorado's."

Hugo stared at him, perhaps surprised by his generous offer. "Why, I…"

"You poor man, you aren't going anyplace." Susanna wagged a finger at him. "You'll spend the night here. We can move the boys around so there's a place for you to sleep in their room."

Evangeline gasped softly. She should have warned Susanna about him. Too late now.

"Mrs. Northam, I accept your kind invitation." Hugo's face was pinched with embarrassment. Obviously he didn't care to be obligated to people whom he considered his inferiors.

"It's settled." Justice didn't appear at all disappointed at this turn of events. "I'll take my leave of you fine folks. Thank you, Susanna, for a fine meal, as always. Good night, all."

He retrieved his hat and fur-lined duster from the mudroom, donned them and strode across the barnyard, where a sprinkling of snow still fell. His silhouette against the barn's lantern light sent an ache through Evangeline. How she wished he were the one sheltering here for the night. A foolish thought. Nothing could come from longing for what could never be, and yet she did.

Justice and Hugo might be her adversaries, but she was her own worst enemy.

Justice rode into the lightly falling snow with no difficulty. He and Thunder had been through more actual snowstorms than he could count. As for the freezing wind blowing through the woolen scarf covering the lower half of his face, he barely felt it. However cold it was, it couldn't diminish the warmth flooding his chest. Evangeline made her own clothes. That surely meant she hadn't run up large bills with New Orleans merchants. The proof would be in her signature on the list in his pocket. He would compare it to the invoices Tolley had locked in his office.

The relief he felt staggered him. Why? Why did her innocence mean more to him than that of any other falsely accused person he'd ever apprehended?

In truth, he feared he was breaking a long ago promise to himself. He was falling in love with the woman who'd destroyed his ability to love, the woman who'd refused even to face him and end their engagement in person. Nothing he'd seen since she came to his town suggested she'd changed or that she cared for him. In fact, she'd been shocked to find him living here, and sometimes she seemed almost afraid of him, even before Giles arrived in town. He didn't understand why because he'd never done anything to hurt her, and he never would. She'd been the one to hurt him. And if he surrendered to this tugging of his emotions in her direction, she would without doubt break his heart again.

Despite his fears, he would do everything in his power to prove she hadn't incurred those debts to the merchants. As for the money Giles claimed she owed to his bank, Justice would investigate further. But the simple fact—if it proved to be fact—that Giles was trying to extort money from her suggested this could be another lie. But what was his ultimate purpose in pursuing her if she didn't actually owe the money?

On the way to his office, Justice turned down a side street to view his new house in the dark. Faint light from the windows of Tolley Northam's house next door illuminated the snow-frosted scene, and his heart warmed again. Would Evangeline find this house as welcoming as he did, even with no light coming from within? Or would she think it small and simple compared to the mansions in New Orleans' Garden District where they'd grown up? If he asked to court her so they could discover if any remnant of their youthful love remained, would she agree? Or would her fear of him forever keep them apart?

Then there was Gerard. Justice had strong reservations about taking on the responsibility of a rebellious boy who seemed determined to cause destruction, one who made clear how much he hated Justice. He still couldn't think of a way to befriend Gerard, especially not while the boy saw his dandified cousin as a hero.

After taking Thunder to the livery stable, where owner Ben Russell insisted upon tending the horse, he hustled down the windy street to his small apartment above the jailhouse. More exhausted than he'd realized, he started a fire in the cold potbellied stove, moved his cot closer to dispel the chill that had seeped into his bones and fell into a dreamless sleep.

Justice had one hour to work on the village while he waited for Tolley to open his office. The list Evangeline had given him last night was in his pocket. It heated him more than the warmth of the library stove where he'd started a fire. Soon he would know whether Evangeline had signed those invoices.

As he worked on the roof of the tiny gazebo, an image of her beautiful face drifted through his mind. Come summer, he could see sitting with her in the real-life gazebo in the town park. It would be the perfect place to propose... Wait! He shouldn't be thinking about a proposal when he still hadn't proved her innocence.

"Good morning."

Justice jumped, and his razor-sharp blade gouged a tiny chunk from the wooden roof and barely missed his left thumb. He turned to see the object of his musings in the doorway looking far too beautiful for his own good. Her cold-reddened cheeks and bright pink nose enhanced rather than detracted from her loveliness.

"Morning, Evangeline." He forced his eyes back to the work at hand. He'd have to glue the chunk back in place or start all over again on the roof. He'd also have to quit these involuntary reactions to this lady. Or quit his job. A lawman needed to be in control of his emotions, a skill he'd begun to lose the day she arrived in Esperanza. "I see you made it to town."

He discarded the ruined piece and picked up another square of wood.

"Yes. Thank you for starting the fire." She removed her gloves, coat and hat and hung them on the rack outside the door. "I still have difficulty doing it." Moving into the back room, she assembled her paints. "What shall I work on?"

He studied the completed pine and applewood carvings. "How about the schoolhouse?"

"Very well." She sat on the stool beside him and opened the jar of white paint.

Her gardenia perfume wafted in his direction, stirring his senses as well as his curiosity because it wasn't listed among her debts. Why not simply ask about it? Because he was afraid of the answer.

"Your perfume reminds me of the gardenia bushes in my mother's garden." Somehow he got the words out without choking on the grief such thoughts always produced.

"It does the same for me." She gave him a sad smile. "Your mother was a dear lady. I'm sure you miss her, as I do mine."

"Yes." He needed to turn the discussion back to the flowers without raising her suspicions.

"I'll be sorry when I use the last of this fragrance." She bent close to her work and narrowed her eyes to touch up a detail on the schoolhouse window. "I don't suppose gardenias grow in this cold climate. I'll have to find local flowers from which to make my perfume."

Despite the giddy feelings pulsing through him, Justice managed not to gouge another chunk from his new piece of wood. So she'd concocted the perfume, not bought it. "Nolan Means has a hothouse. He grows several flowers you may like." His voice shook, but she didn't seem to notice.

"Ah, I didn't know that." She sent a tentative smile his way. Only then did he notice her voice was shaking, too.

My, he was being so conversational. So friendly. Yet, as much as Evangeline longed to trust him, she didn't dare. Not after the sly remarks Hugo whispered to her this morning before they left the house. As she'd feared, he and Justice were in collusion against her. He'd presented the evidence to the sheriff, and as soon as it was verified, he would cart her off to New Orleans, along with the children.

Everything inside her fought against his cruel words. Surely Justice wouldn't have offered to fetch the material for the children's costumes if he intended to send her away with Hugo before the Christmas play. And the two of them had been less than friendly toward each other last night. But no matter what happened, she needed to proceed as if everything was all right. Let them bring their case against her…or not. In the meantime, she would fulfill her assignment for the play.

"I don't suppose you've already been to Mrs. Winsted's."

Still concentrating on his work, he shook his head. "No. I wanted to get to work on this. We still have a few more buildings to make, and we're running out of time."

"Oh. Then you can give me the list." She nodded toward his shirt pocket, assuming he'd keep it there.

"I can get the items on my way to the rehearsal after school."

"Um." He set down his knife and reached up, then paused. "Uh-oh."

"You don't have it?" She felt a pinch of annoyance. Without Susanna's input, which was recorded on the list, she might forget something.

"I'm sorry." He began to clean up his work area. "Did you drive the sleigh to town?"

"Me? Oh, my, no." She managed a laugh, choosing to ignore his deliberate change of subject. He probably felt bad for forgetting the list. "I've never learned to drive two horses, much less a sleigh. Nate drove us to town." She'd been grateful for his company, which prevented Hugo from dishing out more of his poison as he rode alongside them. "With the sun out today, he said the roads should be clear enough to bring home the buggy this evening. If not, he'll come and get us."

"Or I could save him the trip to town and drive you home again." Justice retrieved his coat and hat from the rack and put them on.

"That would be nice." The words were out before she could stop herself. "To save Nate the trouble, I mean."

He gave her a questioning smile. "Would you mind my company?"

Her heart skipped a beat. "No, not at all."

"Then if the roads haven't cleared, I'll take you and the children home after the rehearsal."

She nodded, not trusting her voice. He left the room, and when she heard the front door clicking closed, she began to weep. She didn't know whether it was with fear or with longing.

When Justice entered Tolley's office, the receptionist, Effie Bean, greeted him. "Good morning, Sheriff. How's your house coming? Sure looks good from the outside."

"Almost ready for me to move in." He didn't mind the question. Folks in Esperanza cared about each other's lives, a fact he hoped Giles understood. Although Evangeline hadn't been in town long, she had their loyalty because of her connection to the Northam family.

"Well, I hope you're planning to have a house-warming party, because you know all the ladies will want to take a tour of the inside." She punctuated her comment with a laugh.

Justice put his hand on his chest and groaned dramatically. "Effie, you're the second person to insist I have some short of shindig. I'll have to give it some serious thought."

"Let me know if you need any help. Homer and I will be glad to oblige."

"Maybe I will." Or not. He wasn't sure they and Electra Means would be a good combination to plan such an event for him. Homer and Effie were down-to-earth, while Electra preferred fancier doings.

"Tolley's expecting you." Effie waved toward the short hallway leading to the lawyer's office. "He said to send you on back."

"Thank you." As he walked, he took Evangeline's list from his pocket. She'd almost caught him when she asked for it. Worse, he'd almost handed it to her.

"Morning, Sheriff." Tolley stood to shake his hand. "I think we're well on our way to proving Mrs. Benoit isn't liable for that bank note."

At the unexpected news, a flood of relief overcame Justice, and he dropped into a chair across from Tolley. "Thank You, Lord." He sat forward and leaned his elbows on the desk. "What have you learned? And how did you get it so fast?"

"We live in a wonderful age, my friend, when correspondence travels quickly over the wires instead of days or weeks over land." Tolley pulled a telegram from his desk and set it on top of Giles's portfolio. "And it's always good to have old friends who can investigate matters for you, especially when their integrity is above reproach. Henry Slade and I attended law school in Boston together." He handed the yellow page to Justice. "Read this."

Justice read aloud telegraph operator Charlie Williams's transcription. "'Giles bank not legitimate. Backs gambling dens and worse. LA law says third party not responsible for gambling debts unless she signed note. Will check ownership of Benoit house. Miss Boston seafood.'"

"Ha! That takes care of that." He slapped the telegram on the desk and put the note on top of it. "Now, does this signature look anything like the ones on those bills?"

Tolley pulled the papers from the portfolio, shuffled through them and held the list next to each bill. "Hmm. The capital letters are similar, but look at the *n*'s. On the list, they're rounded. On the bills they have a little point and dip. The dots over the *i*'s here are tiny circles, but on the list they have dots. And there are several other discrepancies." He gave Tolley a triumphant grin. "I would call them obvious forgeries."

"Thank You, Lord." Justice would have whooped with happiness if he weren't indoors. "Now, what about the children's guardianship?"

"Gerard and Isabelle now live in Colorado in a respectable home. I doubt our good Circuit Judge Hartley will allow a scalawag to take an honest widow's children away from her. To be sure, I've sent him a telegram. I expect to hear back from him soon, so let's wait for the final piece of the puzzle before we tell Evangeline what we've learned and before we confront Giles."

Justice tapped his foot impatiently and mulled over the idea. "All right. As much as I'd prefer to get that scalawag out of town before the Pass closes, it's probably a good idea to have the whole matter sewed up first."

"You know what bothers me?" Tolley frowned and shook his head. "It's tragic to think of the anguish Giles has put Evangeline through. I doubt she even knew the laws. Many women don't, especially if they have controlling fathers, husbands or other male relatives. The best thing she did was to leave New Orleans so she couldn't be tricked into paying off these debts." He waved a hand over the stack of bills.

"From the way she seems afraid of him, I'm guessing she does believe she's responsible for them, or at least the bank note." Justice scratched his chin and stared out the window, which faced Main Street.

Merchants were opening their stores, and customers were parking wagons and horses. The business day had begun. He needed to start his rounds of the town soon. "If she doesn't have the money, he could control her and the children by holding the debt over her head. But why would he want to blackmail her? It doesn't make sense."

"I'm hoping Henry can find out for us. Once he catches a scent, he's like a hound dog after his quarry."

"What do you know about hound dogs?" Justice chuckled. His heart felt lighter than it had since before Evangeline arrived at the train station two months ago.

Tolley laughed, too. "Nothing, really. It's something Susanna's father says. You know these Southerners and their quaint sayings."

"Hey, watch it, friend. I'm from the South." Justice stood and shook Tolley's hand. "Thanks for everything."

"My pleasure, Justice. Don't you give this situation another moment of worry. We'll take care of your lady."

"My lady? Well…"

Tolley laughed in earnest now. "Yep. Your lady."

As Justice trekked back to his office next door, he couldn't find any reason to deny the lawyer's assertion. He did care for Evangeline. Perhaps he'd never stopped caring for her.

But how did she feel about him? All the signs pointed to her still being afraid of him, and it was his fault. If he hadn't dwelt on past hurts but instead been friendlier, showed the Lord's forgiveness toward her like he himself received every day, maybe she would have trusted him with her troubles from the start.

Now he must make up for his failure...and pray she would give him another chance.

Chapter Eleven

After a day of milder weather under a pale sun, the roads cleared enough for Evangeline to resume driving the buggy to and from town. By the end of the week, she was enjoying her work and the children's rehearsals so much she refused to let fears of the future destroy her present happiness. Perhaps Justice was delaying her arrest so she could help him complete the Christmas village. Yet when he came each morning to work on the project, he was more solicitous than threatening. Still, each morning as she sat beside him painting the objects he'd carved the day before, she wondered when he would bring up Hugo's claims. Yet he didn't.

If not for Hugo's afternoon visits, she wouldn't worry. But he did come. Further, he insisted upon walking with her to the church for the rehearsals. Like a pesky stray, he dogged her heels, often repeating his threat to take the children away in the middle of the night, as she'd done when she left New Orleans. Of course he never spoke of it in front of anyone else. His torments were for her ears only.

On Friday as she was eating her sandwich, Justice returned to the library with Gerard.

"Evangeline, Miss Prinn has had enough of your son's disobedience." Justice appeared more disappointed than angry, as he'd been the other times Gerard misbehaved. "You'll need to keep him with you. He's been suspended for three school days for deliberately breaking some other students' slates." He tipped his hat and left the building without another word.

"Oh, Gerard." She faced her son. "What am I going to do with you?"

He gave her a smirk that was entirely too much like Hugo's. "Why don't you pay him off?"

She gasped. "What? What are you talking about?"

"Pay him off, and he'll quit bothering me. I heard Father paying off a constable one time so he wouldn't report something."

"I'm sure you misunderstood." And yet, Evangeline didn't doubt it for a moment. "Besides, that's wrong. Sheriffs and constables and other lawmen are our protectors. They help to keep us safe. What would become of us if every man did what was right in his own eyes, as Reverend Thomas spoke about last Sunday? Stronger men would take everything we have and mistreat us terribly." Just as Lucius had done to her. "None of us would be safe. It's why we have laws. Don't you want to keep Isabelle safe?"

He bunched his fists and scowled. "Nobody better hurt my sister…or you. I won't let them."

His bold statement brought tears to her eyes. "See. You do understand." She pulled him into her arms. "There is a right and a wrong. We should always try our best to do what's right. That means in school, too."

He moved away from her, set his dinner bucket on a table and took out his sandwich. "I'm hungry." As usual, he changed the subject when she addressed his behavior.

Evangeline took her food over to the same table and sat beside him. "I'm proud of the way you've been helping Nate at the ranch."

He sat up straighter. "Do you think he'll let me have the new foal? I mean, do you think I could earn it?"

"Hmm. Perhaps. But your being suspended from school might make him think you're not responsible enough to take care of your own horse."

A light seemed to dawn in his eyes. He stared off toward the front windows thoughtfully, then slowly nodded.

Evangeline's heart warmed. Maybe he was beginning to understand.

Several patrons entered the library and searched for books, each appearing surprised to see a child out of school.

"Aren't you feeling well?" every solicitous mother or grandmother asked him.

After one too many ladies put her hand on his forehead to check for fever, Gerard scowled and moved to the back of the room, curling up on the floor beside the stove with *Treasure Island*, his favorite book since she'd begun reading it to his class.

As the afternoon wore on, the influx of readers slowed until only Evangeline and Gerard occupied the large room. A quick look revealed her son had fallen asleep on his coat, so she covered him with her own.

"Lord, please show Gerard his behavior must improve," she whispered, brushing a gentle hand over his cheek.

Back at her desk, she made a list of books due back soon, planning to write notes to remind the borrowers.

"Well, aren't we the busy bee?" Hugo slithered into the library, his snake-like grin making her shudder.

"What do you want, Hugo?" She kept her eyes on her work, but no longer saw the page.

"You know what I want." He removed his hat and pulled up a chair against her desk. "If you and the children don't return to New Orleans with me, I'll have your beau, the sheriff, arrest you and send you back in my custody."

"My what?" Justice certainly wasn't her beau, but she did wish he were her friend.

Hugo chuckled in his evil way. "Oh, come now. If you wanted to, you could wind him around your little finger."

"You're insane." She glared at him but kept her voice low so Gerard wouldn't awaken.

"Then why hasn't he shown you the bills I gave him to prove you ran away from those debts?"

"You know as well as I do those aren't my debts." She wouldn't mention the note Lucius signed to Hugo's bank.

"Of course not." He smirked in his awful way. "Did your dear husband, my dear unlamented cousin, ever tell you about Veronica? No, of course not. Gentlemen never tell their wives about the other special ladies in their lives. Seems Miss Veronica has a taste for fine clothes. When the merchants questioned her right to charge them to Lucius's account, she signed your name, claiming to be Mrs. Benoit. She's such a talented little forger. Now Veronica and I are, shall we say, friends, and she turned those bills over to me to take care of. Naturally, I thought they would be a good tool for getting you to see reason."

"You're insane," she repeated.

"Now, now, you must stop these insults." He leaned close and glared at her through slitted eyes. "You will never be able to prove your innocence. My good friend, Judge Grable, likes to do favors for me because of all the favors I do for him. Once he sends a warrant to your sheriff, good ol' Justice will have no choice but to see *justice* is done." He laughed at the wordplay, sending an icy chill down Evangeline's spine. How like her first thought when she saw Justice two months ago. "Since he's seen the evidence against you, I'm sure he'll help me bring you before the judge. Won't that be something to see?"

Evangeline shuddered again. So Justice knew all about this. Now she had no choice. "Very well. I'll go with you, but Gerard and Isabelle are staying here with Nate and Susanna."

Hugo scoffed. "Do you really think I'll let my little cousins live on a filthy cattle ranch when they can live in a fine mansion in a big city and have every wish and whim granted? That I'd let them miss out on all the delightful enjoyments I have planned for them? No, my dear, the children will go with us, and we need to leave tomorrow. The weather prognosticators tell me a storm is looming over the northern mountains, and snow is likely to block the eastern pass in another day. I hardly want to be stranded in this shabby little town all winter." He stood and gathered his hat and cane. "Pack well tonight, my dear. Soon you and your little darlings will be on your way home."

He strutted out of the library as if the matter were settled. Evangeline felt sick with fear, but she'd never let him take the children. Nate and Susanna would protect them, she was sure of it.

A stirring at the back of the room caught her attention. She turned to see Gerard seated on the floor staring at her, a look on his precious face she'd never seen before. Shock. Horror. Disgust. He must have heard every word that passed between Hugo and her.

Her heart breaking, she held out her arms. "Come here, sweetheart."

He grabbed his coat and dashed past her and out the door, turning down Center Avenue, a small consolation seeing he hadn't chosen to follow Hugo up Main Street.

She hurried to the open door. "Gerard, wait."

She chased him for half a block, but at the corner, she could no longer see him. Where had he gone so quickly? With Nate out at the ranch, who could help her find him? Only one name came to mind.

Justice.

"There goes Giles now." Justice moved quickly from the chair in Tolley's office and motioned for his friend to follow him. "Let's catch him and get this settled."

Tolley's "yee-ha" echoed in Justice's ears and gave him one more cause to smile.

They grabbed their coats, stepped outside into the icy afternoon wind and strode after their quarry.

"Giles. Hold up a minute," Justice called.

The dandy turned, a triumphant sneer on his face. "Ah, Sheriff, good to see you. I'd like to get my portfolio from you. As it turns out, Mrs. Benoit has agreed to go with me—"

"Let's talk about that." Tolley beckoned to him. "Your papers are in my office."

At Giles's hesitation, Justice resisted the urge to grab the man by his collar and drag him back with them.

"Very well." He narrowed his eyes and glanced back and forth between Justice and Tolley, his distrust obvious. Once in the office, he refused the offered chair. "What is this all about?"

"It's about Mrs. Benoit and her children, of course." Tolley sat back in his chair behind the desk.

Mild alarm flitted across Giles's face. "Look, give me my papers, and I will be out of your little town on tomorrow's morning train."

Tolley clicked his tongue. "Can't do that."

"What? Now, see here—"

"No, you see here." Justice stood over the shorter man, causing Giles to drop into the chair after all. "I'm sure you're familiar with the name Arthur Pettigrew."

Giles turned pale, and his jaw dropped. "O-of course. He was my uncle, my mother's brother. What about him?"

Tolley gave Justice a nod, encouraging the sheriff to continue.

"Turns out good old Uncle Arthur had no children, so he left a rather nice bequest to Gerard and Isabelle Benoit, to be managed by a duly appointed guardian until each one comes of age." The amount of the fortune shocked Justice, but it also explained Giles's determination to gain custody of the children. He wanted the money for his own undoubtedly evil purposes.

"And," Tolley said, taking up the story, "since the children already have a competent guardian in their own mother, you won't have to be burdened with rearing someone else's children at your young age."

"Mr. Giles," Justice said, "I suggest you gather your belongings and take this afternoon's train out of town." Still standing over the man, he gave him a deceptively friendly grin. "Do I make myself clear?"

"B-but those other debts. The note to my bank—"

"Tut, tut. How sad for you. Turns out the signatures on the bills are forgeries." Tolley took the portfolio from his desk drawer and shoved it toward Giles. "I've already marked them as such and notarized them. As for your so-called bank, my good friend and fellow attorney in New Orleans informs me it's an illegal enterprise. That alone makes the note worthless. But even if Lucius Benoit did owe you money lost to you in a card game, according to Louisiana state law, no third party can be held liable for someone else's gambling debts."

"Does that clear everything up for you?" Justice adjusted his gun belt, a threatening gesture he'd learned in the Texas Rangers.

It seemed to work. Giles slid out of the chair, snatched up the portfolio and stepped toward the door. "You have not heard the last from me. I will have *my* friend, a judge in New Orleans—"

Justice grabbed the front of Giles's coat and lifted him up on his tiptoes. "You can do as you wish, but our circuit judge has already awarded custody of the children to their mother based on Mr. Northam's and my recommendation. Now, if you don't get yourself over to the train depot right now, you might be spending the winter in my jail, a situation neither one of us would like." He gave the man a little shove. "We'll send your baggage after you."

Wide-eyed, Giles straightened as if trying to regain his dignity. Justice took a step toward him, and he ran from the room like a scared jackrabbit.

Justice gave Tolley a hearty handshake. "Thanks, my friend. I couldn't have done this without you."

"That's what friends are for. When will you tell Evangeline the good news?"

"No time like the present." Then he remembered Gerard's suspension. The boy wouldn't take kindly to Justice's sending his hero out of town. "Then again, I think I'll ride out this evening and tell Nate and Susanna at the same time."

After a little more friendly banter, Justice walked out into the wind again...and right into Evangeline, who appeared to be coming from his office. He caught her before she fell.

"Oh, Justice, there you are. I don't know what to do. Gerard is missing. Please, you've got to help me find him. I'm afraid he's run away."

* * *

Barely able to stand, Evangeline clung to Justice's strong arms to keep from falling.

"Let's go inside." Instead of taking her to the jail-house, he escorted her into Tolley Northam's office, from which he'd just emerged. He seated her beside Effie Bean's reception desk and squatted in front of her, taking hold of her hands.

"What happened? Was he angry about the sus-pension?" The gentleness in his voice brought her to tears. He drew her close and let her weep into his shoulder.

Effie thrust a handkerchief at Evangeline, and Tol-ley emerged from the hallway, both repeating Jus-tice's question.

Through her tears, she choked out a shortened version of her whole sordid story, including Hugo's threats. "And Gerard heard it all. He ran out of the library without saying a word. Please, before you ar-rest me, please go find him."

The puzzled look on Justice's face surprised her. "Arrest you? Why on earth would I do that?"

"B-because of…" She broke down again.

He stood and addressed Tolley. "Will you and Effie take care of her while I find Gerard before he gets into more trouble?"

"Of course." Tolley sent Effie for coffee, then beckoned to Evangeline. "Come on back to my of-fice. We need to have a talk."

Justice frowned. "What are you going to tell her?"

"Trust me. You go find Gerard."

Evangeline gripped Justice's hands. "Please."

"If I can't locate him, I'll ring the fire bell and

round up some folks to help me." Justice exited the building.

Within minutes, Effie brought in a jug of hot coffee from the café, and Tolley escorted Evangeline into his back office.

"Evangeline, I have some things to tell you."

Her heart in her throat, she slowly nodded. What he had to say couldn't be any worse than having her son run away on a bitter cold day in Colorado.

Justice went to his office and apprised his deputy of the situation. "Let's saddle up and start looking." He exchanged his jacket for his lined duster, gathered some equipment and headed for the livery stable, Sean O'Shea right behind him.

"Hello, Sheriff, Deputy." Adam Starling sat on a bale of hay oiling a buggy harness. "Need me to saddle your horses?" He set down his work and moved toward the stalls.

"We can do it." Ordinarily, Justice would let Adam do the job so he could give him a tip. Today he was in too much of a hurry. "Any chance you saw Gerard Benoit in the past hour or so?"

"Yessir." Adam scratched his head. "He said his cousin, that Giles fellow, wanted him to bring Lulabelle over to the hotel. I saddled her, and he took out headed west. He's a good little rider for a boy his age."

As Justice saddled his dappled gray, he considered the situation. From what Evangeline said, he doubted Gerard would seek out Giles. "Did the boy say anything else?"

"No, sir. But he did seem a bit agitated."

"Can you point out Lulabelle's hoofprints?"

"Sure. Those smaller ones over there." Adam pointed to some distinctive prints in the dirt floor. "You gonna track him? Has he done something wrong?"

Justice mounted up. "Yes and yes. Don't worry. I'll bring Lulabelle back safe and sound."

"Yessir. And I know Mr. Russell would want you to make sure the boy is safe and sound first."

Justice waved an acknowledgment of the sentiment, then he and O'Shea followed the little mare's trail in the snowy, muddy street. Sure enough, it led to the hotel and beyond. From there, the deeper, blurred prints showed the pace had picked up.

"Looks like he walked through town to avoid suspicion," O'Shea said, "then took off at a gallop."

Justice exhaled a cloudy breath. "Foolish boy. Where does he think he can go in this weather?"

"Yep." O'Shea snorted. "The kid's wily, but he's not too smart."

"I wouldn't argue with that." Justice urged Thunder into a canter, keeping an eye on the mare's hoofprints. They rode west for some time toward Del Norte. Two miles out of Esperanza, the prints left the road and headed north toward the river.

"Uh-oh. Not good." O'Shea voiced what Justice was thinking.

They hadn't followed the tracks a hundred yards before Lulabelle came galloping toward them, dragging her reins dangerously between her front legs. One step on the straps and she could go down and break her neck or a leg.

Justice snatched his lasso from his saddle's pommel, pivoted Thunder around as the mare passed and flung the loop over her head like she was a maverick calf on the run from branding. As Thunder kept pace with the smaller horse, Justice held the rope loose until she got used to it, then gently tugged. The mare slowed and finally stopped.

He snagged her reins and looped them around the pommel before leading her back toward the river. He found O'Shea riding along the frozen edge of the Rio Grande calling for Gerard. Justice tied the mare to a tree and joined his efforts.

The unmistakable screech of a mountain lion split the air, sending chills down Justice's spine. As he drew his rifle from its sheath, O'Shea called "Cougar!"

"Do you see it?"

"No, sir. The sound came from over there." He pointed toward a small rise.

"Help!" A child screamed in terror.

"We're coming, Gerard." Justice forced his skittish gelding in the direction of the second cat screech. "O'Shea, go back and let the mare loose. She's a sitting target."

"Yessir." The deputy's horse bucked and twisted, all too willing to get away from the danger of a hungry predator. Nonetheless, O'Shea managed to keep his seat.

Justice crested the rise. The sight meeting his eyes sent another shiver down his spine. Gerard had climbed a bare, spindly cottonwood tree and was hanging on for dear life to some flimsy upper branches. The cougar clung to a branch below the sobbing child and swung lethal claws at his foot.

Thunder whinnied in fear and tried to bolt, but Justice held him in check.

"Come on, boy, help me out here," Justice muttered to the horse.

Keeping a tight hold on the reins while lifting the rifle with his left hand, he took off his right glove, put his hand on the trigger and peered down the sight at the deadly cat. "Lord, make this count."

He squeezed the trigger. The loud report echoed throughout the aspen, pine and cottonwoods. Thunder jolted. The cougar screamed again as the branch beneath it broke. Eyes wild, mouth open in another screech, the animal turned its attention to Thunder. The horse whinnied in terror and spun. Justice turned him back. He looked down his sights and squeezed the trigger again. This time, the bullet found its target. The magnificent yet dangerous creature fell lifeless in the snow.

Once he'd subdued Thunder and sheathed his rifle, he rode closer to the tree, where Gerard stared down at him through the branches, his eyes wide.

"Can you climb down?" He tried to keep his tone neutral in spite of the hammering in his chest. This had been entirely too close.

Gerard nodded, but as he descended, his coat snagged on a broken branch. When he tugged at it, the material ripped but didn't come loose. Tugging harder, he sobbed. "Let me go!"

Those were the same words he'd said earlier when Justice had hauled him out of the classroom. But this time his efforts succeeded. The branch released the coat, but the action knocked him off balance.

"Help!"

Arms flailing, he plummeted through the branches right into Justice's arms, smacking one foot into his chest and a hand into his face. With no little difficulty, Justice remained in the saddle and held on to the child, although Thunder stamped the ground and snorted his displeasure. Once Justice reclaimed the wind Gerard had knocked out of him, he righted the weeping, gasping boy and set him in front of him on the saddle.

"Let's go, Thunder." He nudged the still skittish horse back toward the trail beside the river's edge.

Gerard's sobs began to subside by the time they emerged from the woods, but he continued to shake. O'Shea was waiting for them, the lead rope still around Lulabelle's neck.

"You want to ride by yourself?" Justice asked the boy.

He shook his head and leaned back into Justice's chest. Instinctively, Justice tightened his hold. To his surprise, the boy didn't resist.

"O'Shea, head on back to town. We'll be right behind you." This was what he'd been praying for, a chance for a breakthrough with Gerard. Once the deputy rode out of earshot, he said, "You all right?"

Gerard nodded and wiped his nose on his sleeve. Justice pulled a handkerchief from inside his coat and handed it to him.

"Th-thank you." Finally, a pleasant word from the boy.

"You're welcome." He held Thunder to a walk. "You want to tell me where you were headed before you met up with that cougar?"

Sniffing, Gerard shook his head…then started

talking. "I hate Hugo." He hiccuped. "I hate my father."

From what Evangeline had told Justice, the boy had plenty of reasons for his anger at Giles, but what about Lucius Benoit? "Why do you hate your father?"

"He died and left us."

"Hmm. I doubt he wanted to do either one. Most people don't choose when they die."

Gerard nodded, his bare head bobbing against Justice's chest. Justice took off the scarf he used as a face cover against bitter winds and wound it over the boy's head. Gerard shivered as he tugged the woolen garment close.

"He was a bad man. He gambled away his money and lied and…and married another lady besides my mother."

No doubt he referred to the woman—probably Benoit's mistress—who'd forged Evangeline's signature. Justice's heart ached over a young boy knowing such a terrible thing about his father.

"He left us poor, and Mother had to sell my pony and my dog. I had to leave my house and my friends."

Justice thought about using this opportunity to discourage his friendship with Deely and Cart, but better sense prevailed. When Gerard came to town, he was a desperate little boy aching over what he'd lost. No wonder he fell in with boys whose mischief gave him an outlet for his anger. Justice tried to see him through new, more understanding eyes.

"I understand how you feel. My father died when I was pretty young, too, and I also lost everything I cared about."

Gerard twisted around to look at him. "What did your mother do? Did she take you away from your friends?"

A deep ache filled Justice, and he gazed across the landscape while he gathered his emotions. "No, my mother had already died. I was left alone." If Evangeline had waited for him... No, he wouldn't think about that.

Gerard stared at him for a moment before facing front again. "At least I have Mother and Isabelle." He glanced back again. "What did you do?"

Justice managed a shrug that was more of a shiver. The icy, cutting wind had picked up, and the sun was nearing the peaks of the San Juan Mountains. "I left my hometown and looked for a new future. I worked as a cowboy for a few years, then became a Texas Ranger. After a while, I decided to come to Colorado."

"Were you lonely?" An interesting question coming from a ten-year-old.

"Yep. Sure was." An icy blast hit them from the north. Justice opened his coat and enfolded the boy inside its furry warmth. "Then I met a fellow named Jubal Tucker, another Texas Ranger. He talked to me about God." Just as his father used to do. But he wouldn't say it, seeing as how Gerard's father was a crook, and the boy knew it. "He reminded me of what I'd learned in church as a boy. God loves me even though I'm a sinner. His Son Jesus Christ died to pay for my sins. If I accept Him as my Savior, I'll be saved."

"Like Reverend Thomas talks about."

"Right." Good. The boy had a head start on understanding salvation.

"I got mad when he preached about it." Gerard wiped the handkerchief across his nose.

Lord, should I say something else or wait for him to speak? Riding quietly seemed the better option, so Justice held his peace.

"That cougar could have killed you," Gerard said in a small voice after a few moments.

"Yep. You, too."

Another silence.

"Hugo wouldn't have helped me." Gerard snorted. "He'd be scared of a spider."

Justice tried to grin, but the icy wind had frozen his face.

"You saved my life."

"Probably."

"No. You did." Gerard faced him again. "Like Jesus."

Again Justice subdued his emotions before speaking. "I may have saved your life in the here and now, but Jesus can save your soul and give you everlasting life." The words were getting harder to form, but he couldn't lose this moment. "All you have to do is admit you're a sinner and ask Him to save you."

Gerard managed a nod before facing front again. In the following silence, he relaxed more and more against Justice until he fell asleep.

Snow began to fall, so Justice kicked Thunder into a canter. Thankfulness for the day's events vied with disappointment for preeminence in his thoughts. Yes, he'd saved the boy's life, but he wouldn't be satisfied until Gerard trusted the Lord as his Savior.

Chapter Twelve

At the church after school, Evangeline tried to relax as she watched the children rehearse the play. Marybeth and Electra both had been solicitous when they heard Gerard had run away. Then everyone had rejoiced when Deputy O'Shea had arrived with news of finding him, including a horrifying report about a cougar.

"Don't worry, Mrs. Benoit, your son and the sheriff are on their way," the deputy had said. "He sent me ahead to let you know your boy is safe."

Evangeline had wept with relief, and Marybeth had given her a reassuring hug before continuing the rehearsal, leaving her to sit in the pew and ponder the day's happenings.

Still stunned over Tolley's revelations, she thanked the Lord that Justice had been skeptical about Hugo's claims. Hugo, like Lucius, had a way of winning people over, yet Justice had seen through him. He'd even gone to the trouble of having Tolley investigate the legal issues, including securing a circuit judge's decision to grant her custody of her children. And risked his life in this bitter cold weather to search for her son. Any one of those kind deeds would have been enough to make her grateful. Added together, they changed her gratitude into something stronger. Not love, exactly, because she didn't dare give him her heart, at least not yet. But if he was willing, perhaps they could reclaim their long ago friendship and see where it led. Unlike her father, Lucius, Hugo and almost every other man she'd ever known, Justice was honest and noble. While he'd failed to save her from marrying Lucius, he'd made up for it by saving her son's life.

In the midst of her musings, Justice and Gerard entered the front door of the church, a snowy wind blowing them over the threshold. Evangeline hurried to meet them and pulled her son into a fierce embrace.

"Oh, Gerard, why did you worry me this way?"

"Aw, Mother, you worry too much." His voice sounded sleepy, and the expression on his dear face wasn't that of a boy caught in mischief. Instead, he had a certain assurance about him, perhaps even peacefulness.

"What—" She looked up at Justice, whose frozen cheeks appeared to make it hard for him to smile. Next to his right eye, a bruise was beginning to form. While Gerard had only a small scratch on his cheek, Justice had apparently taken a hard blow to his face. She wouldn't ask about it now, but if Gerard hit him, she'd punish her son for the first time in his life. "Both of you, over to the stove right now." She bustled Gerard over to the potbellied stove in the front corner of the church, expecting Justice to follow.

Instead, he approached Marybeth and spoke stiffly. "Looks like we might be in for a blizzard. You need to send the children home right away. O'Shea, you make sure the ones who live in town get safely home. I'll get the large sleigh from the livery stable and take care of the ones who live farther out."

"Yes, of course," Marybeth said as she and the other mothers gathered the children and bundled them into their coats. "Boys and girls, tell your parents we've cancelled tomorrow's rehearsal. Weather permitting, we'll meet again on Monday after school."

While Electra and some older children put away props and cleared the podium for Sunday services, Deputy O'Shea sorted out his group and herded them from the church.

"I'll be back shortly with the sleigh." Justice headed up the aisle.

"But you're freezing." Evangeline followed him. "Come get warm before you go back out."

He turned to her and managed a tight smile. "Gotta get these youngsters home." His gray eyes twinkled. "I'll take you out to the ranch last. We can talk then." Before she could object, he strode from the building.

"Rand will be here soon." Marybeth sat with her two children on the front pew. "Do you want to ride with us?"

"No, thank you." Evangeline shook her head. "Justice said he'd take care of us." And this time, she knew he would keep his promise.

After delivering several children safely to their homes east of town, Justice drove Evangeline and her charges back to Main Street to connect with the southbound road. When they were halfway to Four Stones Ranch, the snow stopped but the temperature lowered. The four children snuggled between Evangeline and Justice under layers of woolen blankets. Despite the cold, Isabelle, Lizzie and Natty questioned Gerard about his adventures and listened wide-eyed as he told his story. Evangeline was no less enthralled than they, as much for her son's dramatic flair as for Justice's courage.

"After the sheriff shot the cougar, I fell out of the tree and he caught me. I didn't mean to, but I punched him right in the eye."

While the children stared up at the evidence on Justice's face, Evangeline gasped. Gerard weighed at least seventy pounds. Looking at him over the heads of the children, she was rewarded with his wry look.

"All part of the job." He tried to chuckle, but coughed instead.

That was it. She'd tell Nate to hogtie him and not let him return to town until the morning. If he became ill because of Gerard, she'd blame herself for letting Hugo influence her son only to disappoint him. Gerard never would have fled into danger if not for his anger against his cousin. Even more, she should have trusted Justice from the moment she arrived in Esperanza. Yet she'd let Hugo's lies consume her.

When Tolley had told her all those supposed debts were a sham, an attempt to both extort money from her and force her to surrender custody of the children, she'd been overwhelmed with relief. Then he added the astounding news of Arthur Pettigrew's bequest. She never would have imagined the austere, reclusive old man thought so kindly of her children. She knew he'd despised both of his nephews, Lucius and Hugo, so he must have changed his will after her husband died.

With this information in hand, Tolley promised to tie up any loose legal ends and see their futures were secure. Among other things, his lawyer friend felt certain Hugo had mishandled the sale of the house and Lucius's valuables, meaning Evangeline and the children would perhaps receive more good news. She permitted herself to hope at least part of her late husband's books belonged to her, for she would have them sent to Esperanza for its library.

Justice coughed again but tried to hide it by turning away from her. Good thing they soon turned down the lane to Nate and Susanna's house so he could get inside where it was warm. The jingle of the bells on the harness announced their arrival. Nate and Wes met them in the barnyard and sent the whole party into the house while they tended the sleigh and horses. Susanna greeted them in the mudroom with relief in her eyes. This late homecoming must have worried her. Susanna and Evangeline helped the children remove their wraps and hang them on the pegs, with Susanna clucking over them all like a mother hen.

"Now, Sheriff, don't you even think about leaving." She wagged a finger in his face. "You're staying for supper. Go on, now. Take off that duster and hat."

"Yes, ma'am." Looking too frozen to argue, Justice removed the items and hung them beside the others, then gratefully accepted a cup of hot coffee.

Later over supper, Gerard regaled the other adults and his youngest cousin with the story of his adventures. This time, he added more details, some Evangeline knew were exaggerated.

"And the cougar tried to bite my foot off." He paused for dramatic effect. His sister and cousins listened with rapt attention. "Had it right between his teeth." He clamped his teeth on a chicken drumstick and growled. The other children stared in amazement.

"That's new." Evangeline looked at Justice sitting beside her.

"Let him tell it as he saw it." Justice's cheeks had thawed but still were red. "He has the makings of a pretty good storyteller. The cougar's teeth will get longer with each new listener."

She rewarded his observation with a roll of her eyes.

"Let him be. He's behaving himself." His eyes lit with a familiar twinkle, and she felt a little kick near her heart.

Of course, it was merely admiration for the man he'd become. He may have failed to save her from marriage to Lucius, but he'd risked his own life to save her son. If she hadn't already respected him, she would now. Not only for what he'd done but because of what he was: a good, honest Christian gentleman who thought of others before himself. Unlike her father, Lucius and Hugo, who'd sought wealth and position for themselves, he'd become a sheriff to protect people. How could she not highly esteem him and regard him as a good friend?

After supper, the weary children were put to bed,

and the adults gathered around the fireplace in the parlor. Susanna served hot chocolate, and then she and Evangeline sat on the settee and picked up their sewing baskets to work on the day's mending. Gerard's coat needed a patch, but if that was the worst to come of his encounter with the cougar, Evangeline was grateful.

"What I don't understand," said Nate, "is why Gerard was over by the river on a school day."

Evangeline traded a look with Justice. Then, between the two of them, they explained Gerard's suspension and Hugo's purpose in coming to Esperanza.

"If not for Justice and Tolley, I don't know what I would have done." Evangeline gazed across the room at the man who'd done so much for her and her children. The smile he returned hinted at something she couldn't quite read.

"Oh, my dear." Susanna wiped a tear away and hugged her. "Why didn't you tell us what you were going through? We could have helped you."

"I'd have run that crook out of town days ago," Nate growled, his green eyes blazing. "Evangeline, you're family, and nobody hurts a Northam relation and gets away with it."

"I should have known that." She sniffed back annoying tears. "After the way you rescued Susanna and Uncle Edward all those years ago, I should have trusted you."

"It's all settled now," Justice said. "Giles is gone, and he knows better than to show his face around here again. I told O'Shea to check at the train station and make sure he left. If he didn't, he'll be spending the winter in my jail."

His reassuring words settled something deep inside Evangeline. If nothing more came of this situation than their friendship, she would treasure it. Oddly, against all reason, she couldn't help but wish for more.

"Sheriff, you've had a busy day," Nate said. "Instead of riding back to town, why don't you stay the night. Wes and I brushed down Thunder and the sleigh horses and fed them. You can bed down in the bunkhouse or sleep on a cot in the boys' room."

Justice hesitated, glancing at Evangeline. He must have seen the hope in her eyes, because he nodded. "I appreciate it, Nate. O'Shea is on duty tonight, so I'm not concerned about getting back to town."

"I'll go make up the cot." Susanna set down her mending basket and stood. "Evie, you stay here. Nate, I need your help." She gave him a meaningful look.

"Uh, sure."

Nate followed her, and silence descended on the room.

"Justice—" Evangeline began.

"Evangeline—" He spoke at the same time.

They both laughed.

"You first." Justice propped his elbow on the chair arm and his chin on his hand. The look of interest in his eyes warmed her more than Susanna's fried chicken and mashed potatoes.

"Where to begin?" She blew out a breath. This was so hard. "I will always be grateful for everything you've done for me. Not only for saving Gerard's life, although that was more than enough. Tolley told me you were skeptical about Hugo from the beginning.

Thank you for trusting your instincts. For trusting in me." She laughed softly even as tears came to her eyes. "And to think all this time, I expected you to arrest me and send me back to New Orleans."

A mock-wounded look came over his face, and he put a hand on his chest. "Oh, the miseries of being a lawman. Even innocent people feel guilty around me."

She tried to laugh, but more tears came. "You heard what I said to Susanna and Nate. I didn't know I was innocent. Hugo convinced me I had to pay those debts and leaving town was a crime. Lucius always told me I was wrong about everything, so it wasn't hard to believe." The memory of her husband's brutality brought more tears, but she had to know one more thing. "Lucius claimed your father embezzled money from their business."

Justice joined her on the settee, where he took her in his strong arms and gently pressed her head to his chest. His tender gesture broke the dam of her emotions, and she wept harder.

"Shh. It's all right."

He brushed a rough thumb across her cheek, but somehow it didn't hurt. "My father was a man of integrity. It was Lucius who embezzled the money to cover his gambling debts. A friend told me about it before I left New Orleans, but I was too young, too inexperienced to do anything about it."

She sighed. "I never could understand how such a godly man could have done something so wrong."

They sat quietly for a few moments, her head still resting against his chest. If she closed her eyes, maybe eleven years would disappear, and they'd be young again, and this time he'd rescue her from Lucius. Such a foolish thought. She sat up and wiped away her tears with her handkerchief. "Why didn't you come for me?" She hadn't meant to give voice to the question, but there it was.

"What do you mean?" Frowning, he released her and moved back on the settee. "Why didn't you wait for me? You knew I was coming home to marry you that June, as we'd planned. I reminded you in my letters."

"What letters?"

Understanding dawned on Justice's face the same instant Evangeline realized how far her father had gone to prevent their marriage.

"I never received your letters." Grief over lost years of happiness brought her to tears again. "My father must have found out when you were coming home and wanted me to think you'd forgotten me so I would willingly marry Lucius. When I refused, he locked me in my room, then forced me to go through with the wedding."

He stared off, the ripple in his jaw the only indication he sought to control his own grief and anger.

"You didn't answer my question. Why didn't you come for me? I sent word to your father through a trusted friend and begged him to send you to rescue me as soon as you came home." More memories of those days returned. "I'm not being fair. He died the day you returned, didn't he? I didn't learn of it until months later when I found a newspaper Lucius had forbidden me to read. He probably died before he could tell you about my plea." She reached across the divide between them to squeeze his hand, puzzled by the furious frown he wore. Didn't he believe her? If not, then they couldn't be friends. And that would break her heart all over again.

The day had worn Justice down, but Evangeline's revelation reignited his energy as only anger could.

"Father tried to tell me something about you. All he could manage was your name. I didn't understand how close to death he was, or I would have begged him to tell me more. Instead, I let him sleep. He never woke up."

Evangeline rested her delicate hand on his rough one and squeezed again. "Oh, Justice, I'm so sorry. Poor Mr. Gareau. Trying with his last breath to save our future for us." More tears fell, but at least this time she didn't weep as before. Seeing her cry tore at his soul as much as seeing Gerard up a tree with a cougar reaching for his heels.

"If I'd known your father imprisoned you in your own home, I'd have broken down the doors to reach you. All I ever wanted was to spend my life with you." He pulled her into his arms again and kissed the top of her head. Her golden curls tickled his nose. In the midst of their shared grief, this bit of humor lightened the burden on his heart, while her gardenia perfume evoked sweet memories. How endearing was the trusting way she lay against his chest, she who had been so badly treated by the men in her life, including him. Somehow he must repair the damage, if only his part.

"Evangeline, maybe it's not too late for us."

She gazed up at him through tear-filled eyes. "Maybe not." She touched his face, which still stung as it thawed from icy windburn. "Where do we go from here?"

"Would you permit me to court you?"

"Court?" Her eyes widened, and color brightened her face. "Oh." Her forehead wrinkled as she appeared to ponder the question. His pulse began to race at her hesitation...until she smiled. "Yes. I'd like that."

He slowly exhaled with relief. "Good." He cradled her face again, taking care not to scrape her with his dry, rough hand.

As she leaned against him, he felt happiness was just within reach. All he needed to do was take hold of it. Tomorrow he would show her his house, maybe ask her advice on draperies and such. If all went well, he would take the next step. Or, rather, he'd ask the Lord to direct his next step.

After several years of making his home above the jail, Justice enjoyed sleeping in a real bedroom in a house filled with warmth and love, even with three small boys snoring in harmony in the other beds. Being here at the Northams' reinforced Justice's belief he'd done right to ask Evangeline's permission to court her. Yes, they still must sort out a few things, but he awoke on Saturday morning fully thawed-out from yesterday and ready to take another step with her. Although they'd both been too tired to discuss the future last night, he now felt both nervous and excited about showing her his almost completed house. If their courtship led to marriage and she didn't like the house, he'd sell it and build one she did like.

After helping Nate with the morning chores, he

found his lady in the kitchen helping Susanna prepare breakfast. Her beauty stole his breath away just as the impact of Gerard landing on his chest had the day before. He rubbed the spot where a bruise had formed to match the one near his right eye. When finally able to speak, he addressed his hostess.

"Susanna, would you mind watching Gerard and Isabelle today? I'd like to take Evangeline to town for a little while." He glanced at her. "That is, if you'll go with me."

"Of course she will." Susanna laughed in her sweet way. "And of course I will. It's about time." She muttered her last remark.

Nate chuckled. "Sheriff, you may as well admit it. You were a goner the moment Evangeline stepped off of that train. Once Susanna sets her sights on matchmaking, nobody's safe."

While the others laughed, Evangeline's face turned a becoming shade of pink. Justice couldn't tell whether she was embarrassed or pleased by the teasing, but he did notice the wariness in her eyes had disappeared. Winning her trust meant a great deal to him.

"Coffee?" She placed a china cup on a matching saucer, poured coffee and handed it to him with the grace of a society lady serving a guest. "Do you still prefer it black?"

"Yes, thank you." He managed to brush her hand as he took the saucer. A pleasant sensation skittered up his arm, and he shivered, causing the cup to rattle on the saucer.

"Are you all right?" The loving concern in her expression warmed his heart.

For most of his life, especially since coming to Esperanza, he hadn't lacked friends who cared about him. Yet this was something deeper, something between just the two of them. Could they truly move beyond the past and into that special relationship between a man and a woman?

"I couldn't be better." He set down his coffee and grasped her hand. "Do you mind going to town on a Saturday?"

"I'd love to."

"Love to what?" Gerard entered the kitchen rubbing sleep from his eyes. The other children filed in behind him and took their places at the table.

Evangeline brought them plates of scrambled eggs and biscuits. "Sheriff Gareau has asked me to go to town with him for a while. You children are going to stay home and bake cookies with Cousin Susanna."

"Oh."

Justice watched with dismay as a familiar frown darkened the boy's face. Hadn't they gotten past this animosity?

"Gerard." Nate must have noticed his mood, because he spoke in a too-cheerful tone. "Would you help me with that new foal today?"

His eyebrows rose, but he didn't smile. "Yessir."

Could be the cookie baking idea he didn't like. Justice would have to proceed cautiously with the boy so as not to lose the ground he'd gained yesterday. How many times, in how many ways would he have to prove to Gerard he was his friend?

After breakfast, they bade the children goodbye and bundled up in the sleigh. The sun shone dimly through a winter haze, the expected blizzard having spent itself on the Sangre de Cristo Range. The sleigh runners shooshed along the tracks they'd made the night before, and the horses kept a brisk pace, probably eager to get back to the warmth of the livery stable.

The closer they got to town, the tighter Justice's chest grew. What if she didn't like the house?

Chapter Thirteen

Unable to talk because of the wind blowing against their faces, Evangeline snuggled close to Justice, feeling true happiness for the first time in many years. She hadn't slept much last night for the myriad of thoughts churning through her mind. Permitting Justice to court her was a dream come true, but during their courtship, they would have some practical matters to sort out.

The first, of course, concerned the children. While Gerard had shown gratitude toward Justice last night, this morning he seemed less than cheerful toward the man who'd saved his life. Isabelle, on the other hand, had been her usual sweet self, gazing at Justice as if he were her favorite person in the world.

Another problem involved where they would live if the courtship led to marriage. She knew Justice resided above the jail in what must be a small apartment, probably one with insufficient room for her and the children to join him there. Still, they'd make do. She didn't know how much money a sheriff earned, but again, whatever amount it was, she'd make the best of it. She'd continue her work at the library, of course, and perhaps take in sewing.

Her biggest concern was cooking, assuming he had some sort of stove in his apartment. Even after two months of Susanna's tutelage, she still hadn't been able to comprehend the secrets for preparing tasty, nourishing food. Her cousin never measured anything. A dash of this, a pinch of that, a handful of something else and delicious meals came into being. Evangeline couldn't catch on no matter how hard she tried. But she was getting ahead of herself. If they couldn't resolve the other issues, she'd never have to confess her deficiency.

Beside her, Justice continued to drive with his usual skill, apparently untroubled by such concerns. They reached the outskirts of town, and instead of driving to the livery stable on Main Street, he reined the horses down a side street with lovely two-story residences on either side. To her surprise, he pulled the horses to a stop in front of a particularly pretty red brick house with a wide, fenced-in front yard. Like several of its neighbors, it boasted a broad, covered wraparound porch with a balcony above it. The front door had an oval etched-glass window, with rectangular sidelights on either side.

"What do you think?" As Justice nodded toward the house, his expression was unreadable, and yet she sensed a little tremor in his voice. Here was a man who could face a cougar to save her son, and yet he seemed afraid of her reaction to this place.

"What a lovely house, Justice. Do you know who lives there?" Yes, she was deliberately being coy. She hoped he didn't mind her teasing.

"Maybe we will." The raw vulnerability in his voice almost made the statement a question.

"Oh, my." She didn't have to pretend to be enthusiastic. "Justice, it's—" Tears choked off the rest of her words. *Bother.* Why couldn't she stop crying?

"You don't like it?" His laughter showed he was taking a turn at teasing her…and that he was relieved.

She tossed off the woolen blankets. "Take me inside."

He climbed from the sleigh and stomped through the snow to her side. There he lifted her in his arms and carried her through the gate and up the front walk, where he set her down.

"If we get married, I'll carry you all the way inside."

"Yes, you will." She gave him a saucy look.

These past two months with Susanna and Nate had shown her what a happy marriage could be. No fear of speaking her mind. No cringing when he lifted his hand toward her, no matter how hard it was to retrain her reactions. Plenty of light-hearted teasing.

She grasped his offered forearm and walked up the three steps to the porch.

"Madame." Justice opened the door and bowed like a footman. "My domicile awaits your approval." He waggled his eyebrows. "Or disapproval, whatever the case may be."

"I love it already." She stepped over the threshold into the spacious entryway.

"May I take your coat?"

She relinquished her wraps, and he hung them and his own on the large mahogany hall tree, a magnificent piece with a leather seat, rectangular mirror and umbrella holders.

In the center of the entry, a wide staircase with mahogany banisters beckoned. Rooms on either side held miscellaneous furniture set about randomly, awaiting arrangement. The front parlor on the right was furnished with an exquisite Persian rug, a damask settee and several chairs. A roaring fire filled the hearth. She entered the room, appreciating the warmth but curious about who'd started the fire. "What a grand place for family gatherings in the evening." She turned to Justice. "I love it all."

"You don't have to say that." He moved to her side and put an arm around her waist. "If we marry, you can change anything you don't like."

"Yes, ma'am." A man appeared from the next room, possibly the dining room. "You say the word, and we'll change anything you don't like." He shook hands with Justice. "Sheriff, I hope you don't mind our fires in the fireplaces. It's a mite hard to work in the cold."

"Certainly. I'd expect it. Evangeline, meet Joe Wilkins." Justice clapped the man on the shoulder. "He's my building supervisor. Joe, this is Mrs. Benoit."

"How d'ya do, ma'am." The middle-aged man gave her a respectful nod.

"I'm pleased to meet you, Joe." She returned a warm smile.

Judging from Justice's pleased expression, he didn't fault her for it. Lucius had forbidden her to smile at the servants and workmen. He'd always said she should treat them as inferiors, as he did. How good it felt to be friendly with those whose services made life easier. And from the looks of this house, Justice's wife would have a much easier life than if she lived over a jailhouse. Once Joe returned to work in the other room, she looped an arm in Justice's.

"Would you be so kind as to give me the grand tour?" Right away, she regretted using the term. The last time they'd spoken of a *grand tour*, it had brought him only pain.

This time, he seemed not to notice, if his wide smile was any indication. "I'd be delighted, my lady."

He led her through the dining room and into the kitchen, where a wooden icebox, a work table, a cabinet, a center table and chairs and various cooking implements offered a homey welcome. However, an enormous enamel and cast-iron range gave her pause.

"My, my. That's quite a cook stove."

Justice smiled with pride. "Do you like it?"

"I suppose a woman who cooks would like it very much." She gave him an apologetic shrug. "I've never learned, and even Susanna, who cooks so well, hasn't managed to teach me."

"Hmm." He cleared his throat dramatically. "Well, I planned to hire a cook. No reason to change that plan…if we get married."

"That's quite an expense. Are you sure you don't want me to try to learn—"

He stopped her with a kiss. A long kiss that made her knees weak and made her forget why she was worried. When he finally released her, he brushed a hand down her cheek.

"Sweetheart, I have something to tell you that may ease your worries, at least about finances." He led her to the table and seated her in one of the ladder-back chairs. "After I left the Texas Rangers, I didn't come directly to Esperanza. I went farther west, deep into the San Juan Mountains, where I found a nice little vein of gold, and it's still producing."

"What?" She gaped at him, unable to comprehend his words.

He shrugged and gave her his cockeyed grin. "Let's just say, if we decide to get married, you won't have to worry about learning to cook. Or cleaning house. Or washing clothes. We'll hire a housekeeper, and you can spend your days as you like."

Evangeline jumped up and walked to the back window, staring for several moments at the snow-covered yard and several outbuildings. A gold mine. Spending her days as she liked. Why, she'd be nothing more than a wealthy man's ornament, as she'd been for Lucius. And why did Justice risk his life being a sheriff when he could do whatever he wished? It didn't make sense.

"Is something wrong?" He stepped up behind her and gently touched her shoulders.

She turned around to face him. "I don't want just to sit and be waited on. I've never cared about shopping for the latest fashions or idly drinking tea with other ladies. By working at the library, I finally found something useful to do with my life, and I plan to continue doing it." She gave him a soft scowl. More of a pout, if she were honest with herself.

"Furthermore—" and far more important "—why on earth do you risk your life being a sheriff when you could do whatever *you* like?"

He grasped her shoulders again and stared into

her eyes. "Because I finally found something useful to do with *my* life." He pulled her into his arms, and she didn't resist. "When I couldn't protect my father from his crooked partners, I promised the Lord I'd protect other people from criminals. It's a calling, as you have a calling to encourage folks to read. Look at the way you've put good books into the hands of people like Adam Starling. He can't afford to go to college or buy books, but he's teaching himself through those library books. I would never take that away from you."

He moved back and lifted her chin so she couldn't escape his gaze. "My darling Evangeline, we've lost so much in this life because of other people's schemes. Now we have the opportunity to make up for the past. Don't let misplaced pride come between us." He tugged her close again.

She willingly rested her head against his chest. She was being silly, of course. Foolish, more like it. "Maybe I'm simply resisting the idea that it's all right for me to be happy."

"I'd like to spend the rest of my life making you the happiest woman in the world."

"And my children?" Isabelle already adored Justice, and Gerard surely regarded him as his new hero.

An odd little grimace crossed his face.

"What is it?"

"Nothing." He took her hand and led her back toward the dining room. "Let me show you the rest of the house."

As they climbed the front staircase, she dismissed the shadow threatening to come over her. If they married, they would be happy—all of them together in this beautiful house.

"We have four bedrooms." Waving a hand toward the center hallway, Justice spoke as if they were already engaged, as if the house were already hers as well as his.

"How grand." She inspected the first two rooms. Isabelle and Gerard could each have a room, and the smallest chamber could be her sewing room. She blushed as she viewed the largest room across the front of the house, which she and Justice would share…if they could resolve all of their problems and marry. He, on the other hand, seemed more interested in her opinion of the shiny new bathroom.

"What do you think?" He crossed his arms and leaned against the doorjamb while she inspected the facilities.

"I think you have the most modern house in Esperanza." She walked across the small space separating them and melted into his arms. "Any woman would be thrilled to enjoy such a luxury."

"I hope you will be that woman." He kissed the top of her head. "Now, would you help me choose the rest of the furniture, the drapes, the rugs—"

She stood on tiptoes and stopped him with a kiss. He responded in kind until the noise of hammering from a nearby room reminded them they were not alone. They gave each other sheepish grins.

"We should probably go back to the ranch." Evangeline took Justice's hand and led him toward the stairs. "Susanna has enough to do without having extra children to watch all day."

"I can't talk you into dinner at the hotel?"

She thought for a moment. "No. I still have some sewing to do. I'd better go back."

They returned to the ranch in time for Evangeline to help Susanna prepare dinner and to regale her and Nate with a description of Justice's fine new house.

"He has a bathroom." She giggled like a school-girl. "Can you imagine?" She took a platter of sandwiches to the kitchen table, where Justice and Nate awaited their dinner. The children were playing outside in the snow, which gave the adults a rare chance to talk without interruptions.

"Are you listening, honey?" Susanna eyed Nate. "Justice installed a bathroom in his new house."

Nate rolled his eyes. "Thanks a lot, Sheriff. First Tolley installs one, now you. You're making it mighty hard for the rest of us menfolk."

"If you other men would follow their good example, it would be easier on your wives." Susanna poured coffee for everyone.

"Sorry to cause you trouble, friend." Justice chuckled in his warm way that suggested he wasn't the least bit sorry.

After Nate offered a prayer of thanks for the meal, he addressed Justice. "When will you tell Gerard and Isabelle you're courting?"

Justice looked at Evangeline, and a shadow crossed his eyes again. "Sweetheart?"

Susanna laughed. "You keep calling her sweetheart, and they'll guess without being told."

Evangeline's giddy happiness vanished. This was something she and Justice should discuss in private. He was concerned about something, probably Gerard. But she was certain her son had changed his opinion of Justice after his rescue from the cougar.

She gave her cousins a wry smile. "I'm sure the right moment will arise. For now, I want Gerard to recover from his ordeal before he faces a potential change in his life."

Justice grunted. "And don't forget he's still under suspension for breaking those slates."

Evangeline's heart dropped. Yes, she'd remembered the suspension, but in her mind, Gerard had suffered enough for his misbehavior. While her son might have changed his opinion of Justice, she wasn't sure Justice had changed his view of Gerard. If she expected him to take on the responsibilities of a father to her children, she must make sure he loved them and would treat them fairly. She quietly sighed. This was why courting was better than an engagement. If both she and Justice still had reservations about important matters, they must not rush into a binding relationship.

The children trooped into the mudroom and shed mittens, hats, coats and boots. Susanna dipped a pitcher of hot water from the tank of the stove and carried it out to the washbowls. Once they'd cleaned up, they filled the kitchen with their chatter.

"We're starving." Gerard gave the platter of sandwiches a hungry look as he took his place beside Natty. The boys jostled each other playfully.

"Hey. Manners." Nate barely raised his voice, but the boys quit their roughhousing right away.

Not meaning to, Evangeline glanced at Justice. He wasn't exactly frowning, but he wasn't smiling either. *Lord, please don't let him be hard on Gerard.*

I can't think of marrying him if he doesn't get along with my son. In truth, Gerard and Isabelle were her first responsibility. But if she married Justice, she would have to let him lead the family. If she didn't see some evidence he and her son would get along, perhaps she should call off the courtship.

As he sat in church with Nate's family and Evangeline, Justice enjoyed their harmonizing as they sang the hymns. They shared smiles of agreement over several points in Reverend Thomas's sermon. And yet he felt as if a pall had been cast between Evangeline and himself at some point yesterday, probably the moment when he'd reminded her about Gerard's suspension. If so, she wasn't being fair to him. Miss Prinn had pronounced his punishment, not he. Even if the boy had a change of heart, he still must pay for destroying someone else's property. Justice hoped Evangeline wouldn't pay for the slates with Gerard's inheritance. He needed to experience some tangible loss for his wrongdoing. Until then, Justice doubted the boy would have a change of heart, much less that he'd learn his lesson.

The minister finished his sermon with a clear Gospel message, then offered an invitation to anyone who wanted to accept Christ as their Savior. One man on the other side of the sanctuary stood up and walked to the front. His wife remained in the pew, her face shining with happy tears. Justice prayed Gerard would go speak to the minister as well. After their discussion on horseback on Friday and now Reverend Thomas's sermon, surely the boy understood what it meant to be saved.

He glanced down the row. Gerard and Natty wiggled in their seats as though eager to run outside after sitting still for over an hour. Justice sighed inwardly. He should be pleased to see Gerard with his better-behaved cousin rather than Deely and Cart. Once their suspension was over, it would be a challenge to keep those three apart.

After a final prayer and hymn, the congregation stood to go their separate ways.

"We're expecting you for dinner, Sheriff," Susanna said from the middle of the pew.

"You'll come, won't you?" Evangeline gave him an equally expectant look. Isabelle also gazed up at him with a sweet smile. That little girl had already found an important place in his heart.

Down the row, Gerard and Natty exited the other end, followed by little Frankie, and were running along the wall toward the back door. Always the diligent father, Nate strode after them.

"I'm sorry, ladies. My deputy has done more than his share of the duties these past few days." He gave them a frown of regret. "I need to stay in town so he can rest."

"Oh, but—" Evangeline sighed and nodded. "I understand."

As they filed out of the pew and up the aisle, Justice had the unhappy feeling she didn't understand at all. It wasn't work keeping him from her, but their unspoken disagreement about Gerard. He couldn't spend another afternoon at the ranch pretending everything was all right. Early tomorrow morning when they were alone and working on the Christmas village, they could sort it out. If not, he feared they must call off their courtship, even though his heart would break all over again.

Something deep inside him rebelled against that idea. If he didn't fight for Evangeline's love, her father and Lucius would win from the grave. Somehow he must make this work.

On Monday morning, Evangeline drove the buggy into town and left Isabelle, Lizzie and Natty at the schoolhouse. Gerard gazed longingly at the building, then hung his head as they drove on. She wished Justice could see her son now, full of contrition and depressed because he couldn't join his friends. Of course this suspension meant she wouldn't read to his class today or tomorrow, but on Wednesday, she'd take him back and begin reading Charles Dickens's *A Christmas Carol*, the perfect story for this time of year. That was, if Miss Prinn permitted it.

Another activity she must forgo while Gerard accompanied her was painting the Christmas village. As much as she loved her son, she doubted he could keep the secret from the other children, so she couldn't permit him to see the project in the library's back room. After his suspension ended, she'd have to work quickly to finish the latest figures Justice carved.

Thoughts of Justice had tormented her since yesterday. After he'd asked to court her Friday evening, she'd been so happy. Then on Saturday, despite her delight in the beautiful house he wanted to share with her and the children, she'd begun to wonder whether it was fair to any of them for her to marry him. When he refused Susanna's invitation to Sunday dinner, it had been like Lucius all over again. Her late husband always gave work as an excuse for avoiding situations he didn't want to face. But that, she told herself, was where the comparison ended. After Lucius's death, she'd learned many of those times he'd gone to a gambling hall. Then Hugo confirmed what she'd always suspected about his having a mistress, and more of his absences were accounted for.

No, Justice was nothing like Lucius. He was honest, hardworking, sober. He cared deeply for her. She cared deeply for him. Somehow, some way, they must make things work between them.

As they drove down Main Street, Gerard glanced at Winsted's Mercantile, then gazed up at her, his dark brown eyes exuding innocence. "Mother, may I go to the mercantile and buy some candy?" How quickly he'd forgotten his regrets over missing school.

"Maybe later, my darling." Should she permit him to have a treat when he needed to replace the slates he'd broken? Justice would probably say no. But she still made decisions about her children and must decide whether candy might seem like a reward for his mischief.

They arrived at the library and hurried inside. On these cold days, she was especially grateful for Adam Starling caring for the horse and buggy so she didn't have to walk back and forth those four blocks in the icy wind.

As they entered the library, she heard a soft click in the back corner. Gerard didn't seem to notice either the noise or the roaring fire in the potbellied stove. Justice must be working on the village. She couldn't very well check to see, so she went about her usual routine.

The morning wore on slowly, with few patrons willing to come out on a cold Monday. Gerard grew restless. He'd brought a rubber ball, but tossing it across the room into the trash bin quickly bored him. Then he stood several books upright on a table and took aim.

"Oh, no, you don't." Evangeline held out her hand.

He hung his head and gave her the ball. "Is it time to eat?" He gazed hopefully at the dinner basket she'd set on a table.

"Not yet, my darling." Evangeline sighed. She dug two pennies from her reticule. "Here you go. Run over to Mrs. Winsted's and get some candy for both of us."

"Yes, ma'am." He grinned as he donned his coat and hat.

"Don't dawdle. Come straight back."

"Yes, ma'am." He dashed out the door and across the street.

She laughed at his quick change of mood. Oh, how she loved her children. They were the only good to come from her marriage to Lucius. And now their future was financially secure, thanks to Arthur Pettigrew's generous bequest. Her only concern was their need for a good male influence. Could Justice be the father they needed? Or would his strictness be as bad as Lucius's detachment? Before she agreed to marry him, she must find out.

Justice hadn't expected Evangeline to bring Gerard to the library. If he hadn't looked out the door at the right moment, the boy would have seen him, and the Christmas village would no longer be a secret. He'd managed to close the door and then slip out the back entrance, locking it behind him. He circled around several blocks and returned to his office from the west.

O'Shea was dozing in one of the three jail cells, his long legs hanging over the end of the cot. Envying his deputy's trouble-free sleep, Justice threw logs into the potbellied stoves, one in the cell room, the other in his office. His own sleep for the past two nights had been fitful because of his troubled thoughts and the ache in his heart. With his plans to have a heart-to-heart talk with Evangeline this morning not working out, he'd have to endure his misery for a while longer. In the meantime, he had work to do.

He sat at his desk by the front window and thumbed through the latest pile of wanted posters. None of the outlaws appeared familiar, but Justice would be on the lookout for any of them who dared to come to his town. At least he'd used to think that way. Since Evangeline arrived, he felt as if he'd lost his edge. He also felt frustrated over not being able to finish his carving. With only eleven work days left until Christmas Day, he needed to complete his figures so Evangeline could have time to paint them.

A flash of red across the street caught his attention. Gerard, in his unmistakable red plaid coat, was entering Winsted's Mercantile. Justice huffed out a cross breath. Evangeline shouldn't have let him run free. That wasn't a meaningful suspension. But he couldn't do anything about it unless the boy caused trouble.

Several minutes later, Gerard emerged from the store. To Justice's annoyance, Deely Pine and Cart Fendel followed after him. Each boy held a licorice stick, and they were laughing. He didn't doubt they'd stolen the candy.

He set aside his work, hoping none of those three would end up with their mugs on wanted posters. Right now, it wasn't looking good for any of them. He grabbed his wool jacket and hat, adjusted his gun belt and strode from the building. And spent the next hour trying to find them. Tracking was difficult because their shoe prints mingled with countless others in the patchy snow and mud-covered ground. Concerned they might take revenge against Miss Prinn, he stopped at the schoolhouse. The children in each of the three classes greeted him with their usual smiles, a pleasant reminder he'd always done well with the young ones. None of the teachers had seen the suspended boys. Nor had anyone he spoke to on the street. Unless someone brought a complaint, he didn't know where else to look.

"Lord, please keep those boys out of trouble," he whispered as he headed back to the office.

The words hadn't been out of his mouth for a second when he realized how he'd failed. He hadn't asked Mrs. Winsted if they'd stolen the candy. They might not be guilty after all. He strode up the street toward the mercantile ready to correct his mistake.

And was halted in his tracks by the jarring clang of the fire bell ringing from the corner of Main and Foster Street. His heart jumped to his throat, and he ran toward the alarm. No need to look any further for three little troublemakers.

"What on earth, Gerard?" Evangeline posted fists at her waist. "How could you lose your coat in a simple, fifteen-minute trip to the mercantile?"

Busy eating his licorice stick, he shrugged and blinked those innocent brown eyes. He hadn't liked the red plaid from the beginning. With the black patch she'd sewed on it to cover the tear, he'd balked at even wearing it this morning. Too bad she hadn't completed his new coat, which she planned to give him for Christmas. She'd have to work quickly over the next two evenings so he could wear it to school on Wednesday.

"Furthermore, you weren't supposed to eat your candy until after dinner." She nodded toward the table where she'd set out their food. "And another furthermore, where's my candy?" She held out her hand.

He blinked again. "Uh…it got et."

"Got et?" Her brows rose as she looked down at him. "Where did you learn such poor grammar? Maybe your sandwich should *get et* by me."

While he giggled at her playful wording, she grasped his hand and led him to the table, then took the sticky licorice. "You can finish this after you eat your ham sandwich." She sat with him and offered a prayer of thanks for their food before they began their meal.

Several patrons came in to return books and check out others. Georgia Eberly stopped by to chat. She was planning a trip to England to visit her sister

Beryl and promised to find a replacement to take her shifts at the library. A clanging bell somewhere in town interrupted their conversation.

Georgia gasped. "That's the fire alarm." Looking outside, she pointed to a plume of black smoke rising in the distance over the buildings on the north side of Main Street. She grabbed her coat. "They'll need my help on the bucket line." As if apprehending Evangeline's unspoken fear, she added, "It's not the school. Wrong direction."

"Should I go, too?" Evangeline glanced at Gerard. She couldn't leave him alone, and she wouldn't be much help if she was worried about him at the scene of the fire.

"No. Children get in the way. Y'all stay here and pray." She dashed from the building and up the street, joining other adults running in that direction.

"Wow. A fire. Can I go see it?" Gerard stood at the window staring at the smoke as the wind blew it toward the south.

"Certainly not." Evangeline frowned at him. As a child, she'd seen a devastating fire when a neighbor's home burned to the ground, and the memories sometimes still visited her dreams. "But we can pray for those trying to put it out." He joined her at the table where they held hands and prayed for everyone to be safe and for the fire to be quenched quickly. "Now, I'm going to mark these books as returned, and I want you to return them to the right shelves."

Although he grumbled at the task, he didn't show the rebellious attitude he'd had for the past year, for which she lifted a silent prayer of thanks.

In midafternoon, soot-covered people trudged

back down the street, mingling with school children who'd finished their classes for the day. Evangeline doubted Georgia would return to tend the library so she could attend the children's play rehearsal. Since Gerard had behaved himself over the weekend, maybe she could send him to the church alone.

Before she could make up her mind about the wisdom of such a plan, Justice appeared in the doorway, sootier by far than any of the others she'd seen. Instead of addressing her, he held out Gerard's coat, which was partially burned, and spoke to her son.

"Lose something?"

Gerard's puzzled expression surprised her. "No, sir. I—" He bit his lip and stared down at his hands.

"You're coming with me." Justice approached the table and took Gerard's arm, lifting him from the chair.

Evangeline stomach sickened. "Wait. What are you doing?"

The anguish and anger in Justice's eyes caused her heart to race. "Your son left his coat at the blacksmith shop, which he set on fire, as he tried to do to Colonel Northam's barn two months ago. Remember that little incident? I'm taking him to jail. This town isn't safe with him running loose." He started for the door with Gerard in tow.

"Wait," she repeated. "Gerard couldn't possibly have set the fire. He's been with me the whole day."

Hurt emanated from Justice's eyes. "I can't believe you'd lie for him…to me."

"I'm not lying. He—"

"Don't." Justice opened the door. "You can't make excuses for him anymore, Evangeline. I saw him running around town with Deely and Cart. He was seen by several people in the very act of setting the fire." He shut the door and faced her again. "It's bad enough to have Burt's business in ruins. He's lost his income, and we've lost a service the entire community needs. But with the livery stable being next door, the danger was even worse because of the horses stabled there. If the hay stored in Ben's loft caught on fire, Nate's horse and buggy, my horse, Tolley's horse and several more could have perished. As it was, the horses were terrified by the smoke and didn't want to leave their stalls." He opened the door again. "It's time Gerard paid for his deeds. He's a danger to the community."

"Justice, please." Evangeline couldn't keep the tears from her voice. "Can't you at least let him speak?" She thought she was going mad. No one could have seen her son at the blacksmith shop because he'd been here with her. Yet he wasn't even defending himself. "Gerard, what can you tell us?"

More disappointed than upset, he looked at her with those soulful eyes. "Does this mean I can't be in the Christmas play?"

Chapter Fourteen

The fire at the blacksmith shop wasn't the first one folks in Esperanza had fought. Before Justice came to town, they'd banded together to save the partially built hotel. Not long after he moved here, he'd joined them in a fruitless effort to save Susanna's father's home by the Rio Grande. After that, they bought the alarm bell and hung it on a street corner near the center of town where most people in the community could hear it. Then each month, the people practiced pumping water and passing buckets. Everyone knew what to do, and they worked together like a brigade of well-trained soldiers. It was time to purchase a steam pump fire wagon, like the ones Chicago authorities used to fight the devastating fire of '71. After today's tragedy, during which several people were injured because they got too close to the flames, Justice would gladly donate the equipment anonymously to the town.

As he marched Gerard the half block to the jail-house, Justice felt his future crumble around him. Sadly, his first opinion of the boy was right. He had his father's evil bent. Evangeline's lying defense of her son destroyed Justice's last hope they could still work things out and find happiness as a family. How could she stand there and say to his face the boy was with her all day? He'd seen Gerard running with his friends with his own eyes. Yet he longed to think she didn't lie, that she decided to go into the back room and paint, and Gerard slipped out while she was occupied. But that didn't make sense. She wouldn't so casually risk her son's discovering the secret village.

"What do we have here?" O'Shea met them in the office part of the jailhouse, his hair damp from washing up after the fire.

Justice still needed to clean himself up. "He started the fire. Put him in a cell."

"Sir, I didn't do it." Tears poured down the boy's solemn, sincere face.

"That's what they all say." O'Shea repeated every lawman's favorite response to criminals claiming innocence.

As his deputy marched the boy to the cell, Justice explained to him what had happened from the moment when he saw the boys exit the mercantile to the discovery of the burned coat. Once in the cell with the door locked, Gerard slumped onto the cot looking like a whipped puppy. For a mere second, Justice's heart stirred with pity and doubt. Until Evangeline marched into his office, her blue eyes blazing.

"Uh-oh." O'Shea slipped out the front door.

"I want to see my son."

Justice closed the door between the office and the cells, cutting off Gerard's plaintive cry to his mother. "He needs some time alone to think about what he's done." And to ponder the coming punishment. Justice leaned back against his desk, arms crossed over his chest. Best to let her get out her anger at him before he reminded her of the evidence right behind him.

She paced back and forth across the office, finally turning to him with her own arms crossed. "How can you be so legalistic you refuse to believe the truth?" She paced again. Stopped again. "You want to think the worst of Gerard because he's Lucius's son." More pacing. This time when she stopped, her eyes shone with tears.

He ground his teeth. A woman's tears were a more formidable weapon than any six-shooter. He lifted his own weapon, the burned coat. "Don't you understand? This was found at the fire."

She gasped and reached out to take it. He withheld it.

"It's evidence."

"I'm sure there's an explanation." She glared at him. "You see what you've done by arresting him? You've forced me to choose between you and my son. I cannot and will not abandon Gerard to your bad judgment. If you insist upon keeping him here, I'll talk to Tolley. At least he'll see reason." She tapped her foot as if waiting.

Somehow Justice managed to maintain his stance when he desperately longed to pull her into his arms and hold her until true reason took control of her. The fire in her eyes stopped him.

"Very well." She marched from the office and turned toward Tolley's office next door.

Justice put his hand on his chest to stop the deep ache. He hadn't hurt this badly since Evangeline's father claimed she didn't want to see him all those years ago.

He whispered a prayer. "Lord, I don't know if I can bear this pain again. If I could stop caring for her, I would have long ago. All those years we were apart, something was dead inside me. I started coming back to life when she stepped off of that train. Lord, help me. I guess I never stopped loving her, and I still love her more than my own life. Please show me what to do. Please help Evangeline see her son for what he is. Then we can get some help for him."

A nagging thought wormed into his brain. What if she was right and he was wrong? What if Gerard didn't start the fire? No. Couldn't be. All he needed to do for confirmation was turn around and look at the half-burned red plaid coat on his desk.

Evangeline tried to stop crying, but it was no use. With sweet Effie Bean beside her, she sat in Tolley's office sobbing out her story to the young lawyer.

"He was with me all day except for fifteen minutes when he went to buy candy at Winsted's." She crumpled her wet handkerchief and gratefully accepted a fresh one from Effie.

His eyes filled with kindness, Tolley gazed at her across the desk. "And you say the sheriff claims to have seen him running around town?"

She nodded. How unbearable to have Justice lie about her son, for that was the only explanation for his claim.

Tolley stared out the window for a few moments, then turned back to her. "Some things don't make sense in this situation. I don't believe either you or the sheriff is a liar. Gerard can't be in two places at the same time. And we'll have to find out why his coat was at the blacksmith shop. I'm going to ask you to trust me to work this out. Can you do that?"

She stared down at her hands and released a shuddering sigh. She'd come to him for help, but being Justice's friend, would he truly look out for her son's best interests? "I'll try."

"I appreciate your honesty." He took a sip of the coffee Effie served. "Do you want me to send for Susanna?"

"No. Frankie has the sniffles again and shouldn't be out in the cold."

"Tell you what." He gave her an encouraging smile. "As hard as it will be, why don't you go on over to the church and watch Isabelle in the play rehearsal?"

"Oh, but—"

"Mrs. Benoit—" Effie squeezed Evangeline's hand "—sometimes we parents have to get out of the way so other people can help our children."

Evangeline stared at her, doubt and fear clouding her thoughts. Yet she had no choice but to accept the older woman's advice. "All right. I'll have to close the library first." In her anguish, she'd run from the building without locking the door.

"Good." Tolley stood and came around the desk, his broad stature almost as imposing as Justice's. He took her hands in his larger ones and gave her a warm smile. "We'll get to the truth. And if the matter comes to trial, I'll be happy to represent Gerard."

Even with his assurance, Evangeline had difficulty following his plan. When she walked past the sheriff's office next door, she couldn't keep from glancing through the window. The inner door to the cells was still closed, meaning her poor son was alone and probably crying his little heart out. In the front office, Justice sat at his desk listening to his deputy, a thoughtful look on his handsome face. She desperately wanted to go inside and find out what they were discussing. More than that, she wanted to hold Gerard and reassure him all would be well. Remembering Effie's wise words and her own promise to Tolley that she wouldn't interfere, she forced her feet toward the library.

"Mrs. Winsted says she was about to send Homer over to get one of us this morning." Like any good deputy, Sean O'Shea had initiated his own investigation, the findings of which he was dictating to Justice. "Deely and Cart were causing havoc in her store. Among other things, they almost brought down a shelf of glass Christmas ornaments she ordered all the way from Germany. When Gerard came in, she expected even more trouble. But he bought the boys some candy and talked them into leaving. Said they should go outside and play tag."

Justice felt as though Gerard hit him in the chest again, only this time it was through a good deed... if that was his real purpose in luring his friends outside. His intention might have been to start the fire, and he wanted the other boys' help.

In the corner of his eye, he saw Evangeline walk past his window, hesitate, then march away in the direction of the library. Relief and disappointment fought inside of him. Relief won when Tolley entered the office.

"Got a minute?" Tolley pulled up a chair and made himself at home.

"Always for you." Justice gave O'Shea a signal, and the deputy laid out coffee and a plate of cinnamon rolls he'd brought from Williams's Café. "What did Mrs. Benoit say?"

Tolley waved his hand in a dismissive gesture. "Let's talk about Gerard. Or, rather, let's talk about how much like Gerard I used to be."

Justice grunted. He knew Tolley's story. Youngest of the four Northam children, this third son could never please his father. He'd caused his own share of trouble, some boyish, such as letting chickens out of their coop, some malicious, such as trying to whip up on his sister's sweetheart and drive him out of town. Instead, Colonel Northam had sent him away. Law school had taught him to respect the law. An elderly minister had taught him to love the Lord. Tolley returned home, married Laurie Eberly and became a father, adding yet another child to the growing Northam clan. He also served as Esperanza's only attorney and was respected by one and all, even his formerly distant father.

Justice took a minute to enjoy a bite of cinnamon roll. "Are you saying Gerard shouldn't be punished for starting the fire? We should just wait and see how he turns out?"

"Nope." Tolley shook his head for emphasis. "I'm saying let's apply a little grace here. Let's hear the boy's side of the story."

Justice lifted the damaged coat. "This is his side of the story."

Tolley huffed out a brief sigh. "Are you going to let me talk to my client?"

Justice sat back. "O'Shea, bring the boy in here."

The deputy opened the door to the cell room, revealing a sleeping ten-year-old. He unlocked the cell, and the creak of the iron hinges awoke Gerard.

"The sheriff wants to see you." O'Shea's voice was calm, kind. Justice regretted his own harsh tone the last time he spoke to the boy.

Rubbing sleep from his eyes, Gerard ambled into the office and took the chair beside Tolley. He stared hungrily at the cinnamon rolls.

"Hello, Gerard." Tolley offered him one. "Actually, I'm the one who wants to talk to you. Your mother asked me to be your lawyer, and it's my job to make sure we figure out exactly what happened today."

"Yessir." Gerard took a big bite of the roll and savored it. "These are as good as Cousin Susanna's."

His artless comment gave Justice pause. Either the child had no conscience, or he was innocent. A third option? He was wily as a snake.

"Are you cold, Gerard?" Tolley took the burned coat in hand and set it in Gerard's lap. Then took it back. "Uh-oh. Looks like it's ruined. That will be hard on your mother because coats are hard to come by."

When Tolley mentioned his mother, Justice noticed a flicker in Gerard's eyes, so he joined in. "Your mother works hard to take care of you and Isabelle. As the oldest child, you need to help her, don't you think? When you let your coat get ruined like this, she'll be worried about how to keep you warm."

Tolley nodded his approval of the question. A tilt of his head toward the boy invited him to reply.

"Yessir. I didn't—" Gerard bit his lip.

"Didn't what?" Justice prayed for a breakthrough.

"Mother's making me a new coat for Christmas. She doesn't know I know, but I sneaked out of bed one night and saw her working on it." He took a breath as if his long speech wore him out. "Deely only has a sweater, so I gave him my coat." Simplicity and sincerity were written across his boyish face.

Again, Justice felt slammed in the chest by an undeniable truth. The boy had done a good deed, and it got him in trouble. The two boys resembled each other enough at a distance so other witnesses could have recognized the red coat and assumed Gerard was starting the fire. "O'Shea, see if you can find Deely and Cart. I know Gerard wants to share these cinnamon rolls with his friends. And pick up a few more and some milk at the café on your way back."

The deputy left, a wide grin on his face. A former New York policeman, he'd rounded up many troublesome street boys. They both knew offering them food was the best way to lure them in.

"Gerard, after you bought the candy for your friends, what did you do?" Justice asked.

He didn't seem surprised Justice knew about it. "They wanted me to play with them, but I remembered Mother wanted me back at the library, so I went there."

"I saw you run the other way." Justice tried to keep an accusing tone from his voice.

"I ran around the block." Again, his face exuded guilelessness.

Euphoric relief so engulfed Justice that he wanted to shout. Wanted to run to the library and beg Evangeline's forgiveness. To tell her how much he loved her *and* her children, both of them. Instead, he reined in his emotions and considered how to wind up this investigation.

"Do you know what Deely and Cart did after you left them?"

"No, sir." Gerard finished his roll and looked hungrily at the plate.

Justice reached across the table and pushed it closer to him. "Don't ruin your appetite for supper."

"I won't." Gerard grinned widely. "Cousin Susanna makes real good food." He grimaced comically. "Not like Mother."

Justice laughed out loud and, my, it felt good. "Son, what your mother lacks in cooking, she more than makes up in a hundred other ways." He hadn't meant to say *son*, but it slipped out.

Unlike that first day when Gerard had responded in anger when he said it, this time he grinned. "I know."

"Tell you what. You'll need something to wear in this cold weather." He took a key from his pocket and handed it to the boy. "Go out back and up the stairs to my apartment. You'll find a tan woolen poncho on the coatrack. You can wear it home."

"Yessir." His brown eyes sparkling, he took the key and hurried from the room.

"Well, I'm impressed," Tolley said.

"Me, too." Justice stared after Gerard.

"No, I mean with you. First you put the boy in jail, then you trust him to go inside your home without supervision."

Justice shrugged. If Evangeline could forgive him for his unfairness to Gerard, if their courtship worked out the way he prayed it would, the boy would soon have the run of a home they all shared. He could hardly wait to see this matter finished.

Evangeline sat at the back of the church so Isabelle could see her but not the tear tracks staining her face. She'd told Marybeth that Gerard would miss the rehearsal but not why. Her friend knew about the suspension, so Evangeline hoped she'd assume her son stayed home for the day. At the memory of his cries from the jail cell, her heart broke anew, and her anger rekindled. And yet, if she were honest with herself, she'd admit she had a part in this, too. If she'd scolded Gerard when he accidentally started the fire at the Northams', Justice might be more willing to believe her son wouldn't deliberately start one. Yet, at the time, Gerard was bursting with rebellion, and she'd been afraid to make it worse by trying to correct him. After observing Justice's more than fair treatment of the cowboys who'd shot out Mrs. Winsted's display window, she could see he simply meant to protect his community from troublemakers.

As she tried to reason out their conflict over where Gerard was when the fire began, his burned coat seemed to be the only clue. Later, she'd ask him what happened. For now she watched Isabelle in the little choir and thanked the Lord for her daughter's obedience and sweet disposition.

The door of the church opened behind her, and she turned to see the object of her ruminations. "Gerard." She rushed to embrace him, but he wriggled from her arms.

"I'm late for my part." He pulled an unfamiliar woolen poncho over his head and flung it on a pew, then ran down the aisle in time to take his place in front of the painted inn where Mary and Joseph sought shelter.

"Thank You, Lord," she whispered as she stared after him. What wonderful thing happened to set him free? Was this another example of Justice's grace toward someone he considered a criminal?

Behind her, she felt more than heard a large presence approaching her. A pleasant shiver swept down her back. She turned to see Justice, his expression a mixture of doubt and... Was that joy?

He grasped her hands. "Come with me. Please."

Though confused, she let him lead her into the cloakroom by the front door.

"Evangeline, I was wrong." Contrition emanated from his voice and his eyes. "I assumed Gerard started the fire because his coat was found at the scene, but he didn't leave it there."

That was enough to start her tears flowing all over again. Lucius had never once admitted to being wrong.

"Gerard gave his coat to Deely Pine because Deely said he didn't have one. After Gerard returned to the library, Deely and Cart started the fire." Justice sighed deeply. "I questioned the other two boys and learned Hugo Giles paid them to cause trouble for you, so what Gerard meant as a kindness, they used to get him in trouble. To his credit, Gerard was more angry than hurt by his supposed friends' betrayal. They'd been using him all along."

Not surprised at all by Hugo's evil plan, Evangeline spared him only a moment of anger. Lucius's cousin could never hurt them again.

"I was wrong, too." She gave Justice a watery smile. "I wouldn't confront Gerard when he got into mischief because I knew he was angry about his father's death. I was afraid I'd make matters worse. But after you saved him from the cougar, he changed. I'm not sure why, but he's becoming the happy boy he used to be, and I'm thankful for it."

"I could see that." He chuckled ruefully. "When he was more concerned about missing this rehearsal than going to jail, I should have seen the Lord had changed his heart. Will you forgive me for being harsh with him when it was Lucius and Giles who deserve my anger?"

"I do forgive you." She gazed up into his beloved face and saw love reflected there. "I can see it's your job to be firm with troublemakers. Will you forgive me for my harsh words?"

"I do forgive you." He took her hands in his. "And now I have one more question for you."

"Yes?"

"Will you marry me?"

The question took her by surprise. As it echoed in her mind, she couldn't stop a smile from overtaking her lips. Still, there was much to consider before she accepted. "I—I don't know. Do we have any other matters to discuss before we enter into a permanent bond?" From now on, she'd insist on discussing everything so shadows of the past couldn't come between them.

"You mean before you're trapped in a marriage like your first one?" He didn't give her time to respond. "Evangeline, I promise you now I will love and cherish you and your children until my dying day."

She touched his beloved face, which still bore a remnant of soot in the blond stubble on his cheek. "I know you will."

He likewise caressed her cheek. "Don't keep me in suspense. Will you marry me?"

She smiled at him, and this one she was sure lit up her eyes as well. "I will."

He tugged her into his arms, and she rested her head against his broad chest, giving herself permission at last to love him without reservation.

He lifted her chin and bent to kiss her, a sweet chaste kiss that promised so much more.

Justice would have preferred to take Evangeline and the children home, but he needed to visit Deely's mother and Cart's aunt to explain why their boys would be in jail until the circuit judge came to town. Newly married to a farmer, Cart's aunt was glad to be rid of him and refused even to visit him in jail. Deely's mother broke down in tears, grief-stricken her son was turning out to be as bad as his father, who'd been hanged for stealing horses. Leaving Mrs. Pine's ramshackle house on the edge of town, Justice prayed for some way to help the boys before they were too deeply entrenched in a life of crime. Sending them to prison would put them under the influence of older inmates who would lead them further astray. He'd consult with the Northam brothers before making a decision.

As he rode back to the jail, he passed the hotel, which was festooned for Christmas with evergreen bows and red ribbons. Colorful lamps glowed in the windows, and through the glass front doors, he saw in the lobby a tall Douglas fir tree decorated with candles and blown glass ornaments from Germany. For the first time in many years, he permitted the joy of the Christmas season to flood his heart. Tomorrow he'd buy presents for his soon-to-be family. And Wednesday, after Gerard's suspension was over, Justice would return to work side by side with Evangeline on the Christmas village, their special gift for the town that had reunited them after so many years.

He awoke the next day with another idea. He asked Marybeth to excuse the Benoit children from the rehearsal. Then after school he collected Isabelle from the schoolhouse and Gerard from the library and, with Evangeline's permission, took the children to the ice-cream parlor. With cookies and a steaming cup of hot chocolate in front of each one, he practiced being their father.

After inquiring about their day and learning important details—Isabelle's favorite subject was writing and she liked to play with dolls, and Gerard was interested in arithmetic and guitar playing—he got down to business. Or he would have if Gerard hadn't beat him to it.

"Are you going to marry my mother?"

Justice smiled at the boy's earnest tone. "I want to. Would you like that?"

For several agonizing heartbeats, the boy seemed to be thinking it over. "Then you'd be my father."

"And mine." Isabelle gave her brother a look of annoyance much like her mother might do if she was being ignored.

"I'll actually be your stepfather." As he said the words, they didn't feel right, no matter how accurate the title was.

Gerard sipped his hot drink. "I like Father better. Or maybe Dad."

"I'd like that." A lump formed in Justice's throat. They'd come a long way in the past two months, but they still had a ways to go. "Do you think we can get along?"

The boy smirked, an expression reminiscent of Lucius's. And yet somehow different. "Does that mean I have to mind you?"

"I don't mind minding you." Isabelle blinked blue eyes full of trust, which endeared her to Justice all the more.

"Thank you, sweetheart." He touched her cheek, then turned to her brother. "How about you?"

Gerard thought for a moment, his expression turning serious and a bit sullen. Justice felt a moment of concern. Had he been wrong? Had the boy not changed? Or maybe the boy was simply mulling over an idea.

"What if we don't agree about something?" Gerard asked as he eyed him skeptically. "Will you get mad and make me mind you anyway?"

He deserved that question, considering how angry he'd been about the fire. "I'd prefer to talk things out with you and come to an agreement." He hoped he'd learned his lesson and in the future wouldn't assume the worst about the boy.

"But if we don't agree, will I still have to mind you?"

The answer to this simple question could seal their future relationship, but Justice must respond honestly. "Yes. As your father, it will be my job to guide you and help you become a man. You'll have to trust I know what's best for you."

Instead of adopting his former sulking attitude, Gerard nodded. "I understand. Like Jesus had to obey His Father and die on the cross, even though He didn't want to."

Justice could have explained that in truth Jesus had died willingly, yet he decided to save the explanation for later. For now, he was profoundly moved by Gerard's connecting their impending relationship with the heavenly example. "Something like that."

As Gerard grabbed another cookie and munched it, Justice considered urging him to ask Jesus into his heart right now. But maybe he already had, if his change of attitude was any indication.

"You can marry Mother," Gerard said. "Can't he, Izzy?"

She answered by jumping from her chair and throwing her arms around Justice's neck. "May I call you Daddy?"

He hugged her close. "Nothing could please me more."

Chapter Fifteen

The next ten days passed quickly for Evangeline. With the Christmas village to complete, presents to make, the Christmas pageant to be presented on Christmas Eve and a wedding to plan, she barely had time to think. She and Justice did take time to attend Nolan and Electra's Christmas ball, where everyone congratulated them on their engagement. Surrounded with love on all sides, she dismissed every memory of her past and looked forward to a wonderful new future.

She helped Justice complete the miniature blacksmith shop—an addition to their original plan—on the same day townspeople banded together and rebuilt Burt's business. The anvil and hammer head had survived the fire, along with several other reparable iron tools. When ranchers donated some items and pitched in money to pay for others, the tough, muscular blacksmith almost came to tears. Making tiny replicas of the tools proved a challenge for Justice's large hands, but Evangeline watched in amazement as he whittled them to perfection.

She stayed up late each night working on Gerard's coat, plus the other gifts for her growing number of loved ones. By day, she saw an increase in the number of patrons visiting the library because many ranchers had more time to read in the winter.

Susanna insisted she must make Evangeline a new dress for the wedding. Evangeline agreed, but only if it was a practical blue wool suit she could wear all winter. Her cousin surprised her with a matching suit for Isabelle. Her Singer sewing machine was kept busy for days, with the two of them taking turns using it.

On Christmas Eve morning, Evangeline, Justice and Susanna moved the village from the library to the church reception hall and set it up in the center of the room.

"What a grand surprise," Reverend Thomas said. "Sheriff, this is delightful. Everyone will enjoy it, not only the children."

Justice shrugged as if the effort had been minimal. "My pleasure. If not for Evangeline's excellent painting, it wouldn't look half as good." He put his hand at her waist and gave her a sideways hug. "Let's lock the door so no one will see it until after the play."

Later that evening, the children gathered at the front of the church to present their pageant. Mothers had made costumes, and Nate had refreshed the scenery he'd built for past plays. Evangeline sat in the front row with Marybeth and Electra on one side of her and Justice on the other.

"And it came to pass in those days, that there went out a decree from Caesar Augustus that all the world should be taxed," read fourteen-year-old Kip Bean from the second chapter of Luke's Gospel. As he continued to narrate the story of Mary and Joseph's trip to Bethlehem, the children portraying the holy couple walked down the center aisle, a "donkey" beside them. Fond chuckles filled the room as the little boy wiggled his long, furry ears.

Evangeline held her breath when Gerard's big moment neared. "Joseph" knocked on the door of the inn, and her son emerged.

"Do you have a room for us tonight?" Joseph waved toward Mary, who looked properly weary.

Gerard blinked several times, and Evangeline's heart stood still. He'd forgotten his few simple lines.

"There's no room in my inn," he finally blurted out. "But you can have my room."

The sanctuary was silent for five full seconds. Mary and Joseph gaped at Gerard. Several people coughed, or perhaps cleared their throats to keep from laughing at his mistake. Evangeline opened her mouth to whisper the correct line, but Justice touched her arm. "Let him work it out."

"Or you can stay in the stable." Gerard waved toward the stable setting across the podium. "It's warm out there with all of the animals and quieter than in here."

Several people now chuckled out loud, and Joseph exhaled with relief. "Thank you, kind sir."

Gerard went back inside the inn, and the moment was forgotten as the more important story continued. But to Evangeline, her son's generous offer further revealed his change of heart. After all, he'd been pleased to get the part because he wanted to be mean to Mary and Joseph. Now he wanted only to be kind to someone in need, just as he'd done for Deely in giving him his coat. Justice leaned toward her and squeezed her hand, his gray eyes filled with paternal pride. She could ask for nothing more precious this Christmas or any other.

"Next year we'll add a train." Justice studied the village to be sure nothing else was missing. He reached across the six-by-eight-foot board and righted a bent tree.

Around him, children and their parents identified the various Esperanza buildings.

"That's the church."

"That's the school."

"A blacksmith shop just like the new one."

"The hotel."

"Tiny people with smiles on their faces." This from Marybeth Northam.

"Mrs. Benoit painted those," Justice said.

"Look." Gerard moved to the front of the group. "The livery stable has a Nativity scene. I can see Mary and Joseph and Baby Jesus lying in a manger, just like in the Bible."

"Oh, my." Mrs. Winsted stepped up to the group, tears sparkling in her eyes. "There's my store. Why, Justice, you've made a replica of our town, Christmas decorations and all." The lady hugged him, the privilege of an older matron.

"It was our pleasure." He nodded toward Evangeline, who stood on the other side of the display. She rewarded him with a smile he felt clear down to his toes.

Mrs. Winsted laughed. "Ah, yes. And you two will have another project to attend to next week."

"Yes, ma'am." He'd already experienced plenty of good-natured ribbing from the men around town about his upcoming marriage. The ladies, of course, were quick to offer Evangeline any help she might need. "Tomorrow we celebrate the Lord's birth. Wednesday, we get hitched."

Others came to admire the village and offer their thanks to the artists. Justice hadn't started the project to garner praise, but their graciousness made all the work well worth it. The important idea was that children would appreciate their town, their families.

"Boss, what shall I do with those two?" Deputy O'Shea had brought Deely and Cart to the pageant and now watched over them as they ate cookies with the other children.

Justice sighed. He'd put them in separate cells because they'd fought, each one blaming the other for the fire. "Did you have any trouble with them during the play?"

"No, sir. Rand sat with me to help out." O'Shea shook his head. "Seemed to me Cart enjoyed it, even shed a few tears when the preacher gave the message at the end. Deely sneered through the whole show, especially when Gerard made his mistake."

He wouldn't correct his deputy. Gerard hadn't made a mistake. He'd revealed his change of heart and brought an abundance of joy to both Justice and Evangeline. "You'd better take them back to the jail. We'll keep praying they see the error of their ways."

After a night of community fellowship, the townspeople returned for church on Sunday, Christmas Day.

As always, Reverend Thomas gave a soul-stirring sermon about God's great gift of love in sending His Son to bring salvation to a lost world. At the end of the service, Cart Fendel answered the invitation to accept Jesus as his Savior. While Justice was pleased, he also knew the boy must still pay for his crime. He'd known criminals who'd pretended to have faith to avoid punishment.

After church, Justice and Evangeline joined the Northams at the big house on Four Stones Ranch. After a feast at which everyone ate too much, Justice gathered his soon-to-be family and returned to town.

"This is where we'll live." He drew the horses up to the house he'd never expected to fill.

"Wow." Gerard jumped out of the buggy and ran toward the front porch. "Come on, Izzy. Let's explore."

"Wait—" Evangeline reached out but caught air.

"Let them go." Justice laughed. "It's their home now." He leaned toward her and kissed her. "Merry Christmas, my love."

"Merry Christmas, my darling." Evangeline savored the kiss, looking forward to many more to come. Then she bundled up the burlap sack she'd brought from Susanna's and waited for him to come around to lift her down from the buggy.

"What's in the bag?" Justice took it from her as they walked toward the house.

"You'll see."

"Huh. Well, I have a few secrets of my own." He smirked playfully.

Indeed he did. To Evangeline's surprise, when she

entered the house, Gerard and Isabelle were sitting on the parlor rug playing with an adorable black-and-white puppy like the ones raised by the Northams. Near the roaring hearth sat several other presents wrapped in brown paper.

"Who lit the fire this time?" Evangeline removed her wraps and helped her children do the same.

"Your new housekeeper." Justice grinned as Effie Bean's daughter May entered from the dining room carrying a tray of sweets and coffee.

"Good afternoon, Mrs. Benoit, and Merry Christmas." A sweet girl of about eighteen, May had her mother's cheerful manner. "I hope you don't mind my taking over your kitchen. Sure do like that new cook stove."

Speechless for a few seconds, Evangeline gave Justice a quick hug. "Not at all, May. It's all yours."

"Let's see what's in these packages." Justice gave one to each of the children, then told Evangeline, "Yours is a little heavy." He pointed to a large one by the coffee table.

While the children ripped off their paper, Evangeline carefully unwrapped hers to reveal a new Singer treadle sewing machine. "Oh, Justice, it's perfect." She stood on tiptoes and kissed his cheek.

Isabelle's present was a beautiful blond baby doll with a bisque head, cloth body and a pink silk gown. For Gerard, Justice had selected a guitar. Evangeline had seen both items in Winsted's Mercantile and was pleased he'd known exactly what each child wanted.

"You two can share the puppy," he said, and neither child complained.

Evangeline had already given Gerard his coat to

replace the burned one. Now she brought out her own presents from the burlap sack. Matching shirts for Justice and Gerard and a new blue wool dress for her daughter. With everyone pleased with their gifts, they managed to find room for May's delicious Christmas cookies.

The holiday celebration was bested only by the next day, when Evangeline married Justice. The church was packed with all of the Northams in attendance, even old Colonel Northam in his wheelchair. It was a simple ceremony, and they'd decided not to hold a reception because the town had already done a great deal of celebrating for Christmas. Instead, May and Effie Bean offered to provide refreshments at the new house for those who wanted to stop by with congratulations.

After Reverend Thomas pronounced them man and wife, Fred Brody took their wedding picture. Then Evangeline, Justice and the children walked the three blocks to their new home. As he'd promised, Justice carried Evangeline over the threshold, accompanied by the giggles of Gerard and Isabelle. To the surprise of the whole family, they found the house filled with well-wishers.

"You see, Sheriff, I said you should have a house-warming." Electra Means waved to a stack of presents on the dining room table.

"And I said the same." Effie Bean indicated a beautiful three-tiered white cake on the sideboard.

While the celebrating went on around them, Justice kept Evangeline close to his side. "I don't ever plan to let go of you again," he whispered in her ear, sending a pleasant shiver down her side.

"Don't worry." She snuggled beneath his arm, hoping no one would think her scandalous. "Now that I have you in my clutches, I'll never let you go either."

She gazed around the room, taking in all the friendly and loving gazes sent their way. After so many years of feeling lost and alone with her precious children, she at last had a home and a husband to love and protect them all. With gratitude to the Lord for reuniting Justice and her, she couldn't ask for anything more to complete her happiness.

* * * * *

If you liked this story, pick up these other
FOUR STONES RANCH *books*
by Louise M. Gouge:

COWBOY TO THE RESCUE
COWBOY SEEKS A BRIDE
COWGIRL FOR KEEPS
COWGIRL UNDER THE MISTLETOE
COWBOY HOMECOMING

Available now from Love Inspired!

Find more great reads at www.LoveInspired.com

Dear Reader,

Thank you for choosing *Cowboy Lawman's Christmas Reunion*, the sixth book in my Four Stones Ranch series. I hope you enjoyed the love story of my hero, Justice Gareau, and my heroine, Evangeline Benoit. These two sweethearts waited for a long time for their happily-ever-after.

My series setting is the beautiful San Luis Valley of Colorado, where I lived for many years before moving to Florida thirty-seven years ago. While I've forgotten many things about the Valley, as we call it, my research sources include a helpful book by lifelong Valley resident Emma M. Riggenbach, *A Bridge to Yesterday* (High Valley Press 1982), in which she writes about Monte Vista, Colorado, the inspiration for my series.

If you enjoyed Justice and Evangeline's story, be on the lookout for more stories set in my fictional town of Esperanza. Can you guess who my next hero or heroine will be? Who would you like to see have his or her own happily-ever-after?

I love to hear from my readers. If you have a comment, contact me at:

http://blog.Louisemgouge.com (You can also sign up for my occasional newsletter there.)

https://www.facebook.com/AuthorLouiseMGouge/
Twitter: *@Louisemgouge*

Blessings,
Louise M. Gouge

COMING NEXT MONTH FROM
Love Inspired® Historical

Available November 7, 2017

A LAWMAN FOR CHRISTMAS
Smoky Mountain Matches • by Karen Kirst

After lawman Ben MacGregor and avowed spinster Isabel Flores discover a four-year-old boy abandoned on her property at Christmas, they must work together to care for him. But can their temporary arrangement turn into a forever family?

MAIL-ORDER CHRISTMAS BABY
Montana Courtships • by Sherri Shackelford

When a child arrives with the Wells Fargo delivery with documents listing Heather O'Connor and Sterling Blackwell as the baby's parents, they are forced to marry to give the baby a home—and save their reputations.

THEIR MISTLETOE MATCHMAKERS
by Keli Gwyn

Lavinia Crowne heads to California planning to bring her late sister's orphaned children back east. But Henry Hawthorn, their paternal uncle, is intent on raising them in the only home they know...and three little matchmakers hope their mistletoe-filled schemes will bring their aunt and uncle together.

A CHILD'S CHRISTMAS WISH
by Erica Vetsch

After her home is destroyed in a fire, pregnant widow Kate Amaker and her in-laws take refuge with Oscar Rabb— the widowed farmer next door whose daughter has one holiday wish: a baby for Christmas.

LOOK FOR THESE AND OTHER LOVE INSPIRED BOOKS WHEREVER BOOKS ARE SOLD, INCLUDING MOST BOOKSTORES, SUPERMARKETS, DISCOUNT STORES AND DRUGSTORES.

LIHCNM1017

Get 2 Free Books,

Plus 2 Free Gifts —

just for trying the Reader Service!

Love Inspired HISTORICAL

SPECIAL EXCERPT FROM

Love Inspired HISTORICAL

*When a child arrives with the Wells Fargo delivery
with documents listing Heather O'Connor and
Sterling Blackwell as the baby's parents, they are forced
to marry to give the baby a home—and save
their reputations.*

*Read on for a sneak preview of
MAIL-ORDER CHRISTMAS BABY
by **Sherri Shackelford**, available
November 2017 from Love Inspired Historical!*

"The only way for us to clear our names is to find the real
parents. If Grace's mother made the choice out of necessity,"
Heather said, "then she'll be missing her child terribly.
Perhaps we can help."

Grace reached for her, and Heather folded her into her
arms. By the looks on the gentlemen's faces, the gesture was
further proof against her. But Heather was drawn to the child.
The poor thing was powerless and at the mercy of strangers.
Despite everything she'd been through, the baby appeared
remarkably good-natured. Whatever her origins, she was a
resilient child.

The reverend focused his attention on Grace with searing
intensity, as though she might reveal the secret of her origins
if he just looked hard enough. "Who is going to watch her for
the time being?"

Sterling coughed into his fist and stared at the tips of his
boots. The reverend discovered an intense fascination with
the button on his sleeve.

Heather's pulse picked up speed. Surely they wouldn't leave the baby with her? "I don't think I should be seen with her. The more people connect us, the more they'll gossip."

"It's too late already," Sterling said. "There are half a dozen curious gossips milling outside the door right now."

Heather peered out the church window and immediately jerked back. Sure enough, a half dozen people were out there.

If she didn't take responsibility for the child, who would? "I'll watch her," Heather conceded.

"Thank the Lord for your kindness." The reverend clasped his hands as though in prayer. "The poor child deserves care. I'll do my best to stem the talk," he added. "But I can't make any promises."

Sterling sidled nearer. "Don't worry. I'll find the truth."

"I know you will."

A disturbing sense of intimacy left her light-headed. In the blink of an eye her painstakingly cultivated air of practicality fled. Then he turned his smile on the baby, and the moment was broken.

Heather set her lips in a grim line. His deference was practiced and meant nothing. She must always be on guard around Sterling Blackwell. She must always remember that she was no more special to him than the woman who typed out his telegrams.

He treated everyone with the same indolent consideration, and yet she'd always been susceptible to his charm.

She smoothed her hand over Grace's wild curls. They were both alone, but now they had each other.

At least for the time being.

Don't miss
MAIL-ORDER CHRISTMAS BABY by Sherri Shackelford,
available November 2017 wherever
Love Inspired® Historical books and ebooks are sold.

www.LoveInspired.com

Love Inspired®

Inspirational Romance to Warm Your Heart and Soul

Join our social communities to connect with other readers who share your love!

Sign up for the Love Inspired newsletter at **www.LoveInspired.com** to be the first to find out about upcoming titles, special promotions and exclusive content.

CONNECT WITH US AT:

Harlequin.com/Community

 Facebook.com/LoveInspiredBooks

Twitter.com/LoveInspiredBks

LISOCIAL2017

Once both twins were bundled, snug between Papa and Erica, Jason sent the horses trotting forward. The sun was up now, making millions of diamonds on the snow that stretched across the hills far into the distance. He smelled pine, a sharp, resin-laden sweetness.

When he picked up the pace, the sleigh bells jingled.

"Real sleigh bells!" Erica said, and then, as they approached the white covered bridge decorated with a simple wreath for Christmas, she gasped. "This is the most beautiful place I've ever seen."

Jason glanced back, unable to resist watching her fall in love with his home.

Papa was smiling for the first time since he'd learned of Kimmie's death. And as they crossed the bridge and trotted toward the church, converging with other horse-drawn sleighs, Jason felt a sense of rightness.

Mikey started babbling to Teddy, accompanied by gestures and much repetition of his new word. Teddy tilted his head to one side and burst forth with his own stream of nonsense syllables, seeming to ask a question, batting Mikey on the arm. Mikey waved toward the horses and jabbered some more, as if he were explaining something important.

They were such personalities, even as little as they were. Jason couldn't help smiling as he watched them interact.

Once Papa had the reins set and the horses tied up, Jason jumped out of the sleigh, and then turned to help Erica down. She handed him a twin. "Can you hold Mikey?"

He caught a whiff of baby powder and pulled the little one tight against his shoulder. Then he reached out to help Erica, and she took his hand to climb down, Teddy on her hip.

When he held her hand, something electric seemed to travel right to his heart. Involuntarily he squeezed and held on.

She drew in a sharp breath as she looked at him, some mixture of puzzlement and awareness in her eyes.

What was Erica's secret?

And wasn't it curious that, after all these years, there were twins in the farmhouse again?

Don't miss
SECRET CHRISTMAS TWINS
by Lee Tobin McClain, available November 2017
wherever Love Inspired® books and ebooks are sold.

www.LoveInspired.com

LIEXP1017